ELIZABETH WEBSTER

AND THE CHAMBER OF STOLEN GHOSTS

BY WILLIAM LASHNER

Elizabeth Webster and the Court of Uncommon Pleas

Elizabeth Webster and the Portal of Doom

Elizabeth Webster and the Chamber of Stolen Ghosts

ELIZABETH WEBSTER
AND THE
CHAMBER OF STOLEN GHOSTS

WILLIAM LASHNER

Little, Brown and Company

NEW YORK   BOSTON

Copyright © 2021 by William Lashner

Cover art copyright © 2021 by Karl Kwasny. Cover design by Phil Buchanan and Angelie Yap. Cover copyright © 2021 by Hachette Book Group, Inc.

Little, Brown and Company
Hachette Book Group
1290 Avenue of the Americas, New York, NY 10104
Visit us at LBYR.com

First Edition: October 2021

Little, Brown and Company is a division of Hachette Book Group, Inc.
The Little, Brown name and logo are trademarks of Hachette Book Group, Inc.

The publisher is not responsible for websites (or their content)
that are not owned by the publisher.

Library of Congress Cataloging-in-Publication Data
Names: Lashner, William, author.
Title: Elizabeth Webster and the chamber of stolen ghosts / William Lashner.
Description: First edition. | New York : Little, Brown and Company, 2021. |
Series: Elizabeth Webster ; book 3 | Audience: Ages 8–12. | Summary: Middle schooler
Elizabeth Webster has a new case for the Court of Uncommon Pleas: a fourth grader
who says her sister's ghosts were stolen; the case leads her to the Ramsberger Institute
of the Paranormal, run by Frederick Ramsberger and his grandmother (deceased),
who are imprisoning and controlling ghosts, and who have a connection to
Elizabeth's enemy, the fearsome demon Redwing.
Identifiers: LCCN 2021019240 | ISBN 9780759557727 (hardcover) | ISBN 9780759557741 (ebook)
Subjects: LCSH: Ghost stories. | Legal stories. | Courts—Juvenile fiction. | False
imprisonment—Juvenile fiction. | Fathers and daughters—Juvenile fiction. | Mothers and
daughters—Juvenile fiction. | Detective and mystery stories. | CYAC: Mystery and detective
stories. | Ghosts—Fiction. | Lawyers—Fiction. | Courts—Fiction. | False imprisonment—
Fiction. | Fathers and daughters—Fiction. | Mothers and daughters—Fiction. | LCGFT:
Paranormal fiction. | Detective and mystery fiction.
Classification: LCC PZ7.1.L3725 El 2021 | DDC 813.54 [Fic]—dc23
LC record available at https://lccn.loc.gov/2021019240

ISBNs: 978-0-7595-5772-7 (hardcover), 978-0-7595-5774-1 (ebook)

Printed in the United States of America

LSC-C

Printing 1, 2021

To all those bold enough to object,
in or out of the courtroom

ROBOTS

Hey there, how's it going? Nice shoes.

In case you didn't know, my name is Elizabeth Webster and I have this thing with ghosts. I also deal with a demon or two, the occasional vampire boy, and maybe even a ghoul when the moon is right, but mainly it's the walking spirits of the dead. "Ghosts," my grandfather often says. "Can't live with them, can't make any money without them."

Which is no joke when your family business is to be attorneys for the damned.

As a way-too-young member of the firm of Webster & Spawn, I talk for the dead. I also sometimes sue the dead, which is a little scary because, well, because they're the dead. But that's the life I have now, bouncing between the supernatural Court of Uncommon Pleas, where I try cases against demons and ghosts, and the Willing Middle School West Debate Club.

I'll let you decide which is more horrifying.

"Proposition rebuttal," said the debate judge. "Three minutes. Ms. Webster?"

As I took my place at the lectern on the auditorium stage and looked out at the sparse crowd, my teammates, Charlie and Doug Frayden, tapped our table enthusiastically. That's how you applaud in debate, you tap the table with a closed fist. *Tap! Tap! Tap! Tap! Tap!* The Upper Pattson Middle School Debate Club tapped their table with much less enthusiasm. *tap-tap-tap.*

Ms. Lin, our debate coach, nodded at me encouragingly. The team was on the edge of qualifying for the district tournament and she had bumped me to the cleanup spot for this rematch. Our first contest hadn't gone so well, but I could see the flicker of hope in Ms. Lin's eyes.

I took a moment to calm myself by shuffling the pages of my notes. On the papers I had written down all the pieces of debate advice I had received in the past few days, a series of chores to be checked off my to-do list, if I ever made a to-do list, which I wouldn't, because making a to-do list was never on my to-do list. But I figured if I followed the advice to a T-square, I had this thing covered.

"Resolved," I said in my serious voice, "that every family should have a robot. As our team has shown, robots are fun, robots are educational, and robots can be taught to cook, which would be a winning argument in itself if you ever tasted my mom's cooking."

A spurt of laughter rose from the crowd as Charlie and

Doug Frayden snickered like hyenas and banged the table. *Tap! Tap! Tap! Tap! Tap!* Ms. Lin always said it helped to bring your personal stories into your debating points, and it seemed to be working. Check.

"Now, the opposition has made all kinds of arguments that are easily rebutted. Yes, robots can kill you in your sleep, but so can little brothers. Have you ever met my little brother? I'd rather take my chances with a robot."

More laughter. My grandfather told me humor was a great way to get a judge's attention, and the way the debate judge was staring at me, I had certainly gotten her attention. Check.

"And yes, robots can take a lot of time programming and reprogramming, but I figure that would be nothing compared to the time-sink of listening to my stepfather's stories, especially with that slow voice of his." I began to speak as if my mouth was full of caramel. "*Gosh, Lizzie, have I ever told you about my junior high drama club?*

"And sure, the robot might break down and have to go to the shop, disappearing for days or even weeks at a time. But then at least you'd know where it was, as opposed to my dad, who you never know where he is.

"Let's just say, when I think of being in the warm embrace of my family, having a robot sounds less a perk and more a necessity."

More laughter, more banging from my teammates. *Tap! Tap! Tap! Tap! Tap!* I was on a roll!

One of the Upper Pattson Middle School debaters stood up and reached out her hand as if she was begging for candy. What she was really begging for was a chance to interrupt me and get in a point of her own in the form of a question. Doug Frayden had advised me that a question would only disrupt the flow of my argument. And my flow was flowing.

"Point of order denied," I said, smiling sweetly as the girl sat down in in a pile of her own disappointment. Check.

"Now, the opposition says we'll be spending so much time with our robots we won't have any time for our friends. Have you seen my friends? Charlie and Doug, stand up. Any questions?"

"Shame, shame," said the Upper Pattson Middle School debaters. Calling out *Shame* was the opposite of the fist tap. The nerve!

"Yes, my life is a shame," I said to my opponents. "Thank you for reminding me of that. Robots at least could be programmed not to insult me with the truth."

More laughter. I looked at the judge. Was it going well? From her face, she seemed to be a bit puzzled. She put up a finger. One minute left. My friend Natalie once told me that shameless honesty was a great way to dupe the unsuspecting. I could out-honest Honest Abe and check off another piece of advice. Time to wallop the judge with the truth.

"But as my time expires, I want to get serious and expand on one of the points made by my teammates. Think of the time robots could save us. They could tidy our rooms. They could do our homework, and surely do a better job. We could even call them Cliff and let them read the stupid books we're assigned and summarize the story for us. Thank you, Cliff! And take-home tests? Need I say more? Those hours saved means freedom for all of us.

"And isn't freedom the very idea on which this great

nation was founded? What patriot would deny us our freedom-granting robots? Don't you love America?"

When in doubt, I once heard somewhere, wave the flag. Check.

Now for the big finish. Always try to inspire, said my mother. Time to inspire their socks off.

"But, you may ask, what would we kids do with that freedom? I'll tell you what we would do. We'd suddenly have time to contemplate life, to explore our possibilities, to grow in ways we never before could have imagined. Think of the seed planted in the earth, spreading out its roots, growing healthy and strong, getting a great head of hair—green, true, but distinctive. That would be us. And when finally pulled out of this untroubled youth of freedom, provided to us by the family robot, we would be something grand and colorful, ready to nourish the whole of humanity. We would become like carrots, only human carrots, and not so orange. This is what robots could do for us. That is what robots could do for the world.

"And that is why every family should have a robot."

Check, check, and checkmate.

FAMILY GOOP

"Why so glum, Elizabeth?" said my mother during dinner that night. "Aren't you enjoying the chicken?"

"Yum," I said as I speared a piece with my fork. My mother had cooked chicken bits, mushrooms, and kale in a goo that looked like shoe polish and tasted like it looked. Dolloped over a glop of sticky brown rice, it was a perfect meal to end this perfect day.

"The chicken is delicious, Mrs. Scali," said Keir McGoogan, sucking up as usual. Keir, who lived with us for the time being, was a pale little kid, short and slight with twisted front teeth and an Irish accent. While to all appearances he was a normal sixth grader, in reality he was older than my grandfather and had an unquenchable thirst for human blood. (Remember the vampire boy I mentioned? There he is!) Did we sleep uneasily with a vampire boy in our midst? A little bit, but not as uneasily as the squirrels.

"Thank you, Keir," said my mother.

"It's just that Elizabeth had a tough day at debate," said Keir. "She misjudged the judge."

I gave Keir a look as he took a noisy slurp of the special shake my mom made him every day to keep his blood-hunger at bay.

"So, I gather debate didn't go well," said my mom.

"Did I tell you how much I like the chicken?" I said.

"Lizzie likes it so much she doesn't want to eat it," said my little brother, Petey. "That way it will last longer."

"I'm simply happy you're participating in after-school activities," said my mother. "You used to run away at the final bell as if the school was on fire."

"The good old days," I said.

"You know, extracurriculars can be so enriching," said Stephen, my stepfather, in his slow, boring voice. "Gosh, Lizzie, have I ever told you about my junior high drama club?"

It took me a moment, but then my fork, swirling in the chicken goop, suddenly froze.

"You were at my debate?"

"I might have stopped in to see the contest," said Stephen. "Nothing like a good competitive debate to get the juices flowing."

"And that was nothing like a good competitive debate," said Keir.

"I didn't mean anything," I sputtered. "I got on a roll and I was hearing so many voices and it just—"

"I thought it was an interesting rebuttal," said Stephen, interrupting me and barreling on past my mother's inquiring looks. "Spirited and sure. But it's important to know your audience. Was the judge a teacher?"

"Unfortunately," I said.

"Then the homework thing might have raised a flag," said Stephen. "I try to know a little bit about the judge before I appear in court. But you were funny, Lizzy, and that's a talent. I always wanted to try my hand at comedy."

"Did you ever do it on a stage, Dad?" said Petey. "I mean with people watching?"

"Once."

"And?" said Petey.

"Once was enough," said Stephen.

"I'm sorry I missed your debate," said my mother. "Maybe next time."

"There might not be a next time," I said.

"You're not thinking of quitting, are you?" said Stephen.

"No, but Ms. Lin might quit me. She wasn't so happy when she heard the results."

"She looked like she had swallowed a frog when she heard the results," said Keir helpfully.

"She told me next time I should think before I speak. And that I should try to avoid talking about carrots."

"Carrots?" said my mother.

"Elizabeth argued that every family should have a robot," said Keir, "because they would turn all the kiddies into carrots."

"Aren't carrots a vegetable, Mom?" said Petey.

"Yes, they are," said my mother.

"And aren't vegetables good?"

"They're good for you," said Stephen. "But no one wants to be turned into a vegetable."

"It was a metaphor!" I said.

"Which is what being turned into a vegetable is," said my mother. "A metaphor. But evidently not a winning one."

I swirled the glop on my plate so I didn't have to look at anyone.

"Well, I thought you were great, Elizabeth," said Stephen. He was that way, my stepfather, never wanting me to feel badly however badly I treated him. And I felt, right then, not just like a loser, but a like an ungrateful jerk, too.

Wasn't I having such a great day? As punishment I took a bite of chicken goop. It felt like my teeth were suddenly glued together. But everything was about to take a turn when later that night, while studying for a social studies test in my room, I heard a knock on my door.

A Confession

Yes, you caught me. I was studying for a social studies test. Don't tell anybody, please. I had promised my mother that I would start trying in school, and I was keeping to it. So, you might ask, if I was trying why was I hiding away in my room?

In the past, what little I studied I studied in the kitchen, while my mother graded papers, so she could see me hard at work. I figured what was the point of putting in time if nobody saw? Perfect logic, right? But now that I was actually trying, I didn't want anyone to see. That way I would have an excuse if my grades stunk. Perfect logic again.

Did anyone ever have more perfect logic than me? I think not.

So with my social studies textbook open, I was taking notes on some dead archduke and what was then called the

Great War—seriously misnamed if you asked me, it should have been called the Most-Idiotic-of-All-Time War—when I heard the knock.

"Go away," I said, without knowing who it was.

"Elizabeth?" said my brother.

"Didn't you hear me? I said go away."

He pushed open the door and stepped inside, closing the door behind him. "I heard."

"But you didn't listen. How so very Peter of you."

"I have to tell you something."

"A confession?" I put down my pen. My brother was only in second grade, but he was a troublemaker to the bone. There was no telling what juicy scandal would come out of his mouth. Stolen cupcakes, lost pants, a science experiment gone very wrong. "Go ahead. This ought to be good."

"Remember at the funeral when I saw Beatrice's ghost and then promised I wouldn't tell anybody?"

"I'm not liking this already," I said. Petey was talking of my very first legal case, when Henry Harrison had been haunted by a teen ghost with a missing head, named Beatrice.

"I told somebody," he said.

"But you promised."

"I did, yeah, except Tyler was telling this story about bees that never happened but everyone was clapping and stuff and I couldn't stand it any longer so I interrupted and said I saw a ghost that my sister helped and the ghost smiled at me. I didn't have any choice. I mean, Tyler was going on and on about those stupid bees."

"Did anyone believe you?"

"They just laughed and passed the story around and everyone was making fun of me. *Oooh, Petey, watch out, there goes another ghost. Better call your sister.*"

"Well then, it serves you right. I hope you learned your lesson."

"What lesson is that?"

"Don't break your promises to me," I said, turning back to my social studies textbook. "I forgive you. You can go."

"But there's more," said my brother. "One day at recess, after I said what I said, while I was sitting alone on the swings, sad because everyone was making fun of me, the girl came and sat in the swing next to me."

"The girl?" I put down my pen and slowly turned back around. "Was she a ghost, too?"

"No, worse. Way worse. A fourth grader."

"That is worse."

"She started talking, just babbling away about nothing, and then she asked me if the thing about the ghost was true. And I said it was. And she said she and her sister see them, too. Or saw them, at least, but can't anymore, because their ghosts were stolen."

"Wait a second," I said. "What?"

"Her name is Janelle and she said their ghosts were stolen. And then she said she wanted to know if you could get them back."

"And you said no, I hope, because no one's supposed to know about what I do with my father and grandfather. That's a rule, Petey. You know that."

"But your friends all know."

I shrugged. "So, what did you say?"

"I said you probably could."

"Oh, Petey."

"I'm sorry, Elizabeth. But she was being nice to me. And you can do anything, I know it. And she was a fourth grader, which means she was scary." He scrunched up his face with terror. "Are you going to tell Mom?"

I looked at my little brother's scrunched-up face and tapped the tip of my pen on my notebook. What to do? What to do?

It was one thing having my father's strange profession infecting me. But if my mother and stepfather thought it was somehow infecting Petey, I'd be sent to a boarding school in a Massachusetts minute. (Is that a thing? I think it's a thing.) But then on the other hand, getting Petey in trouble was always so much fun. To see him cringe as my mother gave him her you-are-in-so-much-trouble face could keep my spirits elevated for a week.

But on the other hand (Who knew I had three hands?), there was this fourth-grade girl who had asked my brother to ask me for help. It turns out I'm a sucker for kids who need help. If I told my mother, she would put the kibosh on the whole stolen ghost thing and I wouldn't be able to help this Janelle.

But on the other hand (Four!), did I tell you how much fun it was getting Petey into trouble?

"Don't worry," I said to my little brother after a long moment of consideration. "I won't tell Mom."

"Thank you, Elizabeth," he said, coming over to give me a hug.

I put up a hand, stopping him in his tracks. "But in exchange, you have to do something for me."

"Make your bed for a week?" said Peter. "Bring you snacks at night?"

"Well, yes," I said, taking advantage of the unexpected opening. "That goes without saying. And my sneakers are getting a little dirty."

"I'll get right on it, Elizabeth."

"But most importantly, next time Mom makes that chicken gunk, in addition to your portion, you have to eat my portion, too."

"Not fair," said Petey.

"I know," I said. "That's why it's the perfect punishment. Two extra forkfuls of goop and you'll never blab about ghosts again."

ANOTHER CORNERSTONE

Grandpop?" I said from my little desk in my grandfather's big office. "Can you steal a ghost?"

"Steal a ghost?" said my grandfather behind stacks of papers and books piled so high on his desk I couldn't see him. "Why would anyone want to do that?"

Normally at the offices of Webster & Spawn I swept and filed, at least when I wasn't filing and sweeping. That was part of what my grandfather called my apprenticeship in the law. But today I was learning how to do fancy legal writing with an old-style pen. Barnabas, the chief clerk, was teaching me calligraphy. "It is quite an important skill for any barrister practicing before the Court of Uncommon Pleas," he had said as he showed me how to make my ABCs. That's what I was working on, drawing a fancy capital *A*, a fancy capital *B*, and a fancy capital *C*. I was making a mess of it.

"A girl came up to my little brother talking about ghosts," I said as I botched the curl at the tail of the *B*.

"Nice young lady?" said my grandfather.

"Probably not. She's a fourth grader." A blotch of ink spat out of the pen. "But she told Petey that her ghosts were stolen and she wanted us to get them back."

"She wants us to get them back?" said my grandfather. "Why, Elizabeth, that's astounding."

"I know. Fourth graders are the worst."

"No, I mean astounding in a good way." I heard the scrape of his chair behind the piles of books and papers and then the tap of his cane. "The Case of the Dastardly Ghost Thief. It has a ring, doesn't it?"

"It sort of does," I admitted.

My grandfather appeared now, bent back, black suit, bald head, bushy eyebrows. That's a lot of *B*s I couldn't draw with that stupid pen. And he was bursting with eagerness as he stood beneath the painting of Daniel Webster, our great ancestor.

"Oh, they'll be writing books about it," said my grandfather. "Avis, get in here right away!"

The door swung open and Avis, the firm's secretary, fluttered in, wide and fierce with sequined glasses. "What is it? Who died?"

"Grab hold of yourself, Avis," said my grandfather. "No one died. We might have ourselves a new case. Send in my son and Barnabas, please, we must discuss this immediately. And prepare the usual documents."

"What name do I use?" cawed Avis. "What name?"

"Well?" said my grandfather, turning to me.

"Janelle something?" I said.

"Something?" said my grandfather. "That's an unusual surname. Greek, is it?"

"And she has a sister," I said.

"Get right to it, Avis, no time to waste. Janelle Something and her sister, Somebody Something, could be two new clients when we're in dire need of them."

Avis looked at me and blinked enough for me to know she would be leaving the names blank on the documents, before fluttering away and slamming the door behind her.

"Do we really need to bring my father in on this?" I said.

"Yes indeed," said my grandfather. "He'll be the one handling the case in court."

A few moments later we heard a knock on the door and my stomach tightened. There was a time when I never saw my father. After he divorced my mother, he sort of disappeared from my life, and that was hard to handle. *Why doesn't he love me?* Then, after I rescued him from a demon's dungeon and started working in my grandfather's office, he looked at everything I did with a pained expression, as if it was such a burden for him to have me around. *Why does he hate me?* Now, when he'd finally accepted that I'd be working here, he tried so so hard to be so so supportive that I wanted to scream. *Why can't he just act like a human being instead of a guidance counselor?*

Was it me? Was I the problem? I didn't think so. As far as I can tell I'm never the problem. I mean I was certainly stinking up the thing I had with my stepfather, but my relationship with my father has always been odd. It just seemed like such hard work. I sometimes thought how wonderful it had been when he was trapped on the other side.

"Eli. Barnabas. Come in," said my grandfather. "Elizabeth has brought us such wonderful news."

"Wonderful," echoed my father as he stepped into the office with Barnabas and closed the door behind them. My father's big black glasses and mop of dark hair surrounded the corn-cob smile plastered on his face. Barnabas stood behind him, tall and pale with a long frock coat and a starched collar. Starchy and Husk.

"But before we get to the news, I have something for Elizabeth," said my grandfather. He reached into his vest pocket and pulled out a strange assortment of keys on a brass ring. "This, my dear, is for you."

"Thank you?" I said, taking hold of the brass ring. One of the keys had a human tooth at the end.

"Ivanov, the doorman at the Court of Uncommon Pleas, sent these over. Your very own keys to the courtroom in the City Hall tower."

"Why would I need my own keys? I always go with one of you."

"It is not about need, Elizabeth," said Barnabas. "It is the honor of it. Every barrister gets their own keys."

"But you have keys, too, don't you, Barnabas?"

"Sadly, no. You grandfather lets me use his."

"I guess we should give a cheer," said my father before letting out the most awkward "Hooray" I had ever heard. But his "Hooray" was enough to get "hooray"s from Barnabas and my grandfather. I'm embarrassed to admit it, but it felt pretty good.

"Now, what about this news?" said my father.

"We have a new case!" said my grandfather. "The Case of the Dastardly Ghost Thief. It has a ring, doesn't it?"

"Surprisingly, sir, it actually does," said Barnabas. "And I'm sure if Mistress Elizabeth brought it in, it is a case of the highest quality."

"On the other hand," I said, "one of the possible plaintiffs is a fourth grader."

"That's trouble," said my father.

"I know," I said. "What is it with them? They graduate third grade and then, bam, right off the rails."

"Not to put a damper on the celebration," said Barnabas, "but I'm not sure one can steal a ghost."

"Precisely," said my grandfather. "That's what makes it so intriguing."

"Why can't you steal a ghost?" I said. "You can steal everything else. Jewels, cars, a lollipop."

"To prove a theft in court you need to be able to prove possession by the owner," said my father. "But can anyone possess a ghost?"

"This is all true," said my grandfather. "We've had cases of possession by a ghost, but never possession of a ghost."

"Couldn't it be something like being kidnapped?" I said. "You can be sued for kidnapping, right?"

"Yes, of course," said Barnabas. "But to bring a legal case, Mistress Elizabeth, you need to be able to prove the plaintiffs themselves have a real injury—something like a broken leg, or maybe loss of property or reputation. That is one of the requirements of what is called standing, a cornerstone of the law. Standing proves you aren't wasting the court's time, and also ensures that the issues in the case are argued by parties with real interests at stake."

"If someone puts up an ugly statue," said my father, "you might walk by and want to sue, but where is your injury?"

"Doesn't it depend on how ugly it is?" I said.

"No," said my grandfather. "Unless it turns you into stone, such as the statue of Medusa that was part of a case we had many years ago. Our plaintiff certainly had standing. With knees of stone, he could hardly sit. Very disturbing."

"The ghosts that were stolen would surely have the type of injury that is necessary," said Barnabas, "so they could bring a suit, but it is unclear if any living being would have standing in such a case."

"The question then becomes," said my grandfather, "how have our fourth grader and her sister been injured?"

"If you want me to set up a meeting with them, I could find out," I said.

"I think you should, Elizabeth," said my father with an awkward smile. "If it's not too much of a bother."

"And also find out if they're related to the deceased," said my grandfather. "That might help prove possession."

"How could that help prove possession of a ghost?" said my father.

"A legal principle known as universal succession, my boy," said my grandfather. "A cornerstone of the law since Roman times, thousands of years ago."

"That's a lot of years," I said.

"Indeed," said my grandfather. "Back then, it mostly involved the possession of land, of course. Everything was about land in those days. But this principle allows an heir to take possession over many other things, too. Maybe even the spiritual remains of a fallen ancestor."

My father looked at my grandfather like he had just belched up an apple, but then my father smiled. "That's pretty good. How did you come up with that?"

"My own father taught me that the law has many facets," said my grandfather. "Hold a case up to the light and turn it this way, then that way. Things show up you would never expect."

"This new case has got me thinking," said my father.

"Trouble," I said.

"Didn't you tell me, Dad, that you got a call from Chive Winterbottom asking to withdraw her case from the Court of Uncommon Pleas?"

"It was an action to eject a ghost that had been singing opera in her attic," said my grandfather. "Torture of the worst stripe, if you ask me. But Chive—a wonderful woman, Chive, quite bright and sprightly—called to say she had taken care of the spirit by other means."

"That's peculiar," said Barnabas. "We've received similar calls from two other clients. Both actions in ejectment, both cases withdrawn because the situations were taken care of by other means."

"Chive told me she used a ghost whisperer," said my grandfather. "She even told me the name. I have it here, somewhere."

My grandfather banged his cane over to his desk and started searching through his documents. It looked like a flight of paper doves were flocking around his head.

"Ah, here it is," he said finally. "Ramsberger."

"Ramsberger?" said Barnabas.

"Fred Ramsberger," said my grandfather. "As untrust-worthy a name as one could imagine. Especially if you're a ram. Elizabeth, your case of the stolen ghosts could be bigger than we imagine."

"You sound quite concerned, Mr. Webster," said Barnabas.

"Of course I'm concerned," said my grandfather. "Three such cases gone. And how many never brought to us in the first place? I was wondering why our revenues have been down. I must pay rent, you know, even if I pay it to myself. But the idea of a ghost whisperer in our midst is even more worrying. It is one thing to steal a ghost, but quite another thing if you could whisper away its autonomy at the same time."

"What's autonomy, Grandpop?"

"It is the power to think and act for yourself. It is what the great Justice Cardozo called 'the indispensable condition of nearly every other form of freedom.' If you could control a ghost's thoughts and actions with a whisper, you could do boatloads of mischief. With just one! Now, think about the situation if you have stolen more than one."

"You'd have a gang of ghosts," said Barnabas.

"Precisely," said my grandfather. "And one can only imagine what mischief someone with the name Fred Rams-berger could do with that."

ELECTROPOP

Mr. Armbruster was reading us a poem in social studies class as we discussed World War I. Yeah, really. A poem. About a war. Such fun!

He stood at the front of the class with the book in his hand, bow tie tight, gray Afro high, his arm outstretched dramatically as he read. The poem was about a guy named Flanders and his grandfathers, or something like that. I wasn't really listening until Mr. Armbruster read the following:

> *We are the Dead. Short days ago*
> *We lived, felt dawn, saw sunset glow,*
> *Loved and were loved, and now we lie,*
> *In Flanders fields.*

Whoa! I still didn't know who this Flanders fellow was with all the fields, but those lines certainly poked my head. And frightened me a bit, too. I leaned over to Natalie Delgado and whispered, "Do you want to hear a ghost story?"

"Now?" she said. "I'm trying to sleep."

"Not now, this afternoon."

"Whose is it?"

"Some fourth grader."

"Ahh," she said with an obvious lack of enthusiasm. "I can't."

"Why not?" I whined.

"I'm getting my nails done with Debbie. She found this great new shade of pink. They call it Electropop."

"Wow," I said, meaning it.

"Yeah, it's so bright it has its own rhythm track."

"Natalie," said Mr. Armbruster from the front of the room as he stared at the two of us. "What do you make of Mr. McCrae's poem?"

Natalie gave me an angry look for getting her in trouble and then said, "It's like a ghost story?"

"Yes, exactly. Very good. You were paying attention. I'm impressed."

"As you should be," said Natalie, to laughter from the class.

Natalie had been my best friend since kindergarten and was the best investigator ever. She had this knack of picking up the scent of a story and then following it like a blood-hound until she grabbed the truth in her teeth. I was hoping she would help me judge Janelle's crazy stolen-ghost story. So when Mr. Armbruster got back to boring us with talk of other poems about the war—it seemed as if they did more writing than fighting—I whispered to Natalie, "Please?"

"I told you, I can't," she said.

"Do the whole Electropop thing tomorrow."

"But I promised Debbie. Ask Keir."

I looked to the other side of me, where Keir sat actually paying attention. There was something sad on his face, which made sense since his father died in that war. He didn't seem in the mood for a ghost story. I turned back to Natalie. "He's got soccer practice," I said.

"Then ask Henry."

"He's been a little weird with me lately. I think he realized he's too cool to hang around me anymore."

"About time," said Natalie.

"Come on. I need you," I said.

"You should have thought of that before you made the appointment without asking me first. I'm quite in demand, you know." She looked at me with that Natalie look, eyes bright, smile so sweet it wasn't sweet at all, and said, "Electropop."

Did I feel betrayed? I did. I mean, how were her nails more important than my stolen ghosts? And how did Debbie Benner, who Natalie only became pals with because of my ghost stuff, become more important to her than me? Why couldn't she just go with my flow?

When, after the next bell, I spied her and Debbie Benner walking down the hallway, their heads leaning together as they talked, I felt a buzz in my chest, like a hornet was flying around in there. And later, when I was sitting in a clearing in the woods above Whistler's Creek, looking at my bare, boring nails—a tragic sight, really—I was feeling quite sorry for myself.

"So, can you help us, Elizabeth?" said Petey's fourth grader. "Can you get our ghosts back?"

I shook visions of manicures out of my head and looked up. "It depends on what actually happened."

"What happened is that some thief in a creepy car stole our ghosts."

Janelle Burton was a lively girl with twin braids and a chattery manner. Her sister, Sydney, sitting next to her on the rock, was not so chattery. A sophomore at the high school, she had the same light brown skin as her little sister and was intimidatingly tall and pretty, but her face was expressionless and her voice was flat. Not sad or bored, or anything really, just flat. A graph going nowhere.

I was perched on a rock across from the sisters. Petey, who had set up the meeting by the creek and begged me to let him come, was sitting cross-legged on the ground down a bit on the path, scratching at the dirt with a stick.

"Do you know the name of this ghost thief?" I said.

"Our aunt and uncle hired him, but they won't tell us his name," said Janelle. "But you can't miss his creepy car. It has no roof, the engine is on the outside, and sticking out the back are two huge light bulbs lit up with these crazy bits of color."

"On the side of the car are the letters R, I, and P, if that helps," said Sydney.

"Right after our granddaddy died," said Janelle, "our aunt and uncle moved in. To take care of us, they said, but I think they care more about the house."

"Shush," said Sydney.

"It's true, and you know it. They even used Granddaddy's money to dig up his garden in the back and put in a pool."

"A pool?" I said, with maybe a touch too much enthusiasm.

"We liked the garden," said Sydney.

"But after they made all their fancy changes," said Janelle, "they started to realize the house might be haunted. First, they got some lady with a funny hat to check it out. When she confirmed that the house was haunted, she gave them the card of the ghost thief. I was looking out from the under the stairway and saw her do it. Right after that, I came home from school one afternoon and saw the thief drive away."

"Who was the lady with the hat?" I said.

"Madame something," said Janelle. "Batzky, maybe?"

"Batzky?" I thought on that for a moment, thinking of a story my mom had told me. "Could it be Blavatsky? Madame Blavatsky?"

Sydney lifted her head to look at me and her eyes widened. "Yes, that's it exactly," she said. "How did you know?"

"I think my mom had some business with her a long time ago," I said. "Were the ghosts the ghost thief stole related to you?"

The sisters didn't say anything right off. Sydney looked back down at the ground and Janelle looked at Sydney. For a time, the only sounds were the breeze meandering through the baby leaves of the trees and Petey's stick scratching at the ground.

Then without looking up Sydney said, "Our parents died five years ago."

She said it as flatly as she said everything else, but it registered like a gut punch. What do you say to that? And then, in halts and starts, they told us the story of the magical music box.

THE MUSIC BOX

Janelle and Sydney had been happy children, full of laughter and spirit, until the accident.

Sydney spent her days, when not in school, reading and drawing, playing basketball. Janelle, six years younger and just about to enter kindergarten, ran around like a crazy chipmunk. Their mother taught the girls to climb trees and kick a soccer ball, her short blond hair bouncing as she scampered around with them in the park. Their father sang them to sleep at night, holding them in his strong dark arms and singing in his sweet voice. *Only you can make all this world seem right.* In their small apartment in the city, life was so ordinary and yet so perfect it felt as if it could never be any other way.

Then a rainy night, a curve in the road, a slick of mud, a guardrail that didn't hold.

That the children's parents specified in their will that the girls would be raised by their father's father, a grumpy old gump, had surprised everyone, the girls included. Their grandfather lived in a spooky stone house high on a hill outside the city. On the rare occasions when their father had brought the girls to see their grandfather, the girls would sit with their father on a leather couch in the library as the dour old man looked at them sourly, his mouth working as if he had a piece of gristle between his teeth.

In the middle of the library stood a game table on which sat a sparkly music box. A little statue of a young ballet dancer with butterfly wings was imprisoned in a glass dome on top of the box, her tiny feet barely touching the golden dancefloor. The girls were never, ever allowed to click the golden lever that started the music.

Once, when Janelle bounded off the couch and reached for the music box, her grandfather snapped, "Don't touch that. It's not a toy."

"But it looks like a toy, Grandfadder," Janelle said.

He glared at the sisters before saying to their father, "The girls must be getting tired. Take them home, boy. And maybe you should teach them some manners while you're at it."

The girls' first days in the big stone house after their parents' deaths were awash with sadness. They moved through the rooms and gardens like zombies, touching the old fussy wallpaper with their fingertips to be sure at least something was real. They had separate rooms in the new house, but often Janelle crept into bed with her big sister so neither would be alone.

Dinner each evening was at the long table in the formal dining room. Their grandfather sat at one end, the girls sat at the other. A vase full of bare branches sat between them as Phyllis, the old lady who lived in the house and cooked for the old man, served their meals. In the quiet they could hear the slurp of their grandfather's soup, the way his teeth clacked when he chewed.

"Why did my mommy and daddy give us to you?" said Janelle one night at dinner.

"Eat your soup," said their grandfather.

"It's not fair," said Janelle. "It's too sad here."

"Shush," said Sydney.

"We're done with the soup," called out their grandfather, and Phyllis bustled in with a tray.

The house was a prison of loneliness and grief. The rooms were dim and uncomfortable, the basements were damp and filled with spiders, and there was the ever-present stink of the ointment the old man massaged into his sore muscles and the cheap cigars he smoked. Still, the girls were given the run of the property, allowed to explore every gloomy room in the house, every room but one.

The girls were never, ever allowed in the library.

"Why can't we see the books, Grandfadder?" asked Janelle one night at dinner.

"You want books, go to the public library," said their grandfather. "I pay my taxes."

"But that was the room we went to with Daddy. Why can't we play there? And what about the music box?"

"We're done eating," called out their grandfather. "You can take the dishes now, Phyllis, and there won't be no dessert."

Being kept out of the library seemed so unfair to Janelle that she was constantly trying the library door to see if it was still locked. She so wanted to sit on the couch where her daddy had sat and remember him hugging her tightly in his arms. She dreamed of clicking on that music box and finally hearing its song. But the library door was always locked as if the old man was keeping it shut just to spite them.

"I hate him," said Janelle one night when the sisters were alone in Sydney's room after dinner.

"Shush," said Sydney. "He might be listening."

"I don't care. He's so mean and he hates us."

"He's trying," said Sydney.

"He's not trying very hard."

"Give him time," said Sydney. And that's what they did, because what choice did they have? But nothing changed. Living with her grandfather would have been intolerable for Janelle, if it wasn't for the strange night sightings.

Janelle kept her door open when she slept to let the hallway light in—since her parents' accident she'd been scared of the dark—and sometimes in the middle of the night she would open her eyes and the old man would be in the hall just standing there, staring. It should have set her blood to fizzling, but there was something in his face that comforted Janelle, something that reminded her that the old man had lost someone, too. Eventually, though they still missed their mother and father like they were missing an arm, both girls started to feel things becoming almost normal in that house.

And then their grandfather, clutching at his chest in the middle of dinner, died, too.

That was when their mother's sister and her husband

moved into the house with all the noisy cousins. It didn't take long for the girls to realize that their aunt and uncle seemed to care more about the house than they cared about the girls themselves. The girls now not only missed their father and mother, but their grandfather, too.

On the night Janelle first saw the old man's ghost peering at her through her open door, she smiled at the sight of him, turned over, and fell back to sleep. It was only later that the girl woke up with a start and remembered that her grandfather was dead.

The next morning, when she told Sydney, her sister shook her head and explained that it had been a dream. But Janelle knew what she knew. That night she stayed awake as late as she could, staring through the gap into the hallway. Nothing.

The next night, nothing.

But the evening after that she went right to sleep, tired from all that staying awake, and when she woke again in the middle of the night, there he was, peering in at her with the same sad face he had when he was alive. As she stared at the figure in the doorway, it turned and floated away. Janelle slipped out of bed and carefully stepped into the hallway on her bare feet.

Her grandfather shimmered blue as he floated silently across the floorboards, looking back once to make sure she was following. A breeze that smelled of his pain ointment and cigars darted around the hallway. The old man descended the stairs as smoothly as if he was going down on an escalator. From the top of the stairs she saw him float to the library door and then slip right through it.

The library, locked to them during their time with their grandfather, had remained locked after his death. While the aunt and uncle lavishly renovated the rest of the house with the girls' trust funds, the library remained untouched. According to the strict provisions of their grandfather's will, no one—NO ONE—was permitted in the library.

It was as if there was something monstrous in that room that their grandfather was protecting even past death.

Janelle swallowed her fears and followed the ghost down the stairs. When she tried the knob on the library door, this time it turned easily. When she pushed slightly on the door, it began to open.

Shocked and suddenly terrified, Janelle yanked the door closed and ran back up the stairs to her sister's room. Shaking Sydney awake, she told her everything she had seen and done.

"It's only a dream," said Sydney. "Go back to bed."

"It's not a dream. It's real. Let me show you."

"I'm sleeping."

"Sydney!"

"Okay, okay. Calm down. If I prove to you it's all in your head, then will you let me sleep?"

"Yes, hurry now before Grandfadder locks the door again."

"Oh, Janelle," Sydney said, shaking her head as she slid out of the bed.

Slowly, silently, they crept along the hallway, not wanting to wake up their aunt or uncle or any of the cousins. Leaning on the handrail to lessen the noise, they climbed down the stairs. As they descended, a breeze swirled around them, smelling now not of the old man but of something dank and thick, a soggy field of mud after a rain. The damp breeze whipped their hair as they stepped off the bottom of the stairs and approached the library door.

When Sydney reached for the knob, a spark jumped from the metal and bit her hand.

"Ow!"

"Go on," whispered Janelle, shielding herself behind her big sister as she clutched at Sydney's arms.

Slowly Sydney reached again for the knob and took hold.

The knob turned, almost as if on its own.

The door opened, almost as if on its own.

The girls stepped forward, as if being drawn by some irresistible force.

The room was dark, with no shimmery blue grandfather hovering. Sydney shook her head at Janelle before turning on the light. And that was when they saw it.

The music box was sitting on the game table in the middle of the room, but the ballerina with the butterfly wings was no longer under the glass dome. And she was shimmering in the light from above, shimmering as if she was waiting just for them.

Janelle couldn't help herself. She had to try it. She'd been waiting her entire life to try it. As she stepped forward, Sydney felt a burst of fear and reached out to stop her—what horrible door would they be opening with that little music box?—but Janelle ducked under Sydney's outstretched arm and went right up to the box, took hold, and pushed the lever.

Click.

ONLY YOU

"W hen the ballerina with the butterfly wings began to spin, we didn't recognize the song at first," said Sydney in that clearing above Whistler's Creek. "It was just notes being plucked on the mechanism, something high and stupid. After the buildup it seemed silly. Janelle turned and looked at me and I could see the disappointment in her face. Poor Janelle. And then out of the scraps of notes a song became clear."

"A song we hadn't heard in years but both knew by heart," said Janelle. "From when our family was still whole and we were happy."

"And Janelle wasn't trying so hard," said Sydney.

"And Sydney still knew how to laugh," said Janelle. "As the music box played, we could both hear Daddy singing that song again. And we started singing along. *Only you can make all this world seem right.* And that's when it happened."

That's when it happened.

While the song played, Janelle and Sydney's mother and father appeared. The sisters could see their beautiful faces. They could feel their kisses and their hugs. They could hear their mother and father tell them that they were loved, that they were missed. They could hear them apologize for leaving them alone.

It was all too much to take.

In the middle of a hope and a memory, both sisters broke down and cried. Their parents were in the music, in the room, in their hearts. The song played two or three more times before the box clicked off and the music stopped.

And their parents were gone.

Gone.

Sydney ran over and wound the brass knob on the bottom of the box and clicked to start the song again, but their parents did not come back. They tried again and again, each time to failure. And through their tears and grief the girls began to wonder if it had been real, if they truly had been visited at all.

When the sisters finally gave up for the night, afraid of being caught in the forbidden room by the aunt and uncle, they turned off the light and closed the door behind them. Before they went back up to their rooms, Janelle gave the door a final check.

It was locked.

The next time their grandfather's ghost appeared at Janelle's door, the sisters were ready. Janelle hopped out of bed right into a pair of soft slippers and tiptoed to Sydney's room. At the first shake, Sydney was out of bed and slippered too. Following their grandfather's spirit down the stairs, with the same mud-smelling breeze, they looked back and forth before slipping into the now-unlocked library. Then, while Sydney carefully held the music box in her lap, her fingers on the winding mechanism on the bottom, Janelle clicked the lever.

As the ballerina began to spin and the magical song began to play, Sydney slowly wound the brass knob to keep it playing. And then they waited, but they didn't have to wait for long.

Their parents appeared again with hugs and kisses and, this time, questions. The sisters could see them more clearly now, including their mussed clothes with spots of mud and tangles of vine. The questions the parents asked were silly, so boring as to be funny, questions about school and friends. Janelle tried to ask questions of her own, like how they came back from the dead and what did ghosts eat, but her parents wouldn't answer, they only asked more questions. And so the girls detailed their lives, what was going on in their classes, how it was living with their aunt and uncle, and all the changes that were being made to the big old house.

"A pool?" said their father.

"Where the garden in the back used to be."

"Your grandfather won't like that," said their father.

"Be careful with your aunt and uncle," their mother said. "Don't let them know about us."

"We won't," said Sydney.

The session ended when their mother finally sent them off to bed so they could get some sleep before school. They complained, but even as the song played on, the ghosts kissed their children and disappeared.

The visits began to seem so normal, they became almost boring. Brilliantly boring. Life with their ghost parents became not unlike life when their parents were still alive. They talked about their days, sometimes they were scolded, they made stupid jokes. The dead parents even helped their living children with their homework. The sisters would bring their papers into the room and their mother would work with them on the math, and their father on the essays.

"A comma's not right there," said their father. "Maybe a semicolon."

"What's a semicolon?" said Janelle.

"A semicolon is very dangerous," said their father. "Very adult. Maybe when you're older I can explain it to you."

That made them laugh, all five of them, because by then their grandfather had started taking part, too. He'd be hovering in the corner, smiling as they talked about nothing and everything. Talked like a family. An almost-perfect family. Perfectly ordinary, perfectly strange.

The sisters knew their aunt and uncle suspected something. Their uncle mentioned hearing music playing in the middle of the night and once, when the sisters were sneaking down the hallway, Janelle thought she heard the squeak of a door. Still, whatever the risks, they wouldn't, couldn't stop their midnight visits. Even during the daytime, when the sisters sat in their rooms, or ate in the kitchen, or played in the garden, they could feel their parents' and grandfather's presence and it gave them exactly what they needed to make it through each day.

The feeling was like a soft hug, a kiss on the cheek, a ruffle of the hair. And the sisters knew, both of them, that they were not alone in this world and that they were deeply loved.

Until the ghost thief came and took their ghosts away.

"After our ghosts were stolen," said Janelle, "we didn't know what to do."

"Who could we turn to?" said Sydney. "Our teachers? The police? There was no one."

"And then Peter started talking about seeing a ghost and how his big sister found the ghost's head and saved her," said Janelle.

"My little brother talks a lot," I said, looking at Peter, who was still scratching with that stick.

"I know what that's like," said Sydney.

"We miss our mom and dad and granddaddy so much," said Janelle. "We really need your help, Elizabeth. Can you? Help us?"

I looked at Sydney and Janelle and wondered at all they had been through. A voice inside me was saying, *Help them! Help them!* But another voice was telling me that this whole story might actually be a shared delusion between them and that I might be helping them more if I told them to forget about their ghosts and get on with their lives. But then another voice was telling me that with all the missing ghosts around town, this ghost thief thing might be something we needed to get involved in.

There were a lot of voices pounding around in my head, like during the debate, and I wished I had my friends with me, not only Natalie, but also Henry and Keir. I always seemed stronger and surer about things with them around. But I looked at my little brother, still sitting down the path a ways but now staring up at me with the same pleading look in his eyes that I saw in the girls' eyes, and I knew what I had to do.

"Yes," I said. "I can help you."

I opened my backpack and took out the agreements that would allow Janelle and Sydney to become official clients of the law firm of Webster & Spawn.

It wouldn't be so tough, I figured. My grandfather would handle the procedural parts, my father would handle the trial. All I had to do was find the ghost thief so we would know who to put in the complaint as our defendant and then work on my calligraphy while they won the case. Hooray! Easy peasy pumpkin pie.

But nothing in this world is as easy as putting peas into a pumpkin pie. Getting to the bottom of the story of the ghost thief would be harder and more terrifying than I could ever have imagined. And the path would start with Natalie getting her fortune read, because, well, of course it would.

CRYSTAL BALL

"Somethink is comink," said Madame Blavatsky in her exotic reading room. "Somethink big. Somethink bad."

"What are you seeing?" said Natalie, leaning forward.

"Danger," whispered the woman.

"Yikes alive!"

Madame Blavatsky was old and thin with white-powdered cheeks and a chin that curved out almost far enough to touch her nose. Pinned to the front of her bright blue turban was a silver salamander pin. She sat across from Natalie at a table on which were set a deck of cards, a lit red candle, and a crystal ball. Atop the lace tablecloth she held tightly to one of Natalie's pinkly-manicured hands.

And, I have to say, the pinkly was electric.

Natalie and I had ridden our bikes to the psychic's storefront, with the neon sign advertising palm readings, tarot readings, and séances. It hadn't been hard to convince Natalie to join me on this outing. All I had to mention was the psychic and she was in. "I'll have to cancel with Debbie, we were going miniskirt shopping—can you say pleather?—but I could use a good reading. I have so many questions."

This was a competition I wasn't happy playing, having to win my best friend's attention with ever more elaborate events—what next, a balloon ride?—but I needed someone to sit at the table and suck up Madame Blavatsky's attention while I remained the unnamed friend observing from a distance, with a plan of my own, of course.

"You are right to be concerned," said Madame Blavatsky. "Very concerned. For small sum, I can do consultation."

"How small a sum?"

"For you, and only because you are so younk, twenty dollar."

"It just so happens," said Natalie, "that's all I have in my pocket."

"Zis is not a job for amateurs," said Madame Blavatsky, holding out her hand.

As Natalie forked over her cash and Madame Blavatsky prepared for her consultation, I sat quietly in the corner and examined the psychic reading room. The walls were red, the velvet drapes were closed so tightly not a spark of sunlight slipped into the room. In the fireplace stood a bronze statue of a woman with two scepters and two horns and two fabulous braids of hair that fell well below her waist. For some reason I was thinking of changing my hair once again—how would I look in braids? Good, right? Pippy

LongSpawn—when I noticed a table in the corner covered with pamphlets and business cards.

"We are ready," said Madame Blavatsky. Suddenly the electric chandelier overhead went dark and the only light was the flicker of flame beside the crystal ball.

"Place your hands on ze scryink ball," she said.

"This?" said Natalie, pointing to the crystal ball.

"Zat."

Natalie did as she was told. Madame Blavatsky then raised her gnarled hands to the black ceiling, on which was painted a five-sided star with a goat's head in the middle and a Hebrew letter at each point.

"We seek reflection of ze past," she chanted. "Wisdom's warnink of what will last. Oh, spirits, tell us right and wronk. Show us on which path we belonk."

When she finished her chant, the ball of crystal began to glow dimly. Natalie yanked her hands away as the glowing ball grew brighter and brighter. Madame Blavatsky waved her hands dramatically and then leaned forward to stare into the orb.

Natalie leaned forward, too, and so did I.

"I see...I see...I see you steppink into danger," said Madame Blavatsky. "I see you and your little friend blunderink where you don't belonk. 'Natalie,' I call. 'Other girl,' I call. 'Don't go zere,' I say. 'Stop!' But you two don't listen. You keep goink, goink. And now my warninks are too late. You are trapped."

"Trapped?" said Natalie.

"Trapped, yes. And zere are more of zem zan you can imagine. And zey are hungry for blood."

"Whose blood?" said Natalie.

"Your blood. Zey are ze spirits of ze dead. And the evil spirits are comink closer, closer. You are trapped, I say, trapped, and they are comink closer. Closer. CLOSER! And zen...And zen..."

Madame Blavatsky raised her hands high as she readied to tell us our horrible fate when the light in the crystal ball died and, with a shout, she collapsed, her head smacking the table.

Thwop!

While the Madame's head was still on the lace, I slid over to the collection of pamphlets and cards and checked them out in the dim candlelight. Financial readings by a wealth psychic? Money! Spiritual cleanses by a juicing psychic? Carrot juice! Ajax Plumbing Company? Plumbing! A stack of cards caught my eye. As I grabbed the top card and slipped it into my pocket, I glanced at Madame Blavatsky.

Her head was still on the table, but one eye now was open and aimed right at me. I looked at Natalie to see if she saw what I saw, but she was slumped in her seat.

And then the Madame spoke.

"Elizabeth Webster," she said, her voice frighteningly familiar, three voices actually, mismatched and horrible. "You will interfere with my plans no more. My time is coming, and so is yours. Run away and hide, little girl, before I catch you in my teeth like a toad."

I was frozen in place as if struck by a frying pan, until the Madame's eye snapped closed and I realized I had stopped breathing.

Breathe, I told myself. *Breathe.*

But I had reason to be breathless. I knew that horrible voice, I had heard it before coming from the mouth of a cast-iron Pilgrim and then later from the witness stand in court. It was the voice of the demon Redwing.

I was sitting in the corner, breathing finally but still shaking with fear, when Madame Blavatsky shuddered back to consciousness.

"Oh my," she said as she raised her head and reset her turban. "What happened, my darlinks?"

"I don't know," said Natalie, awake again, apparently without knowing she had been asleep. "You passed out when you were about to tell us our fate? What did you see?"

She looked at Natalie as if through a fog. "I don't remember," she said. "Sometimes it comes over me like a dream, and zen I forget when I'm awake again. Was it bad?"

"It wasn't good," said Natalie.

"If you want another consultation, zat might be more expensive."

"How expensive?"

"Zree hundred dollars."

"That's exactly what I thought you'd say," said Natalie.

"Perhaps you want to learn business?"

"Maybe I do," said Natalie, looking around as if she was already redecorating.

"I could use apprentice," said Madame Blavatsky. "Ze place gets so dusty."

And then Madame Blavatsky turned to stare at me.

"How is your mother doink, young one?" she said. "I haven't seen her in many years. Did it go well with her and her friend?"

I squinted at her to stop my voice from shaking. "No," I said. "It did not."

R.I.P.

"I think I could do it," said Natalie as we walked our bikes away from Madame Blavatsky's storefront. We passed the cheese shop and the French pastry shop, but I was too scared by the demon's warning to think about putting anything in my stomach.

"Do what?" I said, not really listening.

"You know," said Natalie. "Become the old lady's apprentice."

"Don't be silly," I said.

"I'm not being silly. I've always thought I had psychic powers. There was this one time I was certain we were going to have a snow day and you know what?"

"It snowed?" I said.

"Exactly. I could be Madame Natalie, psychic to the stars."

"Either that or a TV weatherperson," I said.

"To be honest," said Natalie as she started waving her free hand back and forth, "with both jobs it's all in the gestures."

"Did you hear anything weird come out of Madame Blavatsky's mouth when she was passed out?"

"Everything coming out of Madame Blavatsky's mouth was weird," said Natalie. "That's why it was so much fun. But she woke up only about a second after she collapsed. Why, what do you think she said?"

"Nothing much," I lied.

"What's that in your pocket?"

"My pocket?"

"You keep patting it to make sure something's still there."

I stopped and looked at Natalie as she walked away. When she turned around, she was smiling sweetly.

"You're getting entirely too good at this detecting thing," I said.

"Thank you. But maybe it's not just detecting." She started waving her hand. "Maybe it is somezink more. Maybe I can see ze truth."

"Yeah, okay, see ze truth in this." I caught up to her, pulled out the card I had swiped off the Madame's table, and handed it over. Natalie gave a squinty look.

"The Ramsberger Institute of the Paranormal?" she read.

"Remember I told you about Janelle and Sydney's story and the initials on the ghost thief's car?"

"Yes," she said, a smile breaking out. "You think?"

"I'm pretty sure," I said. "My grandfather said this Ramsberger guy might have been stealing ghosts all over the city."

"Yikes." She took another look at the card. "Hey, I know where this is. It's not far. Let's go and check it out."

And without even waiting for me to say okay, she popped her helmet on and started off on her bike. It didn't take much to get Natalie hooked on a case, just a crazed medium and a ghostly mystery. She dashed down the commercial strip and then turned right, into a section of the neighborhood with houses and yards and dogs, then left and right again. I pumped the pedals to catch up.

"Remember Amira?" she said when we finally rode side by side.

"The creepy girl in third grade?"

"She wasn't creepy, she was mysterious and cool. We hung out some before she moved to Texas. She lived in the same neighborhood as your Ramsberger thing."

"You hung out with Amira? Sleepovers and stuff?"

"A couple."

"When you were doing this hanging out, why didn't you invite me?"

"Amira thought you were creepy."

"And you told her I was mysterious and cool?"

"Something like that. This is it."

She pressed the brake on her bike and jumped off the seat. I stopped beside her and took a long look at the old house set on a large lot with an iron fence around it.

"Wow," I said. "Talk about creepy."

We walked our bikes farther down the block, laid them on their sides next to the sidewalk, and sat on the curb, pretending we were doing anything other than staring at the house, though that's exactly what we were doing.

It was cockeyed, that house—narrow and tall and blue, with a pointy top, like a church tower. A porch wrapped around the front of the house, and on the steps leading to the porch were two stone statues of dogs with human faces on them. A bunch of landscapers worked on the lawn and the bushes. A painter was high on a ladder painting the wood around the windows.

"It doesn't look like a business," said Natalie.

"What's with those dogs on the steps? They seem to have the face of Martha Washington."

"You're right," said Natalie. "They're Martha Washington dogs."

"And what's with the lawn people?" I said.

There was something truly weird about the lawn people. First, they wore long pants and long-sleeved shirts, with gloves and bandannas over their faces as if they were still in virus quarantine. With their wide hats and safety goggles, you couldn't see a crack of flesh peeking through their outfits. Even the painter up on the ladder wore the same outfit. And all around them was this strange hum.

"They could be invisible, covered up like that," said Natalie.

"Yeah," I said. "Or ghosts."

Natalie turned her head to me. "You don't think..."

"I don't know what I think," I said. "But they do seem to sort of float across the lawn and...Uh-oh."

Natalie slowly turned her face back to the house.

A man had come out of the doorway and now stood on the porch. He was tall and thin with a huge bald head the color of an orange Creamsicle and a pair of round green sunglasses. His brown leather jacket had a fur collar and his heavy boots had high metal shin guards, like he was about to play soccer against a team of Transformers. He stood there puffing away on a short cigar in his teeth and staring at the figures working on his lawn.

"He seems nice," said Natalie.

"A nice vulture," I said.

"With a big head."

"I know, right? You think that's Fred Ramsberger?"

"The name fits," said Natalie.

Ramsberger looked up and down the street, his round glasses aiming at Natalie and me for the quickest moment. We looked away and fake-laughed. When we looked back at the porch he was placing a metal mask over his mouth and a helmet over his bald dome. Now looking like a green-eyed robot, he walked past the Martha Washington dogs, down the stairs, and around the side of the house to the blue garage. A moment later the garage door opened and a strange topless contraption chittered out and turned onto the street, driving away from us.

It was exactly as Janelle had described, with all kinds of hoses and enginelike things covering the outside and two large globes sticking out from what would have been the trunk. The globes now were dark, no swirling lights, but we could read the letters painted on the side.

R.I.P.

"We've got to get into that house," said Natalie when the car was gone.

"I think we're close enough," I said, suddenly terrified, as if the hum around the lawn people had settled into my bones.

"But imagine what's inside. Ghost cooks. Ghost butlers. Cats with Mary Todd Lincoln faces. We have to do it."

"Ask Amira," I said. "She's mysterious and cool, right? She'll go with you."

Natalie looked at me and I gave her my angry face, but it only took a few seconds for me to snort laughter out my nose. We were still laughing when we saw the R.I.P. contraption car driving down the street toward us, the clatter of its engine growing louder and louder.

As it passed, Ramsberger's huge helmeted head peered at us. His round dark glasses were screens showing nothing but darkness. Without a sound being uttered through his metal mask I could hear again the demon's warning.

Run away and hide, little girl, before I catch you in my teeth like a toad.

By the time he turned the corner and was gone, Natalie wasn't laughing anymore, and neither was I.

You ever have that feeling that the world is too big and you are too small and the only safe place is your bed? It's not a good feeling—it spreads through your veins until you are too scared to even peek out from under your covers.

But I had something in my pocket to guide me past the demon's taunt and through the fear. Was it an amulet? Was it an incantation? Was it a little magic mouse of my own, bound to do my bidding? No, though the mouse would be cool. I'd call her Evelyn and feed her smelly cheeses and have her tie my sneakers when I was too tired in the morning to bend over and tie them myself.

But what I had was even more powerful than Evelyn the shoe-tying mouse. What I had was a story my mother had told me, a thrilling and dangerous story that explained how I ended up spinning here on planet Earth. I'm not in it at all, but I still think of it as my origin story, and while there's no radioactive spider involved, there is a salamander, which feeds on spiders, so there's that.

A story might not seem like much, but don't underestimate its power. Stories can topple empires. And maybe this one did.

10

MY MOTHER'S STORY

There once was a girl named Juniper who believed she was madly rich, if only she could find the money.

Juniper's father, Tommy Lee Jelani, had been an unreliable scoundrel and Juniper loved him all the more for it. He mostly lived on the road, playing his trumpet with a traveling jazz band, but when home he never scolded Juniper or reminded her to do her homework, like her mother often did. Instead, when he swept into town he would put his oldest daughter on his lap and laugh and tell her about the treasure. It was buried in his secret place, he said. But when the time was right, *Oh, Junie,* he would say, *we'll have ourselves a party.*

Then he'd flash that smile of his and ask her to sing for him, and she would—Juniper, with the voice of an angel.

The family always had enough money for the mortgage

and food when Juniper's father was alive, even if he wasn't around much to share in it. But after her father died—in mysterious circumstances, Juniper would always say—things grew tight. There were three girls in the family and the youngest had health issues that were only partly covered by insurance from Juniper's mother's work. Juniper's mother sold the house and bought a smaller one and then sold that and the family moved into a rental apartment in a building by the railroad tracks. She took a second job to fill the gaps, but the refrigerator always grew bare by the end of the month.

When Juniper brought up the treasure, her mother would shake her head, saying that it was merely a story, that her father could spin webs of silver with that tongue of his. But Juniper didn't believe her father would have left them high and dry, and so she took long walks in the park and in the woods, searching.

One day, when Juniper was still in middle school, the shifting clouds conspired to send a shaft of sunlight through the treetops, illuminating a little mound of dirt just off the path to Whistler's Creek.

A sign from beyond!

Juniper marked the spot with stones and came back with a shovel and her best friend, Mel, and the two dug and dug but found only roots and dirt and disappointment. Later that summer, the people who now lived in Juniper's old house came back from a vacation to see their yard dug up, as if a deranged dog had been hunting for a missing bone. As the years went on, it felt to Juniper that it wasn't only the money that was buried and lost, it was her future.

Juniper didn't sing anymore.

"Why don't you just ask your father where it is?" said Mel one day after high school, hearing Juniper's complaint for the umpteenth time. They were juniors at the time.

"He's dead, Mel," said Juniper.

"But there might be ways," said Mel, with a sly smile.

Juniper was tall with dark brown skin, a varsity basketball and field hockey player at Willing High School. Mel was short and pale and as athletic as a post, but would have been a future valedictorian if it wasn't for math. They were best friends, the two girls, and had been since meeting as toddlers in the park. Juniper was the shy one. Mel was the bold one. And Mel had a plan.

Madame Blavatsky charged them a small price for an initial conversation with Juniper's father. She had a storefront on the edge of a small commercial strip by the train station near Willing High, its neon signs advertising palm readings, tarot readings, and séances with the dead. Mel had always been intrigued by those signs. The three sat around a table, holding either other's hands. After a clicking sound was followed by a breeze whisking around the room, the medium announced in her heavy accent that Juniper's father was close and had something important to tell her. Then, suddenly, Madame Blavatsky collapsed at the table, her head smacking the tabletop.

Thwop!

(You can't say the Madame wasn't consistent!)

When she regained consciousness, Madame Blavatsky told them it would take more money to continue the conversation. "He so much wants to talk wiz his darlink Junie."

"How do you know he called me that?" said Juniper.

"He told me," said the psychic. "He loves you so, I could feel it. But his spirit is stronk and I must prepare. I will need another payment, in advance. Zree hundred dollars."

"Zree hundred?" said Juniper.

The girls discussed it and decided that if Madame Blavatsky was such a brilliant psychic, she would have known they couldn't come up with zree hundred dollars. That was how they found themselves in the back room of Jack's Cauldron of the Odd.

Jack's was an old store in Olde City Philadelphia, down by the river. There were skulls in the windows, along with skeletons in witches' costumes and a two-headed dog mounted on the wall. But the oddest thing of all was Jack himself, thin and gray, with bushy brows and one eye completely white. He sat behind the counter, smoking and waiting, waiting and smoking.

When the girls opened the door, a little mallet hit a gong.

Jack inhaled and the tip of his cigarette sizzled as he watched the two girls wander about the store, picking up this, looking at that. Finally, Mel turned to the old man and said, "Ouija?"

Jack nodded toward a door in the rear of the main room.

Beyond the door were shelves full of books and geodes and little dried animal feet. Also in the shelves were stacks of Ouija boards of varying prices, some of plastic, some of burnished wood, one with a painting of a naked witch encircled by a snake. But as Juniper examined the boards, Mel's attention was drawn by something else.

There was a bag made of carpet on the floor, its open top a gaping mouth. And to Mel, it was as if something in the bag was calling to her with a high, squeaky voice, the way a mushroom would sound if a mushroom could talk.

I know what you want. Find me. Feed me. Use me.

Inside the bag were leather scraps, animal jaws still with their teeth, and a brown leather notebook with a moonstone embedded in the cover. The words *The Book of Ill Omen* were burned into the notebook's leather.

The notebook smelled old. The moonstone glowed. The pages were covered with spots of mold and hand-scrawled incantations.

I know what you want. Find me. Feed me. Use me.

Mel flicked through the pages until she found written in bold letters **THE KEY OF SOLOMON**, under which a series of entries listed a host of ancient demons, along with a description of each demon's powers. One notation appeared to glow on the page.

> The demon Gaap: He can cause love and hatred. He can answer truly of the past, the present, and things to come. He can carry his summoners from one kingdom to the next. He can discover hidden things and deliver great treasure at great cost. He is a mighty prince and a cruel trickster and the smartest of the demons of Gaul.

Beneath this entry was a slash of dried blood.

When Mel dropped the book on the counter, old Jack stared at her with his milky eye before inhaling from his cigarette. The tip sizzled.

"That ain't no Ouija board," said Jack in a voice as old as time. "This here book was supposed to be burned."

"Then it should be cheap," said Mel. "Five bucks?"

"Ten."

"Sold," she said.

"And I'll take it back from you for fifty," he said, his milky eye laughing like a maniac.

Once Juniper realized what the book held, and what Mel intended to do with it, she was terrified. She told Mel they were dealing with stuff neither of them understood.

"Then it's like calculus," said Mel.

"It's a little more serious than calculus."

"Have you taken calculus?"

"Mel!"

"Look, Juniper. We're going to play around and then have a laugh. Madame Blavatsky didn't work. The Ouija board wasn't going to work. This won't work. It's just for fun. Think of Brad Frayden and his *Dungeons and Dragons* group. They seem to have a good time."

"Why is he always so smiley for no reason?"

"I don't know. I hope his kids don't inherit it, poor things."

"You promise it won't work?"

"I don't know," said Mel. "But I don't want to live my life paralyzed by fear. Let's be bold. Let's be adventurers. Let's swashbuckle."

"I don't even know what that is. Is that a shoe?"

"And let's do it together," said Mel.

And that's how the two girls ended up in the basement of Juniper's apartment building, among the bags of salt and the spiderwebs, one girl hesitant, the other full of determination. A five-sided star with a pentagram in the middle was drawn in chalk on the cracked cement floor, and five black candles burned on the points of the star. To the side was a small bamboo cage in which hunched a salamander they had caught in the creek, with a red stripe on its back.

Both girls wore bathrobes over their jackets and jeans and T-shirts—it was still cold in the basement. Perfume had been dripped around the star, oil had been dabbed on their foreheads—safflower oil because that was all they could find in Juniper's pantry—and a pot full of green wood, barbecue briquettes, and sage had been doused in lighter fluid and set on fire, creating a musky column of smoke in the middle of the pentagram. The salamander turned its head and licked the smoky air.

Standing at the base of the star, Mel coughed from the smoke and then read from the old leather-bound notebook. *"Evoco Gaap, a septem spiritibus de ventis."*

"We conjure thee, Gaap, by the spirits of the seven winds," read Juniper from the same book, looking over Mel's shoulder.

Mel read out loud another mouthful of Latin and Juniper followed with, "We conjure thee, Gaap, that thou appear and be obedient unto us."

"Soluzen," shouted Mel.

"I command thee, oh mighty Gaap, to enter into this pentagram."

"Halliza."

"And appear in human shape."

"Bellator."

"And speak unto us in our mother tongue."

"Belloney."

"And show unto us the treasure that we seek."

When the last words were spoken, they stood at the base of that star and waited. And waited.

The smoke from the pot rose undisturbed. The salamander in its cage was still. Juniper sighed and Mel put up a hand and they waited.

Behind them a sudden whoosh brightened the room. They looked at each other, each recognizing fear in the other's eyes, before slowly turning until they faced the furnace behind them. A controlled blue flame was visible through a small window in the furnace's door. Mel looked at Juniper, and Juniper looked at Mel, and they both laughed at their silliness.

Of the two girls giggling with relief and wearing robes in that basement like they were deranged senators in ancient Rome, the one who would become my mother was Mel. Yes, the daring and swashbuckling Mel, or Melinda. Who could have ever imagined? And my mother was still laughing with her best friend forever when a breeze arose from behind them and started whipping around the basement.

Their eyes widened at the same time.

The two girls turned back to the pentagram and stared in horror as a ghostly hand trembled in the twisting column of smoke before reaching out, reaching out for them.

THE ICE CREAM TRUCK

The afternoon after our visit to Madame Blavatsky, at the end of my last class of the day, Mr. Armbruster was saying something that I wasn't listening to when the oohs and aahs and squeaks got my attention.

"What just happened?" I said to Keir.

"Mr. Armbruster asked if you could stay after class and have a word with him."

"Me? Why?"

"Trouble, most likely," said Keir. "Good luck."

As the bell rang, I looked at Natalie, who made a face and then scampered out of the room with Keir, leaving me to deal with my social studies teacher alone.

"What did I do this time?" I said after waiting for the room to empty.

"How are things going, Elizabeth?" said Mr. Armbruster.

Yikes, right? He was sitting on the edge of his desk. Somehow they think that makes them young and hip, but in Mr. Armbruster's case the bow tie gave him away.

"Fine?" I said.

"You don't sound certain."

"Well, it's an uncertain time for all of us." I shrugged. "Middle school, you know."

He laughed and nodded. "I caught your debate performance the other day."

"Uh-oh," I said.

"I enjoyed it."

"Too bad I forgot the banana peel. Then you would have really had a laugh."

"What I mean, Elizabeth, is that you were good. Really good, really clever. You have a future as a debater."

"But?" I said.

"Yes, well, as you know," he said, "in my class there's always a 'but.' I've dealt with a lot of clever debaters in my time."

"At Harvard?"

"Yes, at Harvard. Sometimes when they get so good at crushing arguments and being clever, they mistake cleverness for substance. It can be an effective debate strategy, and yes, some of these debate types end up in the Senate, but it also cripples something inside them."

"So you're saying I'm clever?"

"Always. But there's something deeper than cleverness, and it lives inside. Find that and learn to express it and you'll be unstoppable."

"In debate, you mean?"

"In everything."

"Uh, thanks?" I said as I started walking away. Then I stopped and turned around. "I kind of think there was an insult in the middle of all those compliments."

"Have a good afternoon, Elizabeth," he said.

I was already too late for the train to think much about what had just happened. I needed to get to the office to tell my grandfather about the terrifying Fred Ramsberger and his dog statues with Martha Washington faces and his strange lawn people. I was actually jogging toward the train station—really, well, not really, but sort of—when I heard the twinkly music of the ice cream truck. I wasn't hungry, but when did that ever matter within earshot of that music, as relentless and cheery as a laughing dog? I followed the tinkling to a white van parked right on my route to the train station.

A couple of kids were already forking over their cash, so I took a moment to check out the menu on the side of the van. Should I go with my usual and always-delicious Strawberry Shortcake bar, or should I go bold with the Choco Taco? And the Powerpuff Girl Pop looked both sickly sweet and stupidly nostalgic. I was still weighing options when the window cleared and I stepped up to the opening.

The ice cream man in his white coat and peaked hat had his back to me when he said in a voice that was rough and rhythmic and shockingly familiar, "What can I do for you today, young Lizbeth?"

When Josiah Goodheart turned around and gave me his

brilliant smile, I had to hold on to the window's ledge to stop from falling back and smacking my head on the curb.

I had always thought Josiah Goodheart, another barrister in the Court of Uncommon Pleas, was my nemesis. In court, representing the demon Redwing, Goodheart had fought my attempts to free my father. Later he destroyed my gremlin case with a very sneaky and, I had to admit, quite brilliant goat gambit that worked out poorly for both my case and the goat. To see Redwing's attorney here, now, facing me within the window of an ice cream truck, absolutely terrified.

But Josiah Goodheart had also, I believed, slipped a document into my briefcase that not only helped my client Mr. Topper become Keeper of the Portal of Doom, but also might have saved the world. That might be a point in his favor, no?

"What are you doing in an ice cream truck, Mr. Goodheart?" I said.

"Selling ice cream, of course." His face was dark and chubby, his eyes bright, his smile blinding. "Which treat will you be having today?"

"Uh...Choco Taco?" I said slowly.

"Are you asking or telling?"

"Telling?"

"Then a Choco Taco it is. And because of our professional relationship, let's say it's on the house."

"Then maybe two Choco Tacos?" I said.

Josiah Goodheart laughed. "You've always been a shrewd one, Lizbeth. You don't mind me calling you Lizbeth, do you? At least outside the courtroom. Ms. Webster is so formal."

"I suppose we can be friends outside the courtroom," I said, remembering the way my father referred to him as Josiah while sitting on the barristers' bench. "But don't let anyone know, I wouldn't want to wreck my reputation."

"And what reputation is that?"

"For general crabbiness."

Goodheart laughed again. He had a good laugh—it came from deep within, as if he was laughing at all the jokes in all the world and he was one of them.

"I didn't realize Redwing was paying you so little to represent him," I said. "It's not every lawyer that needs to moonlight in an ice cream truck."

"Oh, it's not about need, Lizbeth. Nothing brightens the day like the sweet taste of ice cream. I'm simply spreading joy in the world, along with, perhaps, a touch of wisdom." He raised his eyebrows. "I understand you've been sniffing around the Ramsberger Institute of the Paranormal."

"How do you know that?"

"In my professional capacity I have a range, I say, a range of associates that keep me informed of anything that might affect my clients."

"Is Ramsberger your client?"

"Let's say he's in my range of representation. Choco Taco, you say. Let's see if I can find such a thing." He began lifting freezer lids, one, two, three. "Ah, here we go."

He took out the treat and grabbed a napkin. As he handed it all to me through the window he said, "You should know that things are bigger than they seem."

I looked at the Choco Taco. "It's not as big as I had hoped."

"I'm talking about the missing ghosts."

"You know about them?"

"Keep your eyes open and your back to the wall. That is a not a threat, Lizbeth, just a friendly warning between friends."

"Thank you, Mr. Goodheart, but your client Redwing already sent the message."

"He did, did he?" He peered around as if he might be caught at something. "When?"

"Yesterday," I said. "You're a day late."

"And since I treated you to your treat, more than a dollar short."

I couldn't help but laugh myself. I still didn't understand what this ice cream truck maneuver was all about, but I'd waited long enough to get to the important stuff.

I tore open the plastic wrapper and took a bite of my Choco Taco. Choco goodness!

"You got yourself a little ice cream on your lip," said Mr. Goodheart. "Just a smudge right there."

I took the napkin to wipe my lip where he indicated and stopped still for a moment. There was something written on the napkin. I looked at Goodheart as I pressed that napkin to my lip and then put it around the taco.

"You might think of me as an enemy, Lizbeth," said Josiah Goodheart, "but this is my world, too. My people live within it. Sometimes loyalty expands beyond the narrow boundaries others build for you, if you catch my drift."

"I don't think I do."

"You will. Sooner than you think. Now I've tarried here too long. I have a route to finish."

"You really have a route?"

"Of a sort," he said with a smile. "And my brother Uriah will be wanting back his truck. Always a pleasure, Lizbeth. I'll see you soon in court."

"With a goat?"

"Sometimes you bring the goat," he said, "sometimes you are the goat. And sadly, you don't get to choose." And with that, Josiah Goodheart slammed the window shut.

As the truck headed down the road, a couple of kids ran to catch up to it, waving their hands with dollar bills grasped in their fists, but the truck kept on keeping on. Why did their disappointment cheer me up? As they looked on, I took a bite of my ice cream.

I waited until the truck had turned the corner before I sneaked a glance at my napkin. Written in a neat handwriting was an address in the city and then the following:

Phantasm International Industries
Dr. I. L. Shevski

I guess I'd have to pay this Dr. Shevski and the weird-sounding company a visit, but first, I really needed to talk to my grandfather.

12

THE DEMON GAAP

With the unsettling sight of Josiah Goodheart in an ice cream truck still rattling in our brains—a piranha swimming circles in a root beer float, am I right?—I need to return to the basement of that old apartment building by the railroad tracks with the furnace firing and the sage burning and the ghostly hand reaching out from a swirl of smoke. My mother's story is not just important to me personally, but also key to understanding the Case of the Dastardly Ghost Thief, so I'll be going back and forth to give you the full gist of things. Try to keep up.

See them now, Juniper and Mel, digging their fingers into each other's arms. The vision of that ghostly hand was impossible and terrifying and real as steel. The world they knew, with all its simple certainties, was dying a quick death as the hand turned solid and a figure behind it began to form itself from the smoke and flame.

"Who is it that has dared to summon Gaap?" came a high twittery voice from the smoke. "Gaap was in the middle of a nap."

The girls kept clutching tightly to each other and said nothing.

The figure in the smoke became more substantial, more solid, until it was there, right there, standing within the pentagram marked on the cement floor. It shifted in appearance, first a young boy, then a horse-faced woman, a child, a bear, until it finally took the form of a scrawny old man with a red-splotched face, wrapped in a white toga with purple and gold trim.

"Are you standing before Gaap?" said the old man. "How rude. Kneel before Gaap's awesome presence."

The old man lifted his gaze to the two girls, waited for a moment, and then opened his eyes wide with indignation.

Juniper began to lower herself, but Mel, still clutching her arm, pulled her up again.

"We're not going to kneel," said Mel.

"Of course you're going to kneel," said the old man. "That's the way it works. Gaap arrives, you kneel, we dine, and then you do Gaap's bidding."

"But we brought you here to do our bidding," said Mel.

"Mel?" said Juniper without taking her eyes off the old man. "What are you doing?"

"We summoned him," said Mel. "If anyone's kneeling, he should kneel to us."

"Don't be a ridiculous thing," said the old man. "Gaap doesn't kneel. Do you not know how old Gaap is? Do you not know that Gaap is the thirty-third spirit of Solomon and commands sixty-six legions of demons? You will kneel. You. Not me. You!"

"No," said Mel.

"Then you will pay the ultimate—" He stopped abruptly, his attention taken by the salamander in its cage. "Is that for me? It is so adorable."

He reached down and picked up the cage, opening the door and grasping the salamander by its tail. The salamander swished this way and that, its little legs clawing at the air.

"Don't worry, little fellow, Gaap won't hurt you," said the demon Gaap in a soft and comforting voice. Then he opened his mouth unnaturally wide and tossed the salamander in. When he closed his mouth again, the swishing tail and one frantic little salamander leg lay on his lower lip until he sucked it all in and started chewing.

"Maybe we should kneel," whispered Juniper.

"Delicious," said the demon before tossing the cage and sucking his fingertips one at a time. "Gaap admits to feeling a bit peckish whenever he moves from one kingdom to the next. Now, enough of this nonsense. Kneel."

"We won't kneel," said Mel.

"Well, since you provided a suitable offering in deference to Gaap's status, Gaap will allow your insolence to stand this once. We have dined, now let us confer. What is it you seek from Gaap?"

At this, Mel pushed Juniper slightly forward and gave her an encouraging look.

"My father buried a treasure?" said Juniper after a bit of stuttering. "His name was Tommy Lee Jelani, maybe you know him? He died before he could tell me where it was buried. I need to ask him where it is. Is that okay?"

"Treasure you seek," said Gaap. "What could be simpler?"

He waved his hand and a wooden chest appeared on the cement floor beside him inside the pentagram. The top was open, and the chest was filled with golden coins and golden goblets and bracelets encrusted with jewels of every different color.

"Take it and let Gaap go. Gaap has much to do."

Juniper looked at Mel. Mel looked at Juniper. They both looked at the chest and its glistening contents, shining as if from a light hidden beneath the jewels. *The Book of Ill Omen* had said that the demon could deliver great treasure, but at great cost.

"Are there strings attached?" said Mel.

"Gaap sees no strings," said the demon. "Do you see strings?" A pair of scissors appeared in the demon's fingers. "Where? Gaap will snip them right off."

"What I mean to ask, is there a cost to taking it?"

"Ahh, I see," said Gaap. The scissors immediately disappeared. "There is always a cost to gaining a great fortune. You will be able to buy everything, so nothing will be special. You will be able to purchase your dreams, which will kill them for you. Love will become a transaction, no grander than buying a new pair of shoes. Your children will likely be ruined, though some find that a perk. And, of course, you will become insufferable. That can't be avoided."

"I'm not talking about money," said Mel. "We all want money. What about this specific fortune?"

"Oh well, I admit that when Gaap provides such treasure there is a price. A plague upon your family, disasters in love, an early death, accordion music at your funeral, psoriasis. Such a heartbreak, that last one. But you'll be rich, at least until the accordion plays. So, kneel in gratitude and take your fortune. Gaap has given what you seek."

"I don't want your treasure," said Juniper.

"You refuse Gaap's gift? Fie on you, then. Fie." Gaap snapped his fingers and the great chest of gold and jewels disappeared as quick as that. "I'm beginning to be intrigued. Tell me again, girl, what it is you want from Gaap?"

"I want to talk to my father," said Juniper. "I want him to tell me where his treasure is buried. His treasure. I only want what I deserve."

"Oh, and that's what you shall receive, Gaap promises. Tommy Lee Jelani, you say. He's a bit of a raconteur, is he not?"

"He loved telling stories," said Juniper, "if that's what you mean."

"With a talent for jazz, if my memory is correct, and it always is. Your father is on level eight, within the domain of the demon Abezethibou, whom you earthlings might know as Redwing. Interesting." He crossed his arms and tapped a cheek with a finger. "Yes, a meeting can be arranged on the other side. And you, girl, you with the hair."

"Me?" said Mel. "What's wrong with my hair?"

"What's right with it? Would that satisfy you, too?"

"I only want what Juniper wants," said Mel.

"How noble of you. Such a dear friend you must be. Which is good, because be warned, you two, if you journey together to the other world, you must leave together, too. And also know that Juniper's father won't be able to tell you what you seek until you two do something for Gaap. There is always a price."

"What is your price?" said Mel.

"There is an object that I covet. A very rare object. It once belonged to the noble angel Zophiel, the Watchwoman of the Seventh Heaven, but was stolen by an agent of Redwing and taken to the castle in his domain. It is the Lens of Fate, a machine that allows the bearer to examine the world of the living and the dead at will. Redwing has used it for ill. Gaap would have it for his own."

"How are we to get that?"

"That is for you to determine. It is within the domain where your father was placed. There will surely be clues there. It is a simple matter, really, nothing to worry about. I would do it myself, but Redwing and I have a history of sorts. Still, some quests are not for the weak. Gaap understands. You can go on this simple quest with a reward beyond measure or release Gaap and go back to your paltry little lives. Gaap cares not one way or the other. The choice is yours."

"What did you two decide?" I asked my mother while she told me her story at some fancy spa in Massachusetts. We were sitting alone in the hot tub, steam rising all about us.

"What would you do?" asked my mother.

"Run," I said.

"That's what I wanted to do, too," said my mom. "We didn't know what we were doing, dabbling in the dark arts when all we really wanted was to just do something. But this was too much something, wild and frightening and beyond us."

"So, you told that to Juniper."

"That's not what I told her," said my mother. "Instead I plastered a smile on my face and said, 'Let's do it.'"

"I don't understand," I said, flabbergasted at my careful, always-sensible mother.

"I assumed Juniper would say no. That's what Juniper always did. It was why she was my perfect friend. I could pretend to be anything, and she would keep me safe."

And I understood that, the impulse to dream yourself ready to fly to great and dangerous heights, all the time knowing that someone will keep you safely on the ground. We hate the limits put on us even as we wrap them around us like a warm coat on a frigid day. My coat was my mother. I suppose my mother's coat, when she was my age, was Juniper.

"So, what happened?" I said.

"Juniper shocked me. 'If you think it's what we should do, Mel, then let's do it,' she said. And I should have seen it coming."

"I don't understand," I said.

"Well, to me it was like jumping out of a plane without a parachute. I expected Juniper to save me from my worst instincts. But to Juniper, it was a chance to see her father one more time. Who wouldn't leap at that? It's hard to figure out who failed whom, but somehow, without enough thought, we agreed."

They agreed, Juniper and Mel. They agreed and the demon Gaap smiled a malicious, hungry smile as a flame erupted from the sage pot and the smoke began to billow and twist. Within that smoky haze the demon began to change.

His body swelled in size as great bat wings unfurled behind his back. His hands curled into claws. Horns spiraled out of his forehead, and his face twisted into a horrid bat face, with sharp teeth and pointed ears.

"Behold the demon Gaap in his natural form," he said in a booming voice when his great wings stretched out and he had become so large he was forced to bend at the waist so that his horns wouldn't pierce the ceiling. The smoke of the burning sage now curled about him like a cloak. "Step into the pentagram and take hold of my wings, and I will transport you between kingdoms."

Mel and Juniper, each again holding on to the other, shrunk from the dreadful vision. This demon before them was a thing not of dreams but of nightmares. It was a creature to run from, to hide from, to cry out from in the middle of the night.

But then Juniper disentangled her arms from Mel's and stepped forward into the pentagram as if her long-gone father was calling her forward. She winced as she reached for the edge of one wing—winced, but still she took hold.

And now Mel, wanting with all her heart and soul to run screaming from that basement but unable to desert her great friend, stepped into the pentagram and lifted a hand onto the demon's other wing. She looked at Juniper and Juniper looked back with the slightest of smiles, a smile that said, *What have we done?*

The smoked thickened and twisted until it spun around them like a tornado and the girls could feel themselves being lifted off the ground as Gaap laughed. And just that quickly they were gone. Gone. And so was the pentagram, and so were the candles, and so was the pot of burning sage.

The only things left on the cracked cement floor were the empty salamander cage, the two robes, and *The Book of Ill Omen.*

13

THE COMPLAINT

Y ou've come at last," said Avis at the front desk in the offices of Webster & Spawn. She had abruptly stopped her typing when I arrived and peered suspiciously over her glasses. "Where have you been? Where?"

"I stopped for ice cream," I said guiltily, "and missed my train."

"Ice cream, you say?" said Avis. "Then it couldn't be helped. One must always stop for ice cream." She went back to her typing. "Your grandfather is waiting. Go on, go on."

I looked up and saw Barnabas in the corner of the outer office. He was sitting on his seat, as tall as a lifeguard's chair, leaning over his high desk, using a large feather quill to write on the document before him.

"I need to talk to Barnabas first," I said.

"Make it snappy," said Avis. "Your grandfather has the patience of a mosquito."

As I walked through the waiting area to Barnabas's desk, I passed two of our clients. Sandy was tall and blond and hairy as a hairball coughed up by an oversized cat. This cat was a witch named Gwendolyn, who had promised Sandy more lustrous hair. Talk about overdelivering!

Mildred, a little girl in bright red shoes, had asked the same witch for a more youthful appearance. She was actually over twice Sandy's age.

"Hello, Sandy, Mildred," I said. "How go your cases?"

"They're going," said Sandy in her soft, breathless voice. "Today your father wants to review the promises the witch made to each of us. He says he needs to know the exact phrasing, but it's hard to remember."

"It's not so hard," said Mildred, no bigger than a toddler but with a voice like the rasp of a saw cutting through a brick. "I was promised youth, glorious youth."

"Well," I said, "she certainly gave you that. What about you, Sandy?"

"My hair was getting a little thin," said Sandy, brushing her palm across the hair pouring out of her forearm. "She promised me it would be lustrous. Thick and lustrous. But there are limits, don't you think?"

"I do," I said.

"Your father has decided to try our cases together," said Mildred.

"Together?" I said. "Is that allowed?"

"He says yes, so I'm sure it is," said Sandy.

"Your father's a tiger," said Mildred.

"My father?"

"Growl," said Mildred. "If I was only fifty years younger—"

"Or thirty years older," said Sandy.

"Good luck!" I said enthusiastically before heading over to Barnabas. Nothing gets you out of a weird conversation quicker than a false bout of enthusiasm.

Barnabas looked up as I approached. "Mistress Elizabeth, I'm just now working on your stolen-ghost case. I should have the complaint finished shortly, pending a few minor details."

"Like the full name and address of the ghost thief?"

"Precisely."

I took the card I had swiped from Madame Blavatsky and lifted it onto his desk. "Voilà!"

After looking at the card, he said, "I do believe, Mistress Elizabeth, that this Ramsberger fellow has met his match in you."

"Barnabas?" I said. "Are you okay?" He seemed very much less mournful than usual. "You're not pointing me to the broom or making a bad joke about my filing."

"I need make no bad joke about your filing," said Barnabas. "Your filing is enough of a bad joke on its own. Once I put in all the defendant's details, our complaint titled *Burton v. Ramsberger* will be ready for service. I believe your grandfather wanted to speak to you."

"Are you sure you're okay?"

"Of course. Now go on, your grandfather is waiting."

As I walked toward my grandfather's office, I glanced behind me and spied Barnabas gazing at the far corner of the office as if he was gazing at an ocean swell.

"What's going on with Barnabas?" I asked my grandfather when we were alone in his office.

The door was closed, and we were at our usual positions when discussing legal matters. I was sitting behind my little desk, while my grandfather stood with his cane before the fireplace at the far wall. On the shelf above the fireplace was the skull on top of which lay my grandfather's moth-eaten barrister's wig, which was never used anymore.

"Oh, you've picked up on it, Elizabeth. Very good. Yes, the tide seems to have turned for our friend Barnabas. And it is all due to you, Elizabeth."

"Me?"

"Who else? You were the one who found the document which gave our Mr. Topper his Portal Keeper position. And it is our Mr. Topper who has granted Barnabas the greatest of kindnesses."

"What is that?" I asked.

"I told you once of the sad story of Barnabas and his betrothed, Isabel," said my grandfather, "how Barnabas was murdered by Isabel's deranged ex-husband, Cutbush. And I told you how the demon Redwing, using the Lens of Fate, spied the mourning woman in the land of the living, fell in love, and tricked her into traveling to his domain. Once there, she agreed to trade places with Barnabas in the land of the dead, with the promise that once Barnabas himself died, she and he would be together forever. Redwing, of course, being a demon of the worst stripe, gave Barnabas the curse of immortality, so now he and his beloved are kept forever apart by the border between this world and the next."

"I assumed that was the reason Barnabas never smiles."

"Yes, indeed. But our Mr. Topper, having control now of the portal, has allowed for certain meetings between Barnabas and his one true love. Barnabas is not permitted though the portal, nor is Isabel herself, but her spirit is allowed transit back and forth."

"Her ghost?"

"As you know from the story, this is Isabel's natural world and so her spirit is not technically a ghost. Still, on certain nights her spirit haunts Barnabas's chambers and the betrothed are together for a few blessed moments. No contact is allowed, of course—Barnabas is not allowed contact with the spirit world or the demon's bargain is no more—but the time together is much valued by both."

"That is so romantic, Grandpop," I said. "Star-crossed lovers divided by death, able now to meet but forever forbidden to touch. It should be a book. Maybe I should write it."

"Romantic is the word, precisely," said my grandfather. "But you should leave your literary endeavors for another time. We have the Case of the Dastardly Ghost Thief to pursue."

"What claims are we using?"

"Theft of spirit, using the rule of universal succession to prove standing for our two young plaintiffs. Now all we must do is find the defendant."

"I found him," I said.

"You did? Ramsberger?"

"I gave the information to Barnabas."

"Splendid, Elizabeth. We are on the way."

"He lives in a strange house with these weird lawn people and statues of dogs with Martha Washington faces—"

"Martha Washington, you say?" said my grandfather, tapping his cane on the floor. "I always thought her quite attractive for someone who was the mother of an entire country."

"But these lawn people were really weird, and all bundled up as if they were ghosts. And Ramsberger himself had this huge head and weird boots and is terrifying when he looks at you. It was all really frightening."

"Don't worry, young one. Your father's a Webster, and so are you. I have no doubt that a Webster can handle the likes of a ghost thief with the name Fred Ramsberger."

Just then there was a knock on the door.

"Come in," called my grandfather. "Come right in."

My father came through the door clutching a long piece of vellum. "Barnabas finished the complaint and said Elizabeth discovered the address of the defendant."

"That she did," said my grandfather.

"Excellent work, Elizabeth," said my father. My father! "I'll be serving the complaint tomorrow. The sooner we get service, the sooner we can get this mess before the court."

"Take Elizabeth with you," said my grandfather.

"I don't think that's such a good idea," I said at the very same time my father said, "It's probably better I do this by myself."

My father looked at me and I looked at him and for the first time in ages we actually understood each other. He didn't want me to go with him to serve the complaint on Ramsberger because he was scared for me, and I didn't want to go for the very same reason. That weird blue house frightened the gallbladder out of me.

"Nonsense, both of you," said my grandfather. "Elizabeth found the address and apparently has cased the location. She would be invaluable. Tomorrow the two of you must go together."

My grandfather turned and gave me the barest of smiles. He thought he was giving me exactly what I wanted. He was wrong.

14

THE EARTHLY PARADISE

Mel and Juniper's journey to the other side was beautifully strange.

"We arrived in a flash," said my mother in that Massachusetts hot tub with the steam curling around us, "and yet, the trip seemed to take forever."

She tried to explain it all to me but it made no sense. There were colors writhing about, she said, like a psychiatrist at the deli ordering, I don't know, corned beef? And there was something about woods stocked with jimmies? For a time they were lost in an endless sea of light and sound until suddenly they were floating down to a sloping field greener than green, under a purple sky with two suns, surrounded by the scent of flowers.

And vomit, too, because, yes of course, as soon as they landed, Mel and Juniper threw up right there on the grass.

But immediately a flock of birds descended, singing their sweet birdy songs as they pecked at the ground with their sweet birdy beaks. A moment later the birds flew off into the bright purple of the sky and the grass was again pristine and all smelled of flowers.

"Thank you for traveling Air Gaap," said the demon, transformed once again into an old man in a toga as he stood before them on the grassy field. "I hope your journey wasn't too bumpy."

"It was...it was weird," said Mel, overcome, "but amazing, too. Weirdly amazing."

"Except for the vomit thing," said Juniper.

"Yes, except for that."

"Where are we?" said Juniper.

"We're in a dimension that lies on the far side of death," said the demon Gaap. "It is a dimension of levels, not so different from your world, though these levels are dependent not on money or power but on worthiness. This is the highest level I can take you to. I thought it would be a beautiful and calm initiation to this other world."

It was beautiful, yes, but calm? Not really. The field was thronged with people, all dressed in white with flowers in their hair. The young and the old, men and women and laughing children, people of all sizes and colors, in their loose white clothes, walking, or running, or pushing themselves in wheelchairs up the slope toward a bright light at the top of the clearing.

Some in the joyous procession played funny-looking guitars and banged drums. Others danced like waterfalls, tossing flower petals into the air and singing in harmony with the hum that could be heard above everything, a great and glorious sound, as if a hundred thousand angels were singing a hymn with no words and only one note.

The girls, filled with some sort of light themselves, started to dance along, spinning on the grass and chattering to each other about the journey, about the scene, about what it all meant. The light at the top of the hill was so bright and full of impossible color the girls had to shield their eyes when they peered at it.

"Is that where we're going?" said Mel to the demon while they both still spun.

"I am sad to disappoint you," said the demon, "but no, we are not allowed through the Gate of Light. Those making their way up the field have earned their right to those higher levels. You will have to wait until you come to this world by—ahem—more conventional means."

"Is my father through there?" said Juniper.

"No, my dear. We must travel down to reach him."

The girls stopped their dancing and looked to the bottom of the field. The lower edge was covered by gray fog. As people in white straggled out of the mist, they coughed and fanned the air from their faces as if the fog smelled of wet dog.

"But before we go any farther," said Gaap, "what say we have some lunch?"

The demon snapped his fingers and a blanket appeared on the ground before them with a picnic basket in the middle. From one end of the basket a salamander peeked out its head, looked around, and dove back down. The demon licked his lips as the girls stared.

Mel's mouth stretched uneasily. "Maybe we should see Juniper's father before we eat."

"I don't know," said Juniper. "I'm a bit hungry, too."

Mel looked at Juniper for a moment, but her friend looked away.

"The daughter is right," said Gaap. "It is always better to eat in the here and the now. One never knows when the next salamander is coming. The suns are not as bright on the lower levels, and the food is certainly not so tasty. There are sandwiches of delight in the basket. And Granny Smith apples, quite delicious if you don't mind her berating you with what life was like when she was young as you chew. Sit down, eat, enjoy."

And they did. Eat, I mean, and yes, enjoy.

Leaning back on the blanket as the dancers swirled and sang around them, they ate the sandwiches of delight, which tasted of joy itself. They drank a lemonade that burst on their tongues like the two suns above, bright and sweet and tingling. They ate a tart green apple that tasted of wisdom and care, with hints of wickedness. They had never experienced such a meal. It was...otherworldly. My mother still dreams of it.

During their feast Gaap pulled a squirming salamander out of the basket and swallowed it whole. "When they wriggle all the way down," he said, his eyes dancing, "it's like a delicate throat massage." He opened one of the basket's flaps and pulled out another.

The girls started laughing, they couldn't help themselves, and it wasn't just Gaap and his dancing eyes. The sandwiches of delight, the wise, caring apples, and the sun-bright lemonade had transported them into a plane of pure joy. They kept laughing, laughing, laughing…

When they woke, the sky had turned a dark violet that vibrated with the humming of the angels, and the two suns were setting behind a mountain in the distance.

"You're awake," said Gaap, squatting now on the grass. "Good. It is time to move on."

Mel shook the fog out of her head. "We're going to see Juniper's father?"

"All in good time, young ones," said the demon.

"But this is a good time," said Mel, jumping to her feet. "Come on, Juniper."

"I don't know," said Juniper, who climbed slowly to standing, as if still drugged by the meal. "Maybe we should wait a bit."

"Juniper?"

"It's nice here, isn't it? Why can't we stay here for a time and explore? Wouldn't that be fun?"

Mel closed one eye and then took hold of Juniper's arm and yanked her away from the grinning Gaap. "What's going on?" she whispered.

"Will he be happy to see me?" said Juniper. "Will I be a disappointment? I was so young when he died. Will he even remember me?"

"You are the most memorable person in the world," said Mel. "The moment your father sees you he's going to wrap you in his arms and tell you how much he loves you. And then he's going to tell you where the treasure is. I'm sure of it."

"At least one of us is," said Juniper.

"One's enough," said Mel. "And I think those sandwiches were drugged."

"They were so good, right?"

"Let's go see your dad," said Mel.

When they told Gaap they were ready, the demon said, "Splendid," before it changed again into its pure form. "Now grab hold of my wings and we'll be off. Seventh level, going down."

In a bright and shocking flash Gaap landed them on an ugly cement bridge overlooking a crowded, smog-covered city that spread out like a stain across the landscape. The sky was gray, the two suns were dim fuzzy spots on the horizon, and the air was damp as a wet rag. Instead of the angelic hum of the higher level, there was a strange indecipherable buzz, as if they were standing over a hive of demented bees. And the river beneath was a slowly moving channel of sludge.

"Behold," said the demon Gaap. "Redwing's domain."

"Why does the other world look like Cleveland?" said Juniper.

"Six hundred years ago it looked like Florence when another living mortal named Dante paid a visit," said Gaap. "Redwing's domain changes constantly, but it is always about a hundred years behind the times in your world. The souls under Redwing's care are kept busy rebuilding and expanding the domain as it grows. In fact, that is all they do, build and suffer, suffer and build."

"Is Juniper's father down there?" said Mel.

"Yes, he is," said Gaap. "But more importantly, do you see way beyond the city, that mountain, with those strange peaks? Those are not peaks, those are towers. And that is not a mountain, it is Redwing's castle. Therein lies the Lens of Fate. Go now and fetch it for me as you promised."

"What about Juniper's father?" said Mel.

"All in due time, my children. Take hold of the lens and summon me. I will then return you to this very bridge. When the Lens of Fate is firmly in my claw, I will grant what you seek and then take you both back to your world. Now go and fetch."

"We're not your trained dogs," said Mel. "We're not going to do anything until Juniper sees her father."

"We're not?" said Juniper.

"No, we are not," said Mel, crossing her arms.

"I guess we're not," said Juniper, also crossing her arms.

"Don't be impertinent," said the demon. "I agreed to bring you here under certain conditions. One condition was that you bring me the Lens of Fate before learning what you came here to learn. And now you dare try to change the agreement? Do you not know that Gaap is the thirty-third spirit of Solomon and commands—"

"Yeah, yeah," said Mel. "We know."

Gap narrowed an eye and stared at the two for a moment. "Is this the kneeling thing all over again?"

"I think so," said Juniper.

"You two are as persistent as statues," said Gaap.

"Thank you," said Mel.

"Fine," said Gaap. "I will send you now to Juniper's father, but your meeting will be quite unsatisfactory until you have fulfilled your quest."

"What do you mean by unsatisfactory?" said Juniper.

"You will see, my persistent friends, oh you will," said the demon, his voice growing suddenly bold and angry. "Now gird thy loins."

Mel began to ask what a loin is, how does one gird it, and what does gird even mean, but before she could get the words out, the demon Gaap raised a hand and—

Snap!

Just that quickly Juniper and Mel were in the middle of a gray city street with a streetcar, large and honking, charging right at them.

Honk! Honk!

Mel stood frozen as the streetcar bore down upon her, the headlights a pair of searching eyes growing ever larger.

Honk! Honk!

No Tea

I was sitting in my father's messy white hybrid, buckled tight and growing ever more frightened as he drove to Ramsberger's house so we could serve the ghost thief with a complaint that would make him tremble with anger. Fun, right?

"When we get to the house, I'll do the talking," said my father. "There are things I need to ask before I serve the complaint. This is no time for clowning around."

"But I brought my little red nose," I said.

"Lizzie Face."

"Don't worry, I'm too scared to be chatty. But if I'm not supposed to say anything, then why did Grandpop make me come?"

"I think he wants us to spend some time together."

"And we couldn't have done dinner instead? Tacos!"

"He thinks the world of you," said my father. "So does Barnabas, actually."

"Two out of three," I said. "A D-plus on my report card. Can I ask you something, Dad?"

"Shoot."

"When we were in court one time, you called Josiah Goodheart by his first name, as if you were friends, even though he represents Redwing, who stuck you in a dungeon and has threatened our whole family. How does that work?"

"We're both lawyers."

"But he works for a demon."

"Well, there is that, yes."

"Would you represent a demon?"

"I became a lawyer to represent people and spirits who need help. Demons are usually what they need help from. But every party deserves representation in the Court of Uncommon Pleas, the good and the bad. That's part of due process."

I wasn't telling my father about my meeting with Josiah Goodheart in the ice cream truck. If Goodheart had wanted to talk to my father he would have picked up the phone, they being such close friends and all. But there was really only one question I needed to ask.

"Do you trust him?" I said.

"Josiah?" said my father. "Well, we're both officers of the court."

"What, with uniforms and marching?"

"No, though that might be fun. It means we can't lie to the judge, we have to follow the rules of the court, and we can't help our clients do anything illegal. And he's never lied to me, if that matters. Yes, I trust him." He leaned forward and peered through the windshield. "Is this it?"

I looked out the window and there it was, the iron gate, the strange blue house, the cement dogs with Martha Washington faces. Even buckled inside the car, I could feel the creep of the place invade my bones.

"That's it," I said.

As I walked with my father and his battered brown briefcase along the stone path and up the steps to the porch, I heard the same strange hum I had heard before.

"What's that sound?" I said.

"I don't know," said my father, looking away from me. "A generator, maybe?"

Passing the two cement dogs with Martha Washington faces on the porch, I stopped and took a closer look as my father pressed the button by the door. I hadn't realized they were wearing cement dresses, too. Who wakes up and decides to buy such a thing? What do you say to the guy at the Wawa? *I think I'll have a cup of coffee, a muffin, and a pair of five-hundred-pound fully dressed cement dogs with Martha Washington faces?*

I was still staring at one of the statues when the door creaked open. As I turned toward the sound, out of the corner of my eye it seemed Martha's face was turning, too.

One of the lawn people stood in the opening, with her hat and mask and goggles and gloves. "What?" she said so softly it was more an exhale than a word.

"We are with the law firm of Webster and Spawn," said my father. "We've come to see Mr. Ramsberger."

"Why?" she said in that same breathy voice.

"Business." My father passed a card to the woman. "He'll want to see us."

The lawn woman took the card and without looking said, "Follow."

As she backed into the house my father gave me a smile, which I understood completely. That smile was his way of telling me that things were about to go off the rails. He liked that, my father—the crazier the better. He was just so weird. Personally, I believed the saner the better, and this, this was not that.

I gave one of the dogs a final glance before we headed in together. When the door closed behind us, I spotted another of the lawn people staring through his goggle glasses. I edged closer to my father.

The room we passed through was old and dusty and over-stuffed with stuff. Every table was covered with bizarre figurines, every shelf was filled with orbs and vampire dolls and plates painted with monstrous faces. Oh yeah, and human skulls. Always a nice touch in a living room, don't you think? Inside the house the hum had grown louder, but now I could hear something within the hum, voices whispering, whispering. It almost sounded like social studies class.

We were led, finally, into a large dark library with walls of books, thick curtains covering the windows, and a fire in the fireplace. Standing beside the fireplace with a drink in his hand was Ramsberger. He was still creepy, still bald, but now, with a fancy maroon jacket and a silk scarf tied around his neck, he wasn't the fearsome, helmeted ghost thief. Instead he looked like someone who had watched too many of those British shows with tuxedos and servants and puddings.

"Thank you for seeing us, Mr. Ramsberger," said my father.

"Professor Ramsberger, if you please," said Ramsberger. "And you are Eli Webster of the law firm of Webster and Spawn, so I gather from your card."

"That I am," said my father.

"And who exactly are you?" he said to me.

"I'm the spawn," I said.

"This is my daughter, Elizabeth," said my father. "You're a professor of what, if I might ask?"

"Parapsychology," said Ramsberger. "I teach at the Barnwell Metaphysical College in Chestnut Hill. Do you know it?"

"We've sued it a number of times," said my father cheerfully.

"Splendid," said Ramsberger. "Then you're familiar with the curriculum. Have a seat, please."

Ramsberger waved at a couch with his glass, and my father and I sat side by side. "Can I get you something to drink?" he said.

"Tea?" I said. "I would love some tea!"

Ramsberger and my father both turned their heads to look at me as if I was a singing goldfish.

"Don't bother with the tea," said my father. "We won't be here long."

Natalie had taught me the ask-for-tea-to-get-more-time-for-questions gambit and I had taught that very gambit to my father.

"No tea?" I said.

"No tea," said my father, giving me a look. You know the look, the stop-talking-Lizard-Face look.

Ramsberger said to me, "You were the girl spying on the house the other day with your friend."

"We weren't spying," I said.

"It appeared you were spying," he said with a smile that made me shiver. He was being oh so polite, but his smile was like the garbage disposal in the kitchen sink. It devoured. "My family certainly knows something about spying. And now I learn you're the famous Elizabeth Webster."

"Not so famous."

"Young and modest," said Ramsberger. "There is no height you can't not achieve with such a combination."

I tilted my head and stared. His snide little comment had a triple negative in it. What did it all add up to? And who talks like that?

"That's quite a picture," I said, pointing at a huge painting that hung above the fireplace. It was a portrait of a woman in a grand red dress. One of her hands dramatically rested on her shoulder as she stared down her long nose at us. Perched on the very same shoulder, its claws clutching her fingers, was a large black bird. Nailed up there high on the wall, the woman seemed to dominate the room, as if she was an irritated queen surveying her kingdom.

"My grandmother, Edwina Ramsberger," said the ghost thief. "Quite a breathtaking woman. This was her house. She worked as a spy in Germany during the war and then later in the CIA. They called her the walking revolution. She overthrew more regimes than you have teeth."

"My grandmom bakes cakes," I said.

"Do you know a Chive Winterbottom, Professor?" said my father.

"I do, yes," said Ramsberger, giving me a careful look before turning back to my father. "She is a client of the Institute."

"The Ramsberger Institute of the Paranormal?"

"That's correct. Why?"

"Apparently, she hired you to take care of a ghosting issue."

"For reasons I'm sure you understand, I don't discuss matters involving my clients."

"You can discuss this one with us." My father opened his briefcase and pulled out a piece of paper, which he handed over. "This is a letter from Ms. Winterbottom authorizing us to investigate your handling of the matter."

As Ramsberger read the letter, he said, "I thought the client was quite satisfied with the Institute's services."

"She subsequently had some concerns about the fate of the ghost," said my father. "She wanted you to get it out of her attic, yes—the opera singing had become tiring—but she expressly told you she didn't want you to harm it. She didn't want you to imprison it."

"And that's what she thinks happened?" said Ramsberger. "Chive Winterbottom thinks I stole her opera-singing ghost and am now putting it on the road? Forcing it to perform, say, the tragic aria when Don Giovanni cries out in terror at the chorus of demons intent on carrying him down to hell?"

"This is not a joke, Professor," said my father.

"I beg to differ," said Ramsberger. "I think it is very much a joke. In the course I teach at Barnwell, I endeavor to debunk all the myths surrounding the paranormal, including the idea that ghosts wander among us. It is a tale told by hucksters and grifters seeking to steal precious pennies from those who believe all too easily."

That was strange thing for a ghost thief to say, and for some reason it angered me. "You don't believe in ghosts?" I said.

"I believe there are those who believe in ghosts, young lady," said Ramsberger. "And that belief is strong and dangerous and can cause all sorts of delusions. But that doesn't make the delusions true. You don't believe in Santa Claus, do you?"

"At the mall, sure," I said. "He smells like beer."

"Ghosts are figments of overactive imaginations," said the professor. "They sell movie tickets, they sell Halloween costumes, they have people lining up to see old haunted prisons, but in the reality of the world they don't exist. And that's what I teach my students. Whenever we study the supposed sightings, behind them we find nothing but frauds played upon the gullible."

"And yet, Professor," said my father, "you charged Ms. Winterbottom to rid her house of her ghost. Who is the huckster and grifter in that transaction?"

"The person who put into her mind that such a thing existed," said Professor Ramsberger. "In fact, Mr. Webster, she was represented by your firm, was she not? And I believe she paid quite a sum as a retainer for your services. The poor woman. You could have kept the till going for years."

I was horrified and appalled at this burst of lies. We were lawyers, not hucksters or grifters. There was a difference, wasn't there? Wasn't there? And ghosts were real. I had seen them. I had talked to them. One had thrown her head at me! The idea that they were mere pieces of some delusion made me want to scream.

"When I got word of Ms. Winterbottom's situation," continued Ramsberger, "I called and told her I might be able to help. She agreed to give me a chance. I arrived in my special ghost-hunting garb and made a grand show of things. After I left, having done nothing but provide a psychological service, she was delighted with the results."

"So, you claim there was no ghost?" said my father.

"No ghost," said Professor Ramsberger.

"Which is peculiar," said my father, "because when I served that ghost with a complaint in the middle of an aria, it wasn't happy, I can assure you. It complained so loudly its voice shattered my glasses."

Ramsberger stared at my father for a moment before saying, "Maybe you have an overactive imagination, too, Mr. Webster."

"He doesn't," I said quickly. "My father is as inventive as white toast."

Ramsberger sighed dramatically. "I suppose you've seen them, too, young Elizabeth."

"More than one," I said. "I know they exist."

"Or you've been brainwashed by your father," said Ramsberger. "Maybe I should call child protective services."

"What did you do with Ms. Winterbottom's ghost, Professor Ramsberger," asked my father, "and where is it now? We won't leave until we get some answers."

"You heard your answer," said Ramsberger. "You simply don't like it. I have already debunked a number of supposedly supernatural enterprises. I suppose the Webster firm will be my next target. It will make quite a lively podcast. But now, I believe, it's time for both of you to go."

The door opened and the two lawn people we had seen inside the house stepped into the room. With them came the hum of whispering voices, along with a whole new level of crazy.

16

An Unexpected Appearance

My father had pretended not to recognize the hum as we walked toward Ramsberger's house, but I suspected what it was because of the story my mother told me at that Massachusetts spa. And, as you'll soon see, my father was actually in that story. So when the lawn people stepped into Ramsberger's library and I saw a smile rise on my father's face, I assumed he had caught onto Ramsberger's fraud, which gave me a shot of courage.

"If you're so certain there are no ghosts," I said, standing and pointing at the two lawn people, "then what about them?"

"What about them?" said Ramsberger

"Have them take off their hats and masks," I said.

"You think they're ghosts, young Elizabeth, is that it?" said Ramsberger with a frightening cheeriness. "Ghosts that I've captured and forced to cut my lawn?"

"Why else would they be hiding their faces?"

"Allergies, perhaps?" he said. "The pollen is terrible this time of year."

"Why else would you bring in the voices?"

"Are you hearing things, young Elizabeth?"

"Have them take off their masks," I said.

"Terrence and Chandra," said Ramsberger, "please show your faces so this young girl can be certain you're not dead."

I had seen the lawn people float across the grass, I knew what they had to be. I was fed up with Ramsberger's lies about the natural and the supernatural. What could be more natural than a banshee or a headless teen ghost in a poodle skirt? Webster & Spawn was all about such things. I couldn't let Ramsberger's voice overpower what I knew to be true. I watched with total confidence as the lawn people took off their hats, their goggles, their masks, and showed themselves to be exactly what they were.

Two. Ordinary. People.

A man and a woman made of flesh and blood and bone. As human and alive as my father and mother, as ordinary as the back of my hand.

"It is time for you to go, Mr. Webster," said Ramsberger. "And take your deluded spawn with you."

Something was wrong. Some trick had been played. We couldn't let this stand. This was the moment when my father would open his briefcase, take out the complaint for the case of *Burton v. Ramsberger*, and serve it on the defendant with a flourish.

My father stood and said, "Yes, it is time to go."

"Wait a second," I said.

"Yes," said my father again, "it is time to go."

He took hold of his briefcase and turned toward the door. The voices were louder, more distinct, and now one sounded like my father's voice. *Yes, it is time for you to go.*

"Yes," said my father as he walked out of the room, past the two lawn people who were decidedly not ghosts, "it is time for us to go."

I looked at Ramsberger, who smiled that devouring smile of his, and then I hurried after my father.

"What about the complaint?" I said as we passed through the room with the human skulls. "We came to serve the complaint."

"Yes," said my father as he kept walking, "it is time to go."

My father didn't stop walking until we were back on the porch with the Martha Washington dogs. And with each step, my certainty grew smaller and smaller. On the porch my father stopped and looked around hesitantly, as if he wasn't sure how he had gotten there. Both Martha Washingtons were smirking at us. I looked around, too, not sure what I believed anymore.

And then I saw her.

Yes, there, across the street, peeking out from behind a hedge. Natalie, who had seen the first of my dead people, the poodle-skirted teen ghost that had thrown her head at me. I had asked Natalie to come, but she had some sort of excursion planned with Debbie Benner for that afternoon and I hadn't thought she would show. Yet there she was, and somehow just the sight of my best friend lifted me out of whatever trance I had fallen into and told me exactly what I needed to do.

I grabbed the briefcase out of my father's hand, snarled at the Marthas, and headed back into the house. I marched past the human skulls and the plates with the monstrous faces. I marched through the hallway and around the lawn people, Terrence and Chandra, with their goggles and masks back in place. I marched right into that library where Ramsberger still stood by the fireplace. The lady in the painting had a horrified expression on her face as if a rat had suddenly scampered into the room.

When Professor Ramsberger saw me, he smiled. "Back, are you? Come to your senses?"

Without a word I plopped the briefcase on the back of the couch, opened it, and started rummaging. While still looking inside, I lifted out a manila envelope and held it toward Ramsberger.

"Could you hold this for me a second, Professor?" I said. "There's something in here I need to show you."

"Of course, my dear," he said as he stepped forward and took hold of the envelope. "I'm wondering what little treat you have for me. I am so excited I can hardly breathe."

"Don't get too excited," I said, snapping closed the briefcase. "You've been served. The case of *Burton v. Ramsberger* is now alive. We'll see you in the Court of Uncommon Pleas."

As he slowly realized what had happened, the devouring smile vanished from his face. About time.

When I left the house, my father was still standing on the front porch, staring at his hands with a dazed expression, as if somebody had stolen his sandwich. When he looked up and saw me, his forehead creased in confusion.

"What are you doing here?" he said.

I grabbed hold of his arm and started pulling him toward the stairs. "Let's go."

"But something happened to my briefcase," said my father. "I seem to have left it somewhere."

"I have it," I said, lifting it in the air. "Let's go."

"How did you get hold of it?"

"Can we go? The dogs are making me nervous."

"What dogs?"

I gestured to the Martha Washingtons, who were staring with tilted and confused faces.

"Nice little puppies," said my father, kneeling down and rubbing one of the cement Marthas' cement fur. "And they're so calm."

"We need to go," I said, giving his arm another pull. This time he stood and let me lead him off the porch and down the stairs. As we walked away from the house, the hum grew softer and my father shook his head, as if to shake a daze out through his ears. When we reached the car, he stopped suddenly.

"We never served the complaint on Ramsberger," he said. "We need to go back."

"I served it," I said.

"You?"

"Someone had to, and you weren't in any condition to do it yourself. Ramsberger wasn't happy."

"No, I expect he wasn't." My father smiled. "Good job, Lizzie Face. I don't know what came over me."

"You don't? Really?"

He looked at me and then looked away, toward the house.

"I might have a sneaking suspicion," he said. "It's too bad we didn't get much information from Ramsberger, but at least the complaint was served, the case is live, and Janelle and Sydney will soon have their day in court. We'll consider it a win."

"Yay for the home team," I said. "Are you okay to drive?"

"I think so. That's why I said no to tea, I worried what a ghost thief might slip into the pot."

"Good thinking," I said. "I'll walk home. I can stop in on Natalie along the way."

I took my pack out of the car as my father slipped into the driver's seat. He pressed the button and the car silently sprang to life. Hybrids, the ninjas of cars. Before he drove off, he leaned out his window.

"Your grandfather was right as usual," he said. "I did need you here with me."

The compliment remained humming in my brain as the car pulled away, along with the memory of how weird he had become when the voices in the house started humming in his. It gave me a lot to think about, but not just then. Because just then Natalie was waving me over from behind the hedge across the street.

I looked back, saw that no one in the house was watching, and then ran down the street a bit, slipped behind the hedge, and knelt next to Natalie.

"You came," I said.

"You knew I would," she said.

"No, I didn't."

"Good," said Natalie. "How was the inside of that house?"

"Creepier than you could imagine. I think the Martha Washington dogs laughed at me. And there were human skulls and weird plates and this big painting of a woman who stared at me with such hatred I could almost taste it."

"What did it taste like?" said Natalie, eyes bright.

"Olives," I said.

"Oooh."

"And that hum we heard? Inside it was louder and clearer and it was made up of voices that invaded my father's mind. But the worst thing was Ramsberger himself. He was in this fancy silk jacket acting all lord-of-the-manor while trying to convince me that ghosts were merely figments of my imagination."

"He didn't."

"He did. And as he spoke, and the voices hummed at me, I began to think he might be right."

"He was gaslighting you," said Natalie.

"What's gaslighting?"

"It's when someone tells a lie over and over again," said Natalie, "until you start doubting something you know to be true. It's from an old movie where this Frenchy guy tried to make his wife think she was crazy."

"What movie is that?" I said.

"*Gaslight*," said Natalie. "What aren't you getting? Speak of the devil."

We lifted our heads so our eyes were just above the top of the hedge, allowing us a clear view of the porch, where the ghost thief now stood in his leather jacket. He looked about angrily before heading around the side to the garage.

It wasn't long before the strange R.I.P. convertible peeked

its nose through the garage door. It clattered and clanked out of the driveway and turned right, passing in front of us.

The globes on the back were all lit up now, with swirling colors of light exactly as Janelle had described. Inside the car Ramsberger was hunched forward, strangling the steering wheel with his grip, staring angrily ahead.

And then, when it passed, I saw the strangest thing, something that looked to be fastened to the pipes and hoses on the back of the car, as if it had dripped right out of those two globes.

Keir?

Of course it was Keir, hanging on to the back for dear life as the car zoomed away from us.

"By the way," said Natalie, "I convinced Keir to come along. I tried to get Henry, too, but he said he was busy."

"Of course he did. Do you think it was something I said?"

"Probably," said Natalie. "But Keir was willing. He had to miss soccer practice, but he said you were worth it. He'll find out where your ghost thief is headed."

Just then Keir, still holding on, turned his head and saw us and smiled his goofy, twisted-tooth smile. He lifted his left hand and gave us a wave as if to say, *Hey, wassup?*

The van veered left. Keir lost his balance and looked to be falling as he grappled with his free hand to get his hold back on the car. He was still flailing around when the car, and Keir, disappeared from our view.

17

CLEVELAND

Honk! Honk!

Mel stood frozen in the middle of the city street as the streetcar charged at her like a gray bull with headlight eyes, until Juniper grabbed her by the arm and yanked. The two girls landed hard on the cement road, outside the trolley tracks.

As they spun away from the hurtling piece of metal, an old-style car, with four headlights and narrow tires, rushed at them from the other direction.

This time both girls scampered away onto the sidewalk as the car clipped by. The driver, a man in a hat, looked at them through the window as if he was looking at two fish in an aquarium.

"That was close," said Juniper.

"You can say that again," said Mel, gasping for breath.

"That was close," repeated Juniper. "Why would Gaap drop us right in the middle of the road?"

Mel thought about it for a moment, remembering the anger in the demon's voice. "It was a message. He really wants that Lens of Fate thing."

"Maybe we should have knelt."

They took a moment to catch their breaths and look around. They were in a canyon of stone and cement, with buildings going up and buildings being taken down. Construction dust covered everything, including the pedestrians who detoured around scaffolds and trudged through puddles. Then Mel pointed at something on the far side of the street and Juniper said, "What the…"

Across the roadway, standing on their hind legs, were two sinister-looking alligators—yes, that's right, alligators! The alligators wore black broad-brimmed hats and black overcoats, and their alligator tails snaked out behind them as they kept watch on the trudging crowd.

"That's so strange," said Mel. "They look like cops," which caused Juniper to snort out a peculiar laugh.

And just as strange as the alligators was the color of everything, or the lack of it. The city was gray, everyone was wearing gray, and everybody's skin had a grayish pallor, even though all the populations of the living world were represented. It was as if even the idea of color was a crime.

Which might be why the girls were being stared at. As pedestrians plodded by in all their grayness, their attention was caught by the blue of Mel's jeans and the deep brown of Juniper's skin and the flush of Mel's cheeks and the pink of Juniper's headband.

In the hubbub of sound that flowed with the walkers, they could actually hear the disapproval. That buzz on the bridge was no longer a buzz but an assembly of voices, as if some sort of invisible person was following everyone in the city, whispering whispering.

Look at what they're wearing. Can you believe it? Just asking for trouble. They better hope the bosses don't see them. Turn away, don't stare or you'll be as guilty as they are.

"Do you hear what I hear?" said Juniper.

"I don't think they like us," said Mel.

"We should have put on nicer pants."

A woman walked by in a gray dress with a gray coat and a gray hat, looking at them with wary gray eyes. *How dare they leave the house dressed like that?* said the voice trailing the woman. *And look at them standing around doing nothing. The nerve.*

As the woman was still looking, Mel took a step forward. "Excuse me, ma'am. We're looking for a man named Tommy Lee Jelani. A trumpet player. Do you know how we could find him?"

"I don't know any such man," said the woman with a tight smile. *You need to report this to a boss. How can they accost people like this? They need to be stopped, stopped.* "Now step aside," said the woman before moving on.

As they watched her go, Juniper said, "She seems nice."

"She seems scared," said Mel. "Of us."

"And she doesn't even know us," said Juniper.

"Imagine if she knew us."

"She'd be terrified."

As they laughed, Mel said, "Do you see any phone booths? Maybe we can find your father's address in the phone book."

I have to stop here and give a history lesson. Mr. Armbruster would be so proud. In my mom's day, when she claims people still had manners, it wasn't considered polite to make calls on the street. Instead, if you wanted to make a call you did it in something called a phone booth. You would slip into the booth, order pizza and a soda from the waitress, and make a call on your cell phone. And in the booth there was something called a phone book. It wasn't a book with all the kinds of phones you could buy—instead it was a book with the numbers and addresses of everyone in the city. Really. Is that a great idea or what? A phone book. And that's what my mother was trying to find.

"Over there," said Juniper. "There's a booth across the street."

They ran to the corner and impatiently waited with the gray crowd as cars and trucks roared by and the voices floated around them. *You're tired, so tired. What is wrong with your hair? You're not good enough, you have to be better. Look at your shoes, they're so dusty. You're so so tired. Why are you always so tired?*

There was an alligator with a black hat standing in the middle of the street. When it raised its stubby arm and put up its fat clawed hand, the traffic squealed to a stop. Then the alligator turned its snout toward the waiting crowd and gestured for the people to cross. The crowd started moving, and Mel had begun walking with them, probably wondering if there was a pizza of delight in the phone booth, when Juniper grabbed hold of her shoulder and yanked her back.

"Hold on," said Juniper.

"What is it?"

"Just hold on," said Juniper, pointing down the sidewalk on their side of the street. "There, in the gray suit."

"They're all wearing gray suits."

"The tall man with the hat."

"They're all wearing hats."

"I think it's him," said Juniper. "I don't know. But the way he's walking. Is it him? I think it's him."

"Gaap sent us to this very street for a reason," said Mel. "It means your father is probably somewhere close. Let's see if you're right."

"Wait."

Mel looked at Juniper, saw the fear in her now-squinty face, and hugged her, right there on the street.

What are they doing? Is that allowed? Someone call someone.

"He's your father," said Mel as she kept hugging. "He'll always be your father and he'll always love you. I know it for a fact. Like I'll always love you. Trust him."

Before Juniper could argue, Mel started heading after the man, weaving through the plodding pedestrians, passing behind an alligator cop in a black hat and long black coat, being careful not to step on its tail. She looked behind her to be sure Juniper was following. She was. And so was the alligator's fierce stare.

"Sir?" said Mel when she had finally caught up to the man. "Mr. Jelani."

The man lifted his head as if he was hearing Mel's voice, but he didn't stop.

"Sir," said Mel. "Excuse me, sir? Are you Mr. Jelani?"

Again there was a strange hesitation, but the man kept walking until he turned to enter a building. As he did, he glanced at Mel, and then behind Mel, a glance full of fear, before he yanked open the door and walked though. The door slammed behind him.

A moment later Juniper caught up to her. "Was it him?" she said.

"I don't know," said Mel. "He didn't answer. But that looks like an apartment building. Let's check it out."

"Are you sure?"

"Sure I'm sure." Mel opened the door and held it open as she saw the alligator, who had been staring, start to walk toward them. "It's probably safer to get off the street for the time being anyway."

Inside the front door was a large array of mailbox slots with names and apartment numbers. They went through the names, Mel starting from the top and Juniper from the bottom. Mel stopped when Juniper inhaled deeply and pointed at one of the boxes.

T. L. Jelani. Fourth floor. Room 424.

Juniper held on to Mel's arm as they climbed the stairs. The fourth floor was a long hallway with so many doors so close together they looked as if they each opened to a closet. The two girls stood together in front of the door with 424 painted on the wood. From the other side they heard the soft murmur of voices.

"He won't remember me," said Juniper.

"Knock," said Mel.

"He's talking to somebody."

"Knock," said Mel.

"He doesn't want to be disturbed."

"Knock," said Mel.

Finally, Juniper raised her hand to the door and rapped on it lightly with her knuckles. *Knock-knock.* And then harder. *Knock!*

When the door finally opened, the man stood before them with his jacket off but his hat still on. He was tall and thin, dark-skinned and handsome, and his wide mouth was pursed with confusion. He looked at Juniper, then at Mel, and then back at Juniper, his eyes glassy as a voice from behind him talked.

Who are these two? What are they wearing and what do they want? Send them away. This is no time for visitors. No time at all. Send them away before trouble comes a-calling.

"Dad?" said Juniper. "It's me, Juniper."

He looked closely at her and then his glassy eyes seemed to focus.

Send them away before the bosses come. Do it now, do it now. Send them away or it will be the Stormlands for you.

"Hello there, Juniper," said Juniper's father in a voice strangely like the voice coming from behind him. "It's nice to see you as always." *They must go. They must go now. The bosses are already on their way. On their way.* "But I'm a little busy right at the moment." He winked and said, "See you on the upside," before giving a sad smile, backing away, and closing the door behind him.

Juniper stared at the door as if she had seen a ghost, which I suppose she had.

"What just happened?" said Mel.

Before Juniper could answer, they heard strange plodding footsteps pounding up the stairs toward them, two sets, three sets, tails included, pounding up the stairs.

The alligators were coming!

The stairs were at one end of the long hallway. On the other end was a window facing a solid brick wall.

"The window," said Mel. "We can jump down."

"Four flights?" said Juniper.

"Then what do we do?"

Juniper looked left, looked right, and then looked at the door in front of them. Her father's door. Sanctuary? Mel stepped forward and was about to knock when Juniper stopped her.

"Keep him out of it," she said.

They stared at each other for a moment before Mel looked at the ceiling.

Without any further discussion they both took off for the stairway. They ran up and around, up and around, two stairs at a time, three stairs at a time as the footsteps pounded after them. The image of the two of them leaping to their freedom from rooftop to rooftop thrilled Juniper and terrified Mel as they raced up the stairs.

They reached the top and smashed right through a doorway onto the black tar of the roof, where beneath the low gray sky an alligator waited for them. At the end of the alligator's stubby little arm, its clawed fist gripped a gun aimed first at Mel, then at Juniper, and then back at Mel.

"Freeze," hissed the alligator.

The girls froze.

THE MCGOOGAN REPORT

Natalie and I waited for Keir to reappear at my house, which meant Natalie suffered through a dinner of my mom's cooking. Tonight's special was turkey-and-tofu meat-loaf. A feast for the senses! My friend looked at me with pity as she tried to eat without choking.

"It's delicious, Mrs. Scali," lied Natalie. "The raisins are a lovely touch."

"Thank you, Natalie," said my mother proudly. "I got the recipe off the internet."

"I guessed that!" said Petey.

"I've never tasted anything like it before," said Natalie.

"Don't rub it in," I said.

"If you want, I could save my piece for Keir," said Petey. "I wouldn't want him to miss out."

"Gosh, that's very kind of you, Peter," said my stepfather. "But I'm sure there's enough."

"I'll put it back on the serving dish anyway," said Petey as he put his piece back on the serving dish anyway. "I don't want to take any chances."

"What kind of field trip is Keir on, again?" said my mother.

"A trip involving fields, I suppose," I said, trying to fill in the details of the cover story I'd given her. "Alfalfa, maybe? A trip to the alfalfa fields is always so educational."

"Nothing like a good field of alfalfa," said my stepfather.

"I know," I said. "Nothing."

"When Keir gets home, tell him there's a plate for him in the fridge," said my mother. "Along with his shake. He mustn't forget his shake."

"No indeed," I said.

After dinner I sat with Natalie on the front steps of the house, playing a game of Would You Rather as darkness fell. It was cold and we were hugging ourselves, but Keir didn't have a phone, so we had no other plan but to wait and worry. I felt responsible and guilty and a little nauseous about it all. I should never have gotten my friends involved in this Ramsberger business. And I should never have eaten that meatloaf.

"The spiders, definitely," said Natalie in response to my would-you-rather.

"I would have thought you'd go with snakes," I said, "considering—"

"But snakes are horrible."

"And spiders are so sweet?" I said.

"They're misunderstood," said Natalie. "All they want

is to knit their webs and not be judged. They're crafters. What's sweeter than that?"

"Maybe something that doesn't catch you and then suck you dry," I said. "I hate spiders more than anything."

"There's nothing wrong with spiders," said a voice in the darkness. "Clever little creatures, they are."

"Keir!" shouted Natalie.

And then there he was, a shadow in the darkness sauntering toward us. Even as he stepped into the light, he stayed a shadow, as if the darkness surrounding him was somehow sticking to him like Velcro. Vampires are weird.

His shadowiness didn't stop us from leaping off the steps to give him hugs and pound him on the back. He huddled into himself as if we were attacking him with pitchforks. And then, tired from his walk, and hungry, he dropped onto the steps. I ran inside and brought out his special shake and we all sat together as he slurped through the straw.

"Do you want something else?" I said.

"What else is there?" said Keir. "The shake cures the hunger, but it doesn't fill the belly."

"Mrs. Scali made a new kind of meatloaf," said Natalie.

"Was it good?"

"Petey saved his entire portion for you," I said.

"Ahh, I know what that means," said Keir. "Did your mam get the recipe off the internet, Elizabeth?"

"Actually, yes," I said.

"Then I'll stick to the shake."

"I'm sorry about your soccer practice," I said.

"It's okay, Elizabeth," he said. "I told the coach I pulled a muscle in my leg. I limped for him pretty, too."

"So?" I said. "Spill. Where did Ramsberger take you?"

"To a bunch of old friends, if you need to know. We visited the old cemetery on the edge of the city. It was where the high and low were buried when I was still a living boy."

"What was Ramsberger doing in a cemetery?" said Natalie.

"Aye, that's the question," said Keir. "He drove up to some old marble mausoleum dug into the hill. His last name was carved right into the stone. As soon as the car stopped, he jumped out, rushed over, and disappeared inside."

"A mausoleum," said Natalie. "How marvelously creepy. Maybe he was merely paying his respects to an old dead relative."

"Sure," I said. "A little cemetery visit after getting served in a lawsuit sounds about right."

"When he came outside a few moments later it was a good thing I had jumped off his car and hid behind a gravestone because he went around the back, unfastened one of the glittering globes sticking out, and brought it inside that crypt. About twenty minutes later he brought it back outside, dark and dead now, screwed it back on, and took the second."

"What was inside the globes?" said Natalie.

"Don't rightly know," said Keir. "And I didn't have time to hitch myself back on his car before he left. When I finally got to the gates they were closed and locked. But one of the iron posts in the fence was gone and I slipped through the gap."

"I would have gotten my stepfather to pick you up if we had known," I said.

"It's okay, Elizabeth. It wasn't very far as the crow flies. And it was nice walking among the tombs, wallowing a bit in my past. I passed the graves of all the rich folk that I remember ruling the city when we were so poor. They strutted around so important in their day, with their top hats and tails, and now they're just spittoons, they are. Maybe if they realized where they were headed, they'd have been a little more kind."

"The end," I said.

Natalie and I laughed, and Keir joined in, because whenever he gives one of his little speeches in school that's how he finishes it.

"By the way," I said, "if my mom asks, you were visiting an alfalfa field."

"Why I would be doing that?"

"A field trip?"

"There's something else," said Keir, before taking another slurp of his shake.

"Go on," I said, my eyes widening as he slurped.

"When I was hiding in that garage, I found me a spot in a closet where I could wait for that Ramsberger to show. And in there I saw a machine like nothing else I had ever before seen. It was something that doctor who made the monster would have invented."

"Dr. Frankenstein?"

"Aye, that's the one. This Frankenstein machine had all kinds of tubes and pipes and vials filled with some purple liquid, along with a globe of its own. And sticking out of it all was a horn like on a Victrola listened to by that dog in the advert."

"What's an advert?" I said.

"What's a Victrola?" said Natalie.

"Think of the end of a trombone," said Keir, "sticking out of the middle of a machine as if some marching song was about to be played. My guess is the machine has something to do with his ghost-thieving. I'd hate for that thing to be used against my mam, I would. And you'll never guess the name of the company that made it."

"Let me try," I said. "Phantasm International Industries."

Keir stared at me for a moment and then he laughed. "The only surprise, Elizabeth," he said, "is that you keep surprising me."

But it wasn't only me who figured it out. You knew it, too. Josiah Goodheart had given us the lead on a slip of napkin, and now it was time to follow it.

19

ETHEL

The cell that held Juniper and Mel in Redwing's domain was cold and colorless, with thick iron bars along the front and a single barred window on the opposite brick wall. The two friends sat on a bench, side by side. On the bench across from them sat one other prisoner, a thick lumpy woman swaddled in gray, clasping her hands and staring down at the floor. And, oh yeah, the place smelled bad, overflowing dumpster bad, stadium bathroom bad, my mother's attempts at clam chowder bad. Bad.

"What are they going to do to us?" said Mel.

"I don't know," said Juniper.

"I've never been in jail before," said Mel.

"Quiet."

"What did we even do?" said Mel.

The woman sitting across from them looked up. "Redwing

doesn't care what we do," she said, her rasp of a voice as gray as her misshapen face. "Only that we stay afraid."

"What did you do?" said Mel.

"I had an independent thought," said the woman. "That's enough of a crime for the Raven Master."

"Who's the Raven Master?"

"The demon's henchwoman. One of the dead, she taught the demon how to control the rest of us. And in turn the demon authorized her to mete out his punishments."

"Like what?" said Mel.

"Quiet," said Juniper.

"Listen to your friend," said the woman. "This is Redwing's domain. No one is to be trusted."

"Even you?"

The woman's lumpy face broke into a smile. "Especially me," she said. "I'm Ethel."

"I'm Mel," said Mel. "This is Juniper."

"Can we not talk, Mel, please?" said Juniper. "The first rule in jail is not to talk to anyone."

"How do you know that?" said Mel.

Juniper glanced at Ethel before saying, "Just be careful."

"What's the second rule?" said Mel.

"Save your spoons," said Juniper.

"She's right about the spoons," said Ethel.

They sat in quiet for a moment, Mel staring at Juniper, who stared at the floor. The sky was dark outside the jail, but the cell was overly bright, with lights that sizzled and hissed.

"What punishments can the Raven Master give us?" said Mel to Ethel finally.

Juniper jabbed her in the side with an elbow.

"But I want to know," said Mel.

Ethel, still looking down at her hands, said, "Whatever evil torture you can dream up, she can do worse. But you girls don't have to worry. The Raven Master won't send the living to the lower depths. You're more useful to her here."

"How do you know we're still living?" said Juniper.

"The color in your cheeks, the clothes you wear. How'd you get to this world, anyway?"

Mel said, "We came with a—Ow!"

The elbow poke from Juniper was hard enough to dent a rib. Mel gave Juniper a shocked expression and then became quiet.

"But the real question is why," said Ethel. "Why would two living girls come to a hellhole like this?"

"It's a funny story," said Mel.

"Which we won't be telling," said Juniper sharply. "Do they have law courts down here?"

"There's a Court of Uncommon Pleas on every level," said Ethel. "But don't expect any mercy from those judges."

"And are there lawyers?" said Juniper.

"There are always lawyers. Like there are boils and locusts. This is the underworld, after all. But I wouldn't trust one of them mouthpieces. They are mostly thieves and liars under Redwing's thumb."

"How do we get a lawyer?" said Juniper.

"You pay for it," said Ethel.

"We don't have any money."

"Well then," said Ethel with a weird half shrug. "But if you let me know how you came and why you're here, I might be able to help."

Juniper tilted her head at Ethel before standing up from the bench and walking toward the wall of iron bars. She grabbed hold of a bar in each hand and started shouting.

"Hey! Who's there? Hey!"

"What are you doing?" said Mel.

"Hey!" shouted Juniper, ignoring her friend. "Whoever's listening. We want a lawyer. Do you hear us?"

"I wouldn't do that if I was you, young'un," said Ethel. "The bosses don't take kindly to being snapped at."

Juniper ignored her and kept on shouting. "We want a lawyer and we won't say anything to anyone until we get a lawyer. Nothing." And then she began to chant. *"What do we want? A lawyer! When do we want it? Now!"*

As Juniper began her chant, Mel glanced at Ethel before standing from the bench and heading over to the bars. She hesitated a moment before taking hold herself and joining in with her friend.

"What do we want? A lawyer!" they both shouted. *"When do we want it? Now! What do we want? A lawyer! When do we want it? Now!"*

As they took a break to catch their breaths, Mel said softly to Juniper, "What about a sandwich? I could also use a—"

That was when they heard it, the strange sucking sound behind them, like the sound of the suction thing the dentist sticks into your mouth. Slowly, Mel and Juniper turned around.

Ethel was standing behind them, her head cocked at a weird angle, her eyes dead, her arms loose at her side, her mouth wide and growing wider, wider as the sucking sound continued. And then something appeared deep in her mouth. A tongue, but not a tongue, no—it was green and scaly and its tendrils were tipped with claws.

It only took a moment for the thing to emerge into the light, an alligator hand reaching out of the ever-stretching mouth. And then a second hand. The two alligator hands pulled and stretched until the mouth became a huge, gaping hole out of which rose first the crown and eyes of an alligator and then the long snout with its yellow pointed teeth. The hands kept pulling and the alligator kept rising until all that was left of Ethel was a pile of clothes and skin, along with a slick of what had been Ethel's face lying on the floor flat as a spilled puddle of paint.

"You should have talked to me," said the alligator boss in a high, nasal voice. "I could have helped. Now you get no mercy."

"We don't want your mercy," said Juniper calmly. "What we want is a lawyer."

20

THE MOUTHPIECE

The girls spent an uneasy night alone in the cell, without food or water or even a shout-out by a guard, sleeping fitfully on the two benches as the dark of night outside the window turned into a hazy gray dawn. They were still lying on the benches, pretending to sleep, when one of the alligators let in the strange boy with the rumpled blue suit and the battered briefcase.

The boy stood for a moment in silence, waiting for the guard to leave. He was tall and thin, with ruddy skin, messy black hair, and horn-rimmed glasses with large round frames. From the flush in his cheeks and the blue in his eyes, right away Mel and Juniper could tell he was not from this world but from theirs.

"Welcome to the alligator house," said Mel. "What demon brought you over?"

"Demon?" said the boy. "Why would I need a demon? I came through the portal."

"There's a portal?" said Mel. "We could have used a token and come through a portal?"

"Remember what I told you before?" said Juniper.

"Yeah, I remember. Don't talk in jail."

"She's right, you know," said the boy. "Can I sit?"

"Sure," said Mel, before quickly shifting over to sit next to Juniper, leaving the boy a free bench.

The boy sat down, put his briefcase on the cement floor, took a deep breath, and winced at the smell. "So, you said a demon brought you guys over to this side. Which one?"

"You want to hear something funny?" said Juniper.

"Sure," he said. "This early in the morning I could use a laugh."

"The last time a prisoner in here asked that question, she turned out to be an alligator in a human costume."

The boy patted his chest and shoulders to see if there was an alligator inside. Juniper stared at the act unamused.

"I don't want to disappoint you, but I'm basically human," said the boy. "And I'm not here as a prisoner. You might have heard of me? My name is Eli Webster?"

The girls looked at him blankly, as if they'd missed the class where his name was supposed to mean something, but you didn't miss it, I'm sure. You knew this was my father the moment he walked into the cell. It was in that pair of awkward glasses, that mop of hair and rumpled suit, that same battered briefcase he still carried, bought, no doubt, at the battered-briefcase store in the mall.

"No recognition?" said my father. "Well, all you need to know is that I'm a lawyer and I've come to help you."

They looked at him incredulously. Then Juniper laughed, and Mel joined in. It was the first time they had laughed since landing in the cell, and it felt good, but the boy didn't react as they would have expected. He didn't argue or get embarrassed, he simply waited until the laughter died.

"Aren't you a little young for all that lawyer jazz?" said Juniper. "What, did you do law school when you were twelve?"

"No law school," said Eli. "Not yet, at least. I'm actually still in high school, and not doing so well, I must say. What is it with math?"

"I know, right?" said Mel.

"Then I don't understand how you claim to be a lawyer," said Juniper.

"It's a family thing," he said with a shrug. "Because of something that happened to some long-dead great-uncle, I'm allowed to pass back and forth and appear before the Court of Uncommon Pleas on both sides. Someone in another cell heard you demanding an attorney, and I happened to be on this side for a court proceeding. When I'm here I give help when it's needed, and from what I can see, you guys need it."

"How much trouble are we in?" said Mel.

"You're accused of illegally entering Redwing's domain, of trespassing on Redwing's property, of running from the bosses, and worst of all, and quite shocking I have to say, of hugging in public."

Mel and Juniper didn't object or deny, they just shrugged.

"Since I'm here as a lawyer, everything you tell me is

confidential," said my father. "So why don't you tell me everything."

After a moment's hesitation, they began to talk, starting with the hidden treasure and ending with that race up the stairs in Juniper's father's building. They included everything except the bit about their promise to steal the Lens of Fate for the demon they refused to name.

When the story was over, Eli looked back and forth at the girls and said simply, "Wow."

"So?" said Juniper. "What can the law do for us?"

"I can't make any promises," said Eli after a moment of thought. "But I'm pretty sure I can have the court send you home through the portal."

"Really?" said Mel. "Just that easy?"

"Well, you'd have to confess. And there'd be a mark on your permanent records. I mean, no matter where we are, there's always paperwork, right? And that mark might affect your placement by the Tribunal of Classification after, you know..."

"After we die," said Mel.

"Yes. But if the mark comes early enough in your life it doesn't have too big an effect."

"Like a suspension from middle school?" said Mel.

"Let's not get carried away," said Eli. "Nothing is as serious as a middle school suspension."

"So, you can help us?" said Juniper.

"I think so," said Eli.

"Your certainty is so comforting," said Mel.

My father looked at my mother like she was a dissatisfied customer at a Starbucks returning a scone. "You put yourselves in this crazy situation," he said. "Don't blame me if I can only promise what I can promise."

"Well, golly gee," said Mel. There was something about this nerd-nosed kid playing at being a lawyer that bothered her. Who was he to be so judgy?

"What about my father?" said Juniper.

"I'll argue that he wasn't involved. That should be enough to protect him."

"But I came over here to talk to him," said Juniper. "I need to talk to him. Can I still do that?"

"I'm sorry, no," said Eli. "The court's in session now. I can file an emergency motion and get us before the judge, but you'd be sent back right away."

"I came here to talk to my father," said Juniper.

"We're in jail," said Mel. "We're not talking to your father from here. The baby lawyer said this is the only way out."

"Baby lawyer?" said my father.

"And even if we do get to see your father again," said Mel, "what good would it do, the way he was acting?"

Juniper shook her head at all of Mel's logic. "I won't go back without seeing him again."

Mel looked at Juniper, and then at the boy, who was looking at her friend with a slight smile, as if the judgy lawyer was liking what he judged. For some reason that smile filled Mel with a strange emotion. It wasn't quite anger, but it was something unpleasant. Like someone else taking the best piece of cake.

"Well then," said Eli to Mel, the smile suddenly gone from his face, "the baby lawyer should be able to get you back on your own."

Mel looked at my father, then at Juniper, then down at her hands. "I won't go back without Juniper," she said finally.

"No?" said Juniper.

Mel shook her head, reluctantly but firmly.

"That's surprising," said Eli. "But then the terms are set, together or not at all."

"What do we do now?" said Juniper.

Eli sat there thinking as the girls looked at each other and then around the cell. How long would they be stuck in here? How many hours, days, centuries? Mel was suddenly wondering why Juniper had gotten them into this mess in the first place.

"I think I have an idea," said Eli before grabbing his brief-case and standing. "Hold tight and let me see what I can do."

After he called for the guard and left the cell, the girls waited. An hour. Two hours. The whole of the day. One of the alligators brought a gray mash for them to eat. It tasted of oatmeal without sugar or milk or even oats. They each could only get down a few swallows. As the evening fell, they lay on their benches, still hungry, and watched the gray light outside the window slowly dim to black. It felt like their entire futures were dimming with the light.

And that was when they heard it.

"Pssst."

A sound through the window.

"Pssst. Hey. You two. Back away."

They jumped off their benches and backed away from the window, backed away until their backs were pressed against the iron. Just then they spotted a metal hook being fastened to one of the window's bars.

The girls looked at each other and then back at the window, wondering what a single metal hook could do about a solid brick wall. They were still wondering when an explosion rocked the room and the edges of the brick wall disintegrated in twin flashes of light and power.

The cell was suddenly filled with dust. So much dust they could barely breathe. Dust so thick they couldn't see far enough to make out the brick wall. It was only when a woman in gray climbed over the rubble and stepped into the cell that they realized the brick wall wasn't there anymore.

She was tall and angular, with a pale gray face, and she held out her hand while saying something they couldn't hear over the din in their ears from the explosions.

Word by word she shouted her message and the meaning finally slipped through the madness. "We need to go."

"Who are you?" said Juniper.

"Does that matter?" said the woman.

"Where are we going?" said Juniper.

"Away," shouted the woman.

And then the sirens started.

21

THE POWER PLANT

I stood in the street along with Natalie and Keir, looking down at the napkin given to me by Josiah Goodheart, then up, then down again. This had to be a mistake.

The building in front of us was an abandoned wreck of weed and brick, surrounded by a metal fence, with ragged ducts and stairwells snaking all around its exterior. Three graffiti-covered smokestacks stuck out the top, the salute of a decrepit, tattooed Boy Scout. I spun around in frustration. We had taken the train into the city after school and walked all this way only to find a derelict shell of a ruined steam plant.

"Sorry about this," I said. "A wasted afternoon."

"And I could have been on South Street trying out earrings with Debbie," said Natalie.

"Maybe not a total waste then," I said.

"Be nice," said Natalie.

"Let's explore," said Keir.

"Let's not," I said. "There won't be anything inside other than rust and rats."

"Perfect, then," said Keir, eyes a little too bright. "What more could we want?"

Natalie and I looked at each other and then followed Keir as he squeezed through a gap in a locked gate and slipped through a barely open door, leading to a world of rust and ruin. Sheets of green filth fell from the pipes. Corrosion covered the fittings like a weed. And then there were the actual weeds. Everything smelled wet and old and foul. We could hear traces of some strange music, as if the same sad melody had been rattling the pipes since before we were born.

"What's that song?" said Natalie.

"What is this, a game show?" I said. "I don't know the name of the stupid song."

"The stupid song is coming from over there," said Natalie before she started walking toward the music like it was the piping of a pied piper.

This time we followed her, past big round furnaces with their doors open, and a coal cart frozen with rust. The sound of little critters scurrying made my skin crawl. We stopped at a set of metal stairs set in a brick alcove. From above us the music dripped down more clearly. Natalie gave us a wide-eyed *uh-oh* glance before she slowly started climbing.

Tink tink tink went the metal beneath her feet as rust drifted down. Keir and I looked at each other for a moment and then we hurried to catch up.

Tink tink tink tink tink.

At the top of the stairs we stood in a row as we looked through a brickwork arch into a large well-lit room with a wall of dusty windows. The other walls were lined with pipes snaking this way and that, all dripping with the vile green sheets, but in the center were a series of workbenches with lamps lit and all kinds of strange machines in various stages of construction. Keir pointed at one of the machines, a strange glob of tubes and vials with the end of a trombone sticking out. He nodded to tell me that was the one he had seen.

Moving among the workbenches were two figures in white coats, one huge, one tiny.

The music was loud enough to hide our presence for a time, but our time was up when the huge figure, a giant with unruly yellow hair, raised his head and stared at us. He pressed a button and the music died.

And then, slowly, he walked toward us, his huge hands held out in front, squeezing at the air with every step as if each held a horn with a red rubber ball. *Honk honk.*

"Cheeldren, cheeldren," he said with an accent like the Count from *Sesame Street*, "you should not be here."

"We're looking for a Dr. Shevski?" I said.

"You have no appointment. Go home."

"How do we get an appointment?" said Natalie.

"There are no appointments."

"Are you Dr. Shevski?" I said.

"I am Ygor. With a Y."

"Igor?" said Natalie. "Really?"

"With a Y. Time for all the little cheeldren to go home."

Ygor's hands started squeezing again as he stepped toward us—*honk honk*—and we looked at each other for a moment, trying to figure out what to do. Run? Argue? All kinds of plots and plans were buzzing in my brain when I saw the tiny figure in the white coat start walking toward us. Her gray hair was tied in a bun. Her hands were clasped behind her back. A huge pair of round glasses perched on her ghostly white nose.

"Dr. Shevski?" I called out.

She didn't answer, but my call caused Ygor to look behind him. When he saw the small figure come toward us, he backed away and bowed slightly.

"The cheeldren have no appointment, Doctor," said Ygor.

Without acknowledging Ygor, she stepped right up to Keir and stared for a long moment. "You," she said to Keir. "Come with me."

Without waiting to see if he followed, she turned and walked back into the workshop, her hands still clasped behind her.

Keir looked at me. I nodded. When he started to follow the old woman, Natalie and I followed, too.

"I guess we got ourselves an appointment, hey, Igor?" said Natalie as she passed him on the way into the workshop.

"With a Y," said Ygor.

It wasn't long before Keir was being examined by the old lady. She opened his eyes wide with her fingers. She put a Popsicle stick into his mouth and aimed a flashlight. She put two fingers on the underside of his wrist as she stared at her watch. It was like he was getting a checkup at the doctor's so he could play field hockey.

"Leave him for a few days," she said as she stared at her watch.

"Why would we leave Keir with you?" I said.

"So I can fix him."

"But we don't want Keir fixed," I said. "He's perfect as he is."

"Hardly perfect," she said. "Have you seen his teeth?"

"What's wrong with my teeth?" said Keir.

"But if you don't want him fixed," said Dr. Shevski, "then why are you here bothering me?"

I spun around and pointed at the machine with the trombone horn attached. "We came because of that?"

"Don't be silly," she said. "The SC107 won't have any effect on him. He'll need more drastic measures."

"How drastic?" said Keir.

"We're not here about Keir," said Natalie. "We're here about ghosts."

"Ghosts?" said Ygor, standing behind us. "You are having problem, yes?"

"You could say that," I said. "My name is Elizabeth Webster and we have questions about your machine."

"Elizabeth Webster?" said the doctor, tapping her nose. "Elizabeth Webster. Why does that name ring a bell? Oh yes, one of my clients mentioned you. A Professor Ramsberger."

"Ding," said Natalie.

"He must have referred you to me," said the doctor. "How kind of him. And you're interested in renting an SC107?"

"The SC107 can catch your ghost with flick of switch," said Ygor. "And we have very generous pricing plan for all our models. Would you want to see?"

"Yes," I said. "Yes, we would."

And we did.

PHANTASM INTERNATIONAL

This is the latest version of Spirit Catcher," said Ygor as he waved a hand before the machine that Keir had pointed out. "Model SC107. Model 106 had flaws, yes, with unfortunate results, but model 107 is perfect."

At the base of the machine was some sort of old-time radio surrounded by a cage of metal ribs supporting a network of pipes and cords and vials of bubbling purple liquid. The trombone horn was connected to the pipes, and a globe sat at the very top, a smaller version of the globes on Ramsberger's ghost-catching car.

"When ghost, it appears," said Ygor, "simply turn switch and—Zap!—ghost is sucked through horn and trapped in globe."

"Yikes alive!" said Natalie.

"Not alive, cheeldren," said Ygor. "Dead."

"How does it work?" I said.

"Physics," said Dr. Shevski, who was looking on with her hands behind her back. "I have been studying the phenomenon of ghosts for half a century. The same magnetic force the spirit uses to create its image can be used to trap the spirit when the particles it is manipulating are captured in the precisely correct manner."

"And is it safe?" said Natalie.

"For the user, yes," said the Dr. Shevski.

"And what do you do with the ghost after you catch it?" said Keir.

"You can release it somewhere else far away, like a raccoon, or store it," said the doctor.

"That is why we recommend, along with SC107," said Ygor, "that you purchase latest version of SS-G, our secure storage solution for all your ghostly problems."

He walked over to a small glass globe attached to a base with a small motor and three vials full of bubbling liquids of different colors. The globe itself looked like something you would pick up at a Disneyland gift shop, except instead of being filled with a perfect little town and a gust of snow, it contained a swirl of multicolored lights.

"Each SS-G holds one spirit," said Ygor.

"Like one of my mom's bottles," said Natalie.

"The SS-M, which is larger, holds up to twenty spirits at a time, but the SS-G is most popular."

"Why is that globe lit up with all the colors?" said Keir.

"Inside this model right now we have ghost named Paola," said Ygor, patting the globe. The lights inside scattered at his touch. "She was scaring cheeldren for pleasure of it. Now she scares no one."

"How long can you keep her inside the globe?" I said.

"For as long as we want," said Ygor.

"Forever?" said Keir.

"Theoretically, yes," said Dr. Shevski, "but I don't expect Paola will be around much longer."

There was something wrong about all this, do you feel it? Something was whispering a warning in my head, adding its voice to the threats of the demon that were still rattling around. Along with a question, which I'm sure you have been wondering about, too.

"When you release Paola," I said, "can you keep her from scaring kids again? Do you have a way, Dr. Shevski, to control these ghosts?"

She peered at me for a moment through her large round glasses and then a slight smile cracked her hard gray face. "As a matter of fact, yes," she said. "Ygor, show our guests the SPD-1."

Ygor looked at the doctor and then bowed before leading us to another table. "This marvel of Phantasm technology," he said, pointing at another of the machines, "is Spirit Psychic Drive, newest product in ghost-catcher line."

The machine he indicated was a sphere about the size of a basketball with twenty or more little horns poking out at all angles. It looked a little like those models they made of that virus that had kept us all out of school and away from our friends. On the very top of the ball was a small dome with a little propeller inside.

"Our technology allows you to implant directions deep into spirit's unconscious mind," said Ygor.

"Wait, what?" I said.

"It is a psychiatric technique developed by the CIA," said Dr. Shevski.

"The CIA?" said Natalie. "Really?"

"Oh yes," said the doctor. "In fact, your friend Professor Ramsberger gave us the theory. It works by playing back the spirit's thoughts and confessions in the spirit's own voice. It is called psychic driving, and it weakens the naughty spirit's will as it opens it up to suggestions of more positive behaviors. Beneficial brainwashing, it has been called."

"Could it get me to do my homework?" said Natalie. "I really need to do my homework."

"No force in the universe is that strong," said Keir.

My friends were laughing, but I wasn't. I remembered the hum of voices in Ramsberger's house and the way my father got all dazed out. Like the way all the voices chattering in my head had caused my debating disaster. And of course, the way, in my mother's story, the dead in Redwing's domain seemed confused all the time.

My grandfather told me that everyone deserved the right of free thought. Didn't that right extend to ghosts? And if not, who would be next to lose that right?

"Under what authority do you do all this?" I said.

"What do you mean?" said Dr. Shevski.

"Well, when our friend Henry was having problems with a ghost," I said, "he didn't willy-nilly capture her and put her in jail and brainwash her. He sued her in the Court of

Uncommon Pleas, where a judge had the power to eject the ghost from his property if the law allowed."

"We believe in a power higher than the law," said Dr. Shevski. "The power of science."

"Science gives you the ability, maybe," I said. "But not the right."

"And what right did Paola have to terrify those children? Her victims are still scarred. Trust me, I know. This is the land of the living. The dead have no place here. You might as well ask a court for the right to swat a mosquito. Why did you come here, then, if not to capture a ghost?"

"We don't want to capture ghosts," I said. "We want to free them."

"Why do that?" said Ygor.

"Because they're nice?" said Natalie.

"Because they're family?" said Keir.

"Because they were once human, like us?" I said.

"They are not nice," said Dr. Shevski. "And they are not family anymore. They are a plague on the living. They need to be eradicated."

"Eradicated?" said Natalie. "I don't think I like that word."

"You do when speaking about insects and vermin, I'd bet," said Dr. Shevski.

"Well, yes, actually," said Natalie. "We had a mouse in the kitchen for a week and I was afraid to get a Popsicle."

"Ghosts are like mice," said Dr. Shevski. "If you don't get rid of them, they only multiply. Tell the children our motto, Ygor."

"Put your ghosts to rest," said Ygor. "Forever."

"So, you plan to kill them," I said.

"It is not quite killing," said Dr. Shevski, "since they are already dead, but yes, we are close to perfecting a landmark device in the battle between the living and the dead."

Ygor walked to another table, where a large silver globe sat, with two strange guns on either side hooked up to another large machine.

"We call this Spirit Elimination Globe," said Ygor. "SEG for short. Very sophisticated. Very effective. This is SEG-P. P is for prototype."

"It uses two intersecting beams of particles within the box to create a momentary black hole," said Dr. Shevski. "The black hole swallows everything the box contains, including the spirit. It uses the most advanced physics to rid us of these pests."

"You're creating a black hole to kill ghosts?"

"Fantastic, no?" said Ygor.

"Paola will be our first attempt," said Dr. Shevski. "And if we succeed, then the plague of ghosts will be no more. Think of it, child."

Think of it, she said, and I did. How could I not? The capture, the storage, the brainwashing, and, of course, the elimination.

This wasn't just about Janelle and Sydney's ghosts anymore, although that would have been enough. This was also about Henry's Beatrice, and Keir's mother and father, and Barnabas's Isabel. It was even about Paola, whoever she was—and why did I think she was the key to our strange little physicist? This case was suddenly about all the spirits in all the lands who were simply trying to finish what they started in this world before settling into the next.

We are the dead. Short days ago we lived, felt dawn, saw sunset glow, loved and were loved.

I had to put a stop to this whole terrible enterprise, somehow, some way. It would seem too big a task for anyone, especially a kid still struggling her way through middle school, but as my mother's story showed, sometimes you have to say no.

The Resistance

As the sirens shrieked, Juniper and Mel followed the tall woman in gray through the cloud of dust, over piles of scattered bricks, and out of the cell.

Finally free, the three raced down the alley behind the jail and then along a crowded street. When an alligator appeared, the woman led them down a stairwell and into the door of a basement apartment. A family stared, jaws slack, as the three ran through the kitchen.

They rushed out the back door and up the rear stairs into another alley, at the end of which they stopped and scanned the street. A bunch of boss alligators were massing in an intersection, pointing in various directions with their stubby green arms. The woman spun around and ran to the other end of the alley before tearing down the street to the right. The girls scampered after her.

They pushed their way through a mob of pedestrians—the outraged thoughts of passersby hammering at them—and ran wildly across a traffic-strewn street before the woman in gray led them into the front door of a diner.

Out of the storm, into the quiet.

There were customers seated at the counter and around the tables, eating silently, the burble of their thoughts the only soundtrack as they listlessly chewed sandwiches and slurped soup. The food they ate was as gray as the clothes they wore.

The woman who had rescued them looked at a bald old man behind the counter, who nodded toward the rear of the restaurant. The girls followed the woman to the end of the dining room, through a pair of swinging doors, and into the small kitchen. Off the side of the kitchen was a room with a table. When the three were inside, the woman shut the door behind them and leaned against it.

Juniper and Mel started talking all at once, peppering the woman with questions, but she looked at them calmly and then gestured for them to sit at the table while she remained at the door.

She looked no different than the other women they had passed in the city. The grayness of death on her skin matched the gray of her clothes, a gray now dusted with the red dust of shattered brick. But there was no voice following her around, and her eyes were so brown and deep they were like a forest of trees. She clasped her hands together as she looked at the girls.

"You two," she said finally in a sharp British accent, "are quite daring and quite foolish."

The two girls looked at each other and then nodded as if they had no choice but to confess the obvious.

"Who are you?" said Juniper.

"Who I am is not important," said the woman. "What is important is that you've been rescued."

"By who?" said Mel.

"By the resistance, my dear," said the woman. "I'll answer all your questions in time, I promise. But perhaps we should wait for the others."

As soon as she said this there was a knock at the door.

The woman opened the door an inch to look through the gap, and then wide enough so that a man and a woman had enough space to slip inside the room before she shut the door behind them. The gray clothes of the two were also speckled with the red dust of the bricks.

"Any trouble?" said the woman at the door.

"Not too much," said the man. He was tall and dark-skinned and smiled as if he liked trouble.

"We split up," said the woman, pale and short and fierce, "and the gators weren't fast enough to nab us."

"What about Wendell?"

"We don't know, General," said the man. "He had to get back to his construction site."

"Astrid and Kofi," said the woman they had referred to as the General, "these are our guests, Juniper and Mel. Astrid and Kofi helped set the explosives and then fled in different directions to confuse the bosses."

"Thank you both," said Mel.

"Wendell's the explosives master," said Kofi with a grin. "We just like to run."

"I hope you all are hungry," said the General, "although with Astrid you never have to worry about that."

It wasn't long before the bald man who had been behind the diner's counter brought in a tray piled with food, not sandwiches of delight, sadly, but dishes levels above the gruel they had been served in the jail. There were a bowl of hummus, green leaves stuffed with rice, a cucumber and tomato salad, a spicy fried eggplant dish, and loaves of pita bread. All five were now seated at the table, digging in.

"Da'ud lived in Lebanon," said Astrid as she dipped a piece of pita in the hummus. "Even though he can only serve the approved cardboard-tasting dishes to the customers, he makes us the good stuff whenever he can."

"He's in the resistance, too?" asked Juniper.

"He is sympathetic," said the General. "That is all most here can allow themselves to be, constantly being badgered with their own thoughts."

"How is it that you're not being badgered with your thoughts?" said Juniper. "When we came into the diner, we could hear the hum of thoughts from the people eating. But we don't hear anything in here."

Astrid and Kofi looked at the General, who shook her head. "We have our ways," she said. "That knowledge is our greatest strength and our most dangerous weakness. If the Raven Master learned how we counteract her voices, the resistance would be mortally wounded."

"I like that name," said Juniper. "The resistance."

"What are you resisting, anyway?" said Mel.

"Everything," said Kofi with a smile that was as welcome in that gray ghost city as a splash of color.

This was the way they explained it, according to my mother as we sat on the balcony of our spa room in Massachusetts, overlooking a lake reflecting the orange streak of the sunset. Redwing controlled his domain by controlling the dead. He worked them to exhaustion, starved them into submission, muddled their thoughts with the voices, and banished them to a wild landscape called the Stormlands if they caused any trouble.

"So they were resisting Redwing," I said to my mother.

"Yes, of course they were resisting Redwing," said my mother. "And his Raven Master. But those two were just an inevitable symptom of a bigger problem."

The Tribunal of Classification determined which level an individual inhabited on the other side after their life on this side came to an end. But the Tribunal seemed to follow no real standards while enacting its punishments, causing great and unmerited misery. Instead of being a body of justice and mercy, the Tribunal had become a tool of those demons, like Redwing, seeking to increase the size of their domains and thus their power.

"What about the Court of Uncommon Pleas?" I said to my mother. "Wasn't the court able to correct any injustices?"

"The law can right individual wrongs," said my mother. "That's why your father traveled to Redwing's domain. But the General and Kofi and Astrid believed that the entire system was corrupt. Your father could petition the court to remedy this grave injustice or that unfair result, but he could never bring a case big enough to bring the whole system down."

"And so, the resistance," I said.

"That's right," said my mother.

And then she described the way the whole hopeless situation in Redwing's domain made her feel. My mother was suddenly desperate to get back home, where her life with her mother and father and brother was not so unfair. Back to America, where the laws made sense. Back to the country that offered her protection and hope.

But Juniper didn't feel the same way, my mother could tell.

Mel could see the excitement in her great friend's face when Juniper said, after hearing their explanations, "You really are resisting everything."

"That about sums it up," said Astrid as she reached for one of the stuffed leaves.

"Do you think you can beat Redwing and the Tribunal in the end?" asked Mel.

Astrid and Kofi both looked at the General, as if looking for hope. The woman smiled back at each of them, the two soldiers in her resistance group and the two lost girls, and the smile was joyful and sad at the same time, like the smile at a funeral.

"No," she said finally.

"Then I don't understand," said Mel. "Why are you resisting?"

"Because what else is there to do?" said Juniper.

"That's right," said Kofi, smiling at Juniper. "You either say yes or no. We can't say yes."

"So we say no," said Astrid.

They kept eating for a while—the eggplant, the salad—with Astrid piling the food on her plate as if she was building a castle. As they ate, Mel looked at the three resistance fighters with a sense of confusion and pity. Why fight a battle you were bound to lose? But she could tell, when she looked at Juniper, that her friend felt only admiration. Mel thought she and Juniper were as close as sisters, but after a night in prison and now at this table, it was like her best friend was someone she had never known.

"Why did you break us out of jail?" said Mel.

"We heard from one of our trusted sources," said the General, "that two from the other side had refused to plead guilty because that would mean abandoning one of their fathers."

"My father," said Juniper.

The General smiled at Juniper. "We admired that and thought we would try to help. Helping those in need is another way to say no. So tell us, Juniper and Mel, what is your need?"

"We need to talk to my father when he isn't mind-controlled," said Juniper. "Then we need to get back home."

"And how do you intend to do that?" said the General.

"We have a way," said Juniper, "though it might be more difficult than we originally thought."

"First we need to enter Redwing's castle," said Mel.

"Then we need to find the Lens of Fate," said Juniper.

"And then we need to summon the demon Gaap and deliver the Lens of Fate to him," said Mel.

"Oh," said the General. "Only that."

They didn't laugh, none of them laughed. They sat for a long quiet moment, which only served to terrify Mel. If the details of their task made brave members of the doomed resistance turn quiet and grave, then what chance did Juniper and Mel have to succeed?

"It won't be easy," said the General, finally, "but I can attest that Redwing has done much damage with the Lens of Fate. The device has allowed it to interfere with your world in terrible ways, and now the Raven Master has used it to spark in the demon a dangerous ambition. It would be safer in the hands of the vain buffoon who brought you here."

"You're going to help us?" said Juniper.

"Your quest is dangerous and foolhardy," said the General. "Of course we will help."

Which explains why, after a difficult night's sleep in that same back room, and a breakfast of baked cheese with a sugary topping, doused with rose water and stuffed into a small sesame pastry—the best breakfast, my mother still claims, she has ever eaten—Juniper and Mel were walking to the far reaches of the city.

Their faces had been powdered gray with makeup and they each wore a long gray coat to cover their more colorful clothes. Along with Astrid, they had taken a streetcar as far as it would take them and were now following their guide past where the roads petered out, through the wild, overgrown section of a park, to the bank of a river. The constant hum of voices had quieted as they moved toward the city's edge, until they could barely hear it.

On the other side of the river was a forest, thick and tall. And rising above it all, but close enough now to inspire a shiver, loomed the mountainous castle of Redwing.

"The river that encircles the city is calm in this stretch

so it's easier to cross," said Astrid. "A raft is in the bushes. Poles are lashed on top."

"Poles?" said Juniper.

"Stand on the raft and push yourself forward with the poles. But be careful not to fall in. There are monsters in the river, half-fish, half-dog. They snatch any swimmers in their jaws. And the water itself is poisonous, so don't try to drink it. In fact, all the water in the Stormlands is tricky. Drink this instead."

She handed Mel a round metal canteen with a leather strap attached.

"What's it like in the Stormlands?" said Juniper.

"Not as gray. You can give me the coats and wipe off the makeup, you won't need all that over there. And it rains a lot. You have the map and the instructions the General gave you?"

"Check," said Juniper, as if she was in a war movie.

"You should memorize the instructions and then bury them somewhere, but you'll need the map," said Astrid. "When you get to the other side of the river, start toward the castle. One of our people will find you and help you cross the forest. Say the word *Dalmatian* to identify yourselves."

"Dalmatian?" said Mel. "Is our contact a dog?"

"Not exactly." Astrid looked at them with friendship and pity when she said, "Good luck. You'll need it."

A few minutes later, balancing on opposite corners of the raft, the girls used long wooden poles to slowly push themselves across the River of the Dogfish. The gray skies above were turning dark and ominous, and the distant hum of city-thoughts was vanishing.

Mel, in the back right corner of the raft, looked ahead to the strange forest on the other side of the river—the Stormlands, Astrid had called it—and then Redwing's castle in the distance. That landscape contained her route home, and no matter how cruel or dangerous that journey might be, she gazed upon it with a longing that caught in her throat.

At the same time, even as she poled the raft toward the same destination, Juniper was glancing behind her, to the gray and ugly city that spread like a weed field across the horizon, the city of pain and bosses, the city of her dead father, the city of the resistance. The city of saying no.

24

THE CLASSY ACTION

Something in my mother's story had been zooming around in my head, trying to find a place to land, and, strangely, it made me think of Mildred and Sandy and their cases against Gwendolyn the witch. The next afternoon, I sat with them in the waiting area at Webster & Spawn and asked them a question.

"The last time we spoke," I said, "you mentioned that my father had decided to try your cases together. How does that even work?"

"We don't know," said Sandy. "Apparently it just does. Your father calls it a joint action, which sounds so official it gives me the chills."

"It also allows us to split the fees," said Mildred in her hoarse voice. "With the price of lawyers these days, we're saving a bundle."

"Which is really quite welcome," said Sandy, "now that I have so much more hair to get styled. Not just anyone can trim the hair growing on your eyeball."

"I would suppose not!" I said.

"You should get it colored," said Mildred.

"You think?" said Sandy.

"Pink, maybe, like Elizabeth had, to match the blue," said Mildred. "It would be adorable."

"It would, actually," I said.

A little later in my grandfather's office, as I sat at my small desk and worked on my calligraphy, I asked my grandfather, in an offhand way, about the whole joint action thing.

"A joint action, you say?" said my grandfather, sitting behind his desk, hidden by the tilting stacks of papers and books as he rummaged around looking for the one necessary page in his piles. "It's a simple thing, but very convenient for all involved. When two plaintiffs have a case against the same defendant on similar facts, they can join their cases and sue together."

"Can you combine more than two plaintiffs?"

"Oh yes, but with too many the whole thing becomes terribly messy. Most judges will split them apart. That's why it's better to keep the number smaller."

"But what about if there's lots of people with the exact same case? What if everyone in a city had the same complaints about, let's say, some demon who was making everyone's life miserable?"

"A demon, is it?" said my grandfather. That's when I heard his chair scrape the floor, the popping of his knees, the tapping of his cane. As he made his way around the desk he asked, "Perhaps you're thinking of Redwing itself?"

"Possibly," I said.

"Who have you been talking to, girl?"

"Maybe my mother?"

"Ah, I see, and about time, too." My grandfather, with his legs bowed out like a pair of parentheses and his back bent like a comma, now stood beneath the portrait of our famous ancestor Daniel Webster and stared at me through the gray brush of his eyebrows. "Melinda has finally told you the tale of her time on the other side."

"It's quite the story."

"Indeed."

"But she said something about how the Court of Uncommon Pleas over there could only handle things on a case-by-case basis even though the whole city was suffering."

"There was a time, long ago, when the courts would hear something called a group litigation," said my grandfather. "Whole villages in medieval England would sue in a group litigation if the local lord was rooting around in each villager's house and field, stealing anything he wanted and calling it a tax. Eventually the nobles didn't want to be held accountable and they put a stop to it."

"How?"

"By passing statutes that forbid such actions. The powerful are quite clever at passing statutes against anyone limiting their power. But in America, we have a statute of our own that allows something quite similar to England's group litigation. It's called a class action."

"A classy action?"

"Oh, it is that, yes, and more. With a class action, a single plaintiff can bring a suit against a defendant on behalf of a whole group. Class actions are quite handy, but the Court of Uncommon Pleas follows only the common law and so that statute doesn't apply."

"No classy action?"

"Well, the judges on the other side are quite fussy and they haven't permitted a group litigation. But I must say, we haven't ever tried to press a group litigation before Judge Jeffries. That proud popinjay is so much the contrarian, he might go for it. Why all the questions, Elizabeth?"

"In researching the Ramsberger case, I found the scientist who made the ghost-stealing machines."

"No!"

"Yes. I just said it."

"Well done, Elizabeth! How did you get such a lead?"

"Ice cream?"

"Oh, splendid. Nothing like a good plate of ice cream to help solve a case. You must tell everything to Barnabas so he can add it all to the complaint."

"This scientist also made a ghost-storing machine. And she gave the impression, Grandpop, that Ramsberger might be storing a lot of ghosts. I mean a lot. With the complaint my father and I served, we might be able to free Janelle and Sydney's ghosts, but what about all the other ghosts? How do we free them?"

"And you think they need to be freed?"

"I do," I said. "Because the scientist can also control them and, even worse, she told us she's also working on a way of killing them off."

"No!"

"Yes. I just said it again. Why do you keep saying no?"

"Why, that's dreadful!"

"We can't let that happen, Grandpop. What if Ramsberger gets rid of Sydney and Janelle's family before the trial? What about the other ghosts he has stolen? I was thinking maybe the classy action thing might be a way to free all the ghosts and keep them safe."

My grandfather stood there for a moment, tapping his cane on the floor and thinking, thinking. He turned around and gazed for a moment at the portrait of Daniel Webster, and then turned around again. He gave the floor one final tap before saying, "By Galahad, girl, you've convinced me. We have no choice but to force that moth-eaten judge to say yes. Tell Barnabas to amend the complaint."

"Amen the complaint? Are we praying?"

"It will take a prayer to win, that's for sure," said my grandfather. "But we must try. We'll add the group litigation to our Ramsberger case, demanding release of all the ghosts captured by the dastardly ghost thief."

"Will it work?" I said.

"We won't know until we try. But the chance of losing won't stop us when we're in the right. Hurry to Barnabas and give him the particulars. He'll draft the new complaint. The court will be in session soon and there is no time to waste."

I grabbed my calligraphy and headed out of my grandfather's office, excited by his decision. I almost felt like a lawyer for once. I had discovered new facts and raised all kinds of legal questions and now our ghost thief case was getting bigger and bolder. I was feeling all kinds of good about myself as I stood before Barnabas, which is usually a mistake.

"Mistress Elizabeth," said Barnabas. "How goes the calligraphy?"

"It's going," I said.

"Let me see what you have. I'm sure you've conquered the task."

"I'm glad you're sure," I said as I showed him my pages, with their blotches and shaky lines.

"Oh my," he said. "Is that an *F* or a swooning swan with an arrow through its chest?"

"My grandfather says we're going to amen the ghost thief complaint."

"Praying over it, are we?"

"That's exactly what I thought."

"I assume what he wants us to do is amend the complaint."

"Ah, that makes more sense. We're supposed to add a classy action."

"All your grandfather's actions are quite classy," said Barnabas with one eyebrow raised.

"Are you laughing at me?"

"No, but if I were of a disposition to laugh, I suppose now would be the time. Why don't you explain what is going on and I'll try to maintain the classiness as I write it up."

I explained it all to Barnabas, our visit to that old power plant and the things my grandfather had said about the claims we might make. Barnabas nodded as he took notes.

"You've done excellent work, Mistress Elizabeth," he said when we were through. "You are exceeding even our high expectations for your progress. Now we'll need two things before we can file our amended complaint. First, we will need a count of the stolen ghosts—it doesn't need to be exact, but it does need to have a basis in fact."

"What does that mean?"

"You can't simply guess a number. You need to be able to explain to the judge how you came by your estimate."

"I think I know how we can do that," I said. "We suspect he's been storing them in a cemetery."

"How uninspired. And then we will need one of the ghosts to sign the complaint."

"Wait a second, what?"

"Remember what we said before about standing?" said Barnabas. "Without the signature of a plaintiff, the judge would surely toss out the group litigation without a second thought. You must find one of the spirits willing to affix its name and sign the complaint. Then we can attach the group action to the claim of Mistress Sydney and Mistress Janelle."

"I'm not sure how my father will be able to do all that, but once he finds the stolen ghosts at the cemetery, I suppose he can figure that out."

"Oh, your father is not the one to do all this. You must do it. You."

"Me?"

"Yes, of course. Your father told us what happened to him at Ramsberger's house. The ghost thief evidently has a way to scramble your father's mind. This task would be too dangerous for him. But you seemed not affected. So it is all up to you."

"Me?"

"The so-called classy action is all up to you, Mistress Elizabeth. Good luck. And let us hope it works out better than your calligraphy."

The Stormlands

Mel and Juniper became helplessly lost in the strange forest on the other side of the river.

The girls had grown up in Willing Township—the suburbs—and had thought it would be a simple thing to keep heading in one direction, like walking down a street to the mall. But without a clear path within the murk of the forest, and amid drenching storms, it wasn't long before they lost track of the river that should have been behind them, or the castle they hoped was in front of them.

They circled forward and circled back and bickered with each other. They guzzled the water from their canteen, and slapped at bugs, and grew ever more tired and wet and anxious. At one point Juniper stopped and looked around.

"Where's the contact that was supposed to help us?" she said.

"Hey, Dalmatian!" yelled Mel.

Juniper put a hand on Mel's arm. "Do you really think we should be shouting out our code word?"

"You have another suggestion?"

Juniper looked at her friend for a moment and then called out, "Dalmatian!"

They kept walking then, shouting out the word into the forest with the rhythm of a marching band. It was fun for a bit, but eventually their mood soured and they lost the spirit. Soaked and miserable, when they passed a big rock, Juniper, instead of continuing on, just sat. Mel sat beside her.

"Now what?" said Juniper.

"Dalmatian?" said Mel softly.

Juniper laughed. Mel offered the canteen with only drops left inside and Juniper drained the last of the water. When Juniper handed it back, Mel looked at the canteen forlornly, as if it embodied the whole of this stupid trip to the other side. Then they heard a rustling behind them.

Both girls spun on the rock and spied an upside-down pair of eyes staring at them through a scrub of bushes.

"Dalmatian?" came a soft, whispery voice from behind the leaves.

"Yes," said Mel, bolting to her feet. "Yes! Dalmatian!"

"They're such pretty dogs," said the voice. "I always wanted a Dalmatian."

Mel looked at Juniper with a puzzled expression. "Are you our contact?" said Juniper.

"I think so. I was asked to help two girls who would definitely become lost. My name is Leonora."

"Pretty name," said Mel. "I'm Mel, this is Juniper. Where have you been all this time?"

"Watching," said Leonora, "and following, and making sure no one else was watching and following. You have to be very careful in the Stormlands."

Slowly, from out of the bushes, came the most remarkable sight. It took Mel and Juniper a moment to understand what they were seeing, and a moment more to choke back the revulsion and fear.

My mother described Leonora as a human crab. Not much older than the two lost girls, she walked on her hands and bare feet even as her torso, covered by a muddy lace dress, faced upward. Somehow her joints had been reconfigured, with her feet facing forward and her knees bending backward, so that crab-walking was not only possible, but inevitable. And though her head faced upward, when she lifted her chin she could look at Mel and Juniper straight-on, though upside down.

"Are you okay?" said Mel.

"What? Is something wrong? Oh, you mean the way I walk. I'm used to it by now. I can't any longer imagine walking on two legs. It seems so unsteady. I don't know how you don't fall right over with the slightest breeze. But this was part of my punishment."

"Punishment for what?" said Juniper.

"Talking. They said I talked too much. Can you believe such a thing? Too much talking? Is that even possible? I was trying to have conversations. Is that such a crime?"

"No," said Mel. "It's not."

"Thank you. But I guess to the bosses it was. It was that way in school, too. I kept on getting my knuckles rapped by the teacher. And for what?"

"Talking?" said Juniper.

"Silly, right? Punished because I like to talk. This happened before the Raven Master taught the demon how to control people with the voices. In the old days, the bosses wanted us all to be quiet so we couldn't conspire against them. They figured a short time walking upside down in the Stormlands would quiet me."

"How long have you been like this?" said Juniper.

"A hundred and thirty-five years or so, give or take."

"I guess they were wrong," said Mel with a laugh.

"So far," said Leonora. "From what I understand, you are trying to get to the castle. I think we can reach it by tomorrow."

"Tomorrow?" said Juniper.

"It's a bit of a journey, and you've already wasted most of the day, but I'll take care of you. Why would you want to visit that creepy old castle, anyway?"

"Just to pick up something," said Juniper. "But first we need water."

"Well, that's convenient because water is right on the way. And do you know what we can do as we walk there? We can talk!"

They watched for a moment as Leonora led them forward, crab-walking so naturally that they felt awkward as they began to follow with their two-legged waddles. Leading them through thick brush and over fallen tree trunks,

Leonora talked about her life growing up on a farm in Canada. She talked about her death in a boating accident while fishing with her father off the Newfoundland coast. She talked about what the city looked like when she arrived, a combination of old Italian buildings and then newer colonial-style wood and brick buildings, without any cars or trolleys but lots of horses.

Eventually, through the cloud of words, the girls could hear the burbling of a stream. They had gone now so long without water that no matter how much Leonora talked, all they could hear was their own thirst. In a clearing they saw two little rivers converging into a deep pool. Mel, who was carrying the canteen, rushed toward the closest stream.

"I wouldn't let your friend drink from that one, if I were you," said Leonora.

"Hold up, Mel!" called out Juniper, but Mel had already stopped. There was a sound rising above the rush of water over rock. It was soft but insistent, like a moan rising from the water itself, mourning the loss of youth, the loss of love, the loss of hope.

"That first stream carries the water of heartbreak," said Leonora. "If you drink from it, the water fills you with a sadness so deep it can crush your heart."

"Pass," said Mel. "What about the second stream?"

"That's even worse. It carries the water of joy."

"Why is that worse?" said Juniper. "That actually sounds pretty good. Have you ever had a sandwich of delight?"

"No. How are they?"

"Delightful!" said Mel.

"Well, once you satisfy your thirst with the water of joy,"

said Leonora, "all you care about is filling your belly with it again and again. Those who drink it never leave this part of the forest. They become its prisoners. Look."

As the three watched, a man crawled out of the forest to the stream. He was filthy, dressed in rags, and bone-thin except for his belly, which seemed bloated. He clawed his way to the stream before dunking his whole head in the water. When he finally emerged, his belly was even more bloated, as if he was pregnant, but he had a soft smile on his face as he crawled back to the forest.

"Pass on that, too," said Juniper. "But where can we get something to drink?"

"Follow me," said Leonora, leading them down to the deep pool.

"This is where the waters of joy and heartbreak combine into the water of regret," said Leonora. "At first it was painful to drink, but I've grown to enjoy it."

They watched as Leonora walked to the edge of the pool and gracefully put her upside-down face in the water. Again, the movement seemed so natural that Mel felt awkward holding the canteen. But her thirst was strong enough that she filled it to the top and took a long drink before handing it to Juniper, who drank most of what was left.

And then, my mother told me, the regrets hit in a rising wave of emotion that threatened to drown her. She felt remorse and defiance and joy and guilt and shame. Why had she given up piano? Why didn't she try harder in math? Why hadn't she kissed Tommy Carmichael when she had the chance? (Of course I looked him up on the internet— no great loss there!) The wave crested with an intensely beautiful aching before it passed through her and the emotions began to subside.

Mel looked over at Juniper, who had tears in her eyes, and then at Leonora, lying on her back, a sad little smile on her face. Still thirsty, Mel took another long gulp.

"And I just left him in that apartment building, all befuddled with the voices," said Juniper later, as the three of them were lying on the grass, recovering from the water of regret. "The bosses came and all I did was run. We need to get into the castle and find the Lens of Fate so I can see him again. I need to tell him how much I love him. That's why I really came here, to tell him all the things I never told him when he was still alive."

It was the most Mel had ever heard Juniper speak about her father, and again it was as if a stranger was talking. Mel was regretting all the ways she had never really known Juniper and all the ways she had failed her, when Leonora gave a loud "SHUSH!"

That was when they heard the steps coming through the forest, accompanied by the harsh clanking of metal on metal.

Leonora sprang into the air and landed in perfect crab-walking position before scuttling into a clump of bushes. Juniper and Mel had to climb around to the back of the bushes and tunnel in to kneel beside her. The three of them, hidden now in the leaves and branches, waited as the clanking and the steps grew ever closer.

It was a platoon of men and women in tan uniforms with little tan caps and red armbands with a horn in a circle of white, carrying nets and ropes and poles. Metal handcuffs hung off their belts, jangling as they marched. The three girls remained silent as the marchers detoured around the bushes in which they hid.

"Who are they?" whispered Juniper when the platoon had passed and now stood around the Pool of Regret.

"Stormland Rangers," whispered back Leonora.

"What happens to the people they catch?"

"If they're lucky, they get sent down," said Leonora.

"What's worse than getting sent down?" said Juniper.

"Not getting sent down," said Leonora.

They spent the night at the Pit of Inertia, a large lake filled with tar. The surface of the pit was studded with fabulous jewels that turned light into rainbows. It was hard to resist the temptation to step forward and reach down and examine the precious little things. But one step too many, Leonora warned, and you were caught in the tar, which was almost alive. The harder you struggled to free yourself, the harder the tar pulled back.

It would seem the worst kind of trap, and yet the dead stuck in the pit—Leonora called them Pitters—seemed quite content, playing with their little jewels, talking with the others.

"Welcome, welcome," said a portly man in a pale green suit standing in the tar up to his pink tie. "Care to join us? It is quite warm and cozy."

"We're good," said Juniper.

"Oh, I understand. The pit may look unpleasant, but I can assure you it is more agreeable than you can imagine." Right then he picked up a toad that had gotten trapped in the tar and held the squirming creature up by one of its legs.

"There is so much to eat, a buffet of possibilities, and the jewels are so beautiful. I can stare at them for hours, for days."

"How long have you been in there?" said Mel.

"Oh, fifty or sixty years," said the man. "It's hard to be sure when you're having so much fun. I keep hoping Leonora will join us. She is such a vibrant conversationalist, unlike"—and here he lowered his voice and looked around—"some in here. But don't worry, I expect to be out any day now. I have places to go, things to do. Excuse me for a moment," he said before turning around and dropping the toad into his mouth.

"They keep wanting me to get trapped with them," said Leonora as the man chewed. "And I am tempted. Those in the Pit of Inertia are the happiest people in the entire domain."

"Why is that?" said Juniper.

"Everything is here for them. The tar is gooey and soft, the jewels are so pretty, you're never alone, and there is plenty to eat. For the Pitters, time flies away like a sparrow through the air. What could be more pleasant?"

"Then why don't you join them?" said Mel.

"I guess I'm just not a joiner," said Leonora.

Far from the pit, Mel and Juniper made beds for themselves with pine needles and leaves beneath the triple moons that presided over the darkness of Redwing's domain. They fell asleep to the sound of Leonora talking and woke up to the same thing.

In the morning, as the rainstorms began again, they continued on their way through the forest, being led as much by

Leonora's voice as her crablike body. "The news from the pit was very worrying," said Leonora as she scurried forward at a faster pace than the day before. "Word has gone out that the rangers are searching quite hard for you two."

"That's bad," said Juniper.

"There has been a bounty placed on your heads," said Leonora.

"Why are they making such a fuss about us?" said Juniper.

"The Raven Master thinks you two can lead her to the legendary leader of the resistance known as the General."

Mel and Juniper looked at each other and gulped.

"Have you ever met her?" said Mel.

"No, never," said Leonora. "In fact, I didn't even know the General was a she."

Juniper gave Mel her be-quiet-you-fool face before saying, "We haven't met him or her, either. Are you in the resistance, Leonora?"

"Oh no," said Leonora. "Like I said, I'm not a joiner."

"Then why are you helping us?" said Mel.

"Because you needed help," said Leonora. "And you're such pleasant company. Now let's hurry, we still have a long way to go. Have I told you yet about the Canyon of Depravity?"

As Leonora wove this way and that way through the forest, detouring to avoid ranger platoons on the way to the castle, she was a tour guide showing off the horrors of the Stormlands.

The Canyon of Depravity was a gash in the middle of the forest with sides too steep to climb, where couples held tight to each other as frigid winds blasted them back and forth across the rocky bottom.

"You're not allowed to fall in love in the city," said Leonora. "If they catch you, they send you into the canyon together. I have friends down there. They say it's worth it, but they beg for blankets."

"How does Redwing invent these punishments?" said Mel.

"Those who know say Redwing has re-created all the terrors created by the other demons and put them in its own forest."

The Lake of Forlorn Hope was so beautiful the dead could stare at it for hours, for decades, Leonora told them. "In it they can see all the dreams and hopes they failed to achieve in their former lives. Eventually they can't resist walking into it, until they are submerged completely. Once on the bottom they grow gills in their necks and wander aimlessly with the other lake creatures.

"If you listen closely you can hear the cries of sorrow rising in the bubbles of air," she went on. "They wander and drift until they reach that island there in the middle of the lake, do you see it? The Island of Lost Souls. Once on the island, they're not allowed back into the lake. All they can do is stare out at the life they left behind."

At the very edge of the forest, as the three stood in the shadows and peered out, they finally saw it, in the hills beyond a long grassy plane.

Redwing's castle.

"Who are all those people working in the middle of the plain?" said Juniper.

"Remember when I told you there was a punishment worse than being sent down?" said Leonora. "That is what I meant. Flowing across the plain is the River of Retribution, in which thousands toil for crimes against the Lord Demon."

"What's that smell?" said Mel.

"The river is not really a river. It's more an open sewer. Along its bed the waste from the entire domain flows. And the workers are forced to stand in it with paddles, keeping it moving so it doesn't overflow the banks. It's the foulest job in the domain. Redwing could build a machine to do the work, but it wouldn't be as cruel."

"How do we get across?" said Juniper.

"We're not swimming," said Mel.

"There's a bridge," said Leonora.

"Phew," said Mel.

"The crews and overseers change shifts at night, and in between one group leaving and one group coming, the bridge is unmanned. That's your moment."

"Are you coming with us?"

"As part of my punishment, I'm not allowed to leave the forest," said Leonora. "We'll hide until it gets dark and then I'll send you on your way. But we have time until then. What should we do?"

"How about we talk?" said Juniper.

"I would like that," said Leonora. "I have so much still to tell you."

As they made their way to a hidden spot where Leonora knew they could wait for nightfall without being found, my mother took a moment to stop and stare at the castle. It was a huge, towering thing, with stone spires that split the dusky sky. Its shape and size projected such a terror that it seized her throat. Inside was their ticket home, but also inside was the demon Redwing. And at that moment, with the castle towering, and the smell sickening, and platoons of rangers marching this way and that across the plain, she didn't need to drink the water of her canteen to feel a crushing wave of regret.

This whole landscape had been a warning. If you think, you are punished. If you talk, you are punished. If you hope, you are punished. If you love, you are punished. If you try to escape, you are punished.

The task was too much and she was not enough and the only thing that awaited them on the other side of the River of Retribution was doom.

NIGHT AT THE CEMETERY

I was walking through the middle school hallway with my head down, pretending I didn't hear or see anything—which is frankly the only safe way to walk through a middle school hallway—when I heard my last name being called. Of course I continued on my way, head down, as if I had heard nothing.

"Hey, Webster, come on," said a familiar voice. "Wait up. You mad at me or something?"

When I recognized the voice I finally stopped and turned around to see Henry Harrison fake-jogging toward me. Henry, tall, Black, and sharp as a knife, was the king of the eighth grade, a star swimmer with a blinding smile that he was now aiming at me. Behind him a group of his eighth-grade friends were gawking at the sight of someone like Henry Harrison running to catch up with someone like me. I saw one of the group doing a little robot dance.

"So, Webster," said Henry when he finally reached me. "Where've you been?"

"One of your friends is doing a robot dance," I said.

Henry turned and looked. "That's Regina. She's just joking. You know, about the whole debate thing?"

"I'm laughing, Henry," I said. "Can't you see me laughing?"

"I heard you got yourself another ghost case."

"So?"

"So why am I not involved?"

"I figured you were too busy. And anyway, when Natalie asked you the other day, you said you had stuff. What, were you dancing the robot with Regina?"

"I've been a bit busy, yeah," he said, rubbing his hand across the top of his high fade. "But you know, ghosts! That's my thing."

"Natalie, Keir, and I have it covered. Thanks, though."

"Webster, come on." He was wearing his Henry face, cocky and pleading at the same time.

"Why do you care?" I said.

"I don't know," he said. "Maybe because I still think of her."

"It's time to get over it, Henry. Beatrice has."

"But it's not only that." He moved closer, glanced at his friends, and then lowered his voice. "I get it, I've been distracted by…things and we haven't been hanging. But you know why I like working with you, Webster? Because you help. You helped me and Beatrice. You helped Keir with that countess. And now, according to Natalie, you're helping these ghosts. You step up. I admire that. I want to be that."

"You want to be me?" I said.

"Well, you know, not in every way," he said, before he did a little robot dance himself.

I could see his pals laughing in a pack on the other side of the hallway. That was fun. But I also had to wonder who was being the jerk here. It didn't take me long to think it might have been me. Like maybe I was being the jerk with Natalie, too. Henry was being sincere, I knew, the same way I knew he was someone I could truly rely on.

"You busy tonight?" I said finally.

All of which explained how the old gang had finally gotten back together when late that night we all slipped through the gap Keir had found between the iron bars in the fence surrounding the cemetery at the edge of the city.

A half-moon was shining brightly through the haze of city light, painting the features of the rolling landscape with a dim and eerie glow, the weeping trees, the tall stone spires, the aboveground cement coffins surrounded by low stone walls. It smelled of cut grass and wood smoke, the cold air felt prickly, something flapped in a circle overhead.

"Is that a bird?" said Natalie.

"No," said Keir. "It's not a bird."

"I think it's a bat," said Henry.

"Nothing to worry about," said Keir, as if talking about an auntie. "Harmless little critters."

In my backpack was a copy of the complaint Barnabas had drafted for the group litigation, with the name of the action still unwritten, a blank spot for the number of stolen and stored ghosts, and a line for the signature of our designated plaintiff. I was hoping I'd be able to fill in the blanks by the end of the night, along with the fee agreement my grandfather had given me. Not too much of an ask, right? But my friends had reassembled themselves around me. Was I wrong to sense that whatever came my way, they would get me through it?

Keir, wearing his red plaid jacket, waved his lantern as he led us across a field of graves. The rest of us had normal flashlights, but Keir had brought a lantern with a propane flame he had grabbed from the camping gear in our garage. Keir was going old-school, which somehow seemed right. We followed him along paved walkways and across grassy paths, the beams of our flashlights snagging on the stone markers. I recognized some of the names. Rich guys, politicians, a famous army general who I think won the Battle of Gettysburg.

Finally, Keir led us down a set of stairs and then along a cemetery road to a marble mausoleum built right into the hill. With its Moorish-type decorations, it looked like the outhouse of some long-dead sheik. Two green urns on stone posts flanked the entrance.

"That's where the ghost thief went," said Keir, waving his lantern at the mausoleum. I aimed my flashlight at the door, a solid piece of stone with no knob, no handle, no apparent way to open it. Above the door, carved into the stone, was the year 1861, and then the name RAMSBERGER.

And—wait a second. What was that behind the pillars on either side of the door?

"Look," I said to Natalie. "The Martha Washington dogs!"

"What are they doing there?" said Natalie.

"Were those cement dogs with the human faces here when you came before?" I asked Keir.

"I don't remember them," said Keir. "And I sure would have."

"Uh-oh," I said.

Henry ignored my concerned "Uh-oh" and headed up the stairs and past the dogs. We had briefed him on the whole twisted story when we met up after dinner, so he knew what we suspected was behind the stone door. He tapped it with his knuckles, tried pushing the marble slab open. It didn't budge.

"Did you see how Ramsberger opened it?" I said.

"Not exactly," said Keir. "But the first thing he did was head over to that urn on the right."

The four of us surrounded the stone post with the fancy green urn on top. What were we looking for? Anything—a button, a lever—

"A hinge," said Natalie, pointing her flashlight at the bottom rim of the green urn.

Henry, the tallest of us, grabbed hold of the top of the urn on the side opposite the hinge and tilted it up. While we were all looking underneath the now-raised urn for a button or a lever, we heard a strange grinding sound behind us.

Slowly we turned to see the marble door slide open and the inside of the mausoleum click bright. Henry lowered the urn and the door stayed open. We looked at each other, wondering if we should go in.

"Raise it again," said Natalie.

Henry raised the urn and the light inside the mausoleum darkened as the door, with a grinding sound, slid shut.

"Once it opens it stays open until we close it back here," said Natalie.

"Good to know," said Henry, and he once more tilted up the urn, causing the door to again grind open. "Let's find us some ghosts."

With Henry in the lead, we headed up the stairs, through the door, and into the lighted mausoleum. As I passed the dogs, I could have sworn one of them tilted her head at me. When I stopped and looked at her, Martha was smiling her usual mild smile. And then, quick as that, we switched off our lights and stepped inside.

"Whoa," said Henry.

We were in a small damp room with marble walls on either side, a light fixture within an iron cage overhead, and a green panel at the far end with a fancy relief sculpture of a long-nosed woman. I recognized her right off. Maybe it was the way she clutched her shoulder, or the way she stared down at me as if I was one of the worms scavenging the dead bodies beneath the ground. But mostly it was the large bird perched on her shoulder.

"I know that woman," I said.

"A relative of yours?" said Keir.

"Ramsberger's grandmother. Her name was Edwina or something. CIA, apparently."

"Here she is," said Natalie, pointing at one of the walls.

On each wall were two rows of four marble panels the

size of a coffin. Some of the panels were blank, others had names spelled out with large brass letters. On one panel, the brass letters spelled out:

R. EDWINᗄ RAMSBERGER

The letter A in Edwina was strangely flipped around. Beneath the name were the dates **1899–1979**.

"I wonder if she's watching us," said Natalie.

"I doubt it," said Henry. "No windows."

"The CIA would find a way," said Natalie.

"But if this is where Ramsberger is keeping the ghosts in those storage machines," I said, "where are they?"

"In the crypts behind the walls?" said Henry.

"Under the floor?" said Keir.

"This all seems a little small, doesn't it?" I said.

"Wait a second," said Natalie. "Wait. Wait. Wait."

"What? What? What?" I said.

"Look at Edwina's name," said Natalie. "Look at it carefully. What do you see?"

The three of us gave the brass letters a careful look. I didn't see anything other than a bunch of letters. But then Keir started laughing.

"Aye, there it is," he said. "It's as obvious as a thumb in the eye."

"What's so obvious?" I said. "What am I missing?"

Keir walked over and, starting with the first R in Ramsberger, flipped all the letters in Edwina's last name to match the upside-down A, all except for the G.

R. EDWIN~A ЯƎ⅁ᴚƎᴮ ꟽⱯЯ A

As the final R in Ramsberger was turned, leaving the rest of the letters to spell out the demon's name, we heard a grinding noise to our left. We looked at each other before we darted to the closing marble door, but by then the narrowing gap was too thin to get safely through.

Henry tried to push the door open, but when his feet started sliding, he let go and pulled his hands in just before the door slammed shut and the light turned off.

"Uh-oh," said Natalie in the darkness. "Now what?"

As soon as we switched on our flashlights, another grinding sound filled the mausoleum. We spun our lights to the back of the room as the sculptural panel of the ghost thief's grandmother slid to the left, revealing a doorway into some sort of chamber dug into the hill. On the other side of the doorway, overhead lights switched on, one after another, with a *click-thud click-thud click-thud*, traveling in a line going back back back.

But it wasn't the overhead lights that frightened us so, or even the ever-growing length of that seemingly endless tunnel illuminated by the lights. No, it was what the tunnel contained, on the shelves lining either side—machines, an uncountable number of machines, Dr. Shevski's spirit storage machines, model SS-G, each with a globe imprisoning a swirl of light and color.

The two rows of globes vanished deep and deeper into the very guts of the earth, lined up like two columns of a great and terrible army ready to march.

The Chamber of Stolen Ghosts

The chamber we opened was breathtakingly beautiful, with its columns of globes swirling with frantic multi-colored lights. I would have been swept away by the beauty if I hadn't understood right off what it meant.

From my first adventure in the Court of Uncommon Pleas I had been told that Redwing was a danger that needed to be stopped by the Websters. And now, using a ghost thief, a brilliant physicist, and a mind-control technique learned from the Raven Master, Redwing had created an army of obedient ghosts on this side of the line, an army awaiting only the demon's command before its terror was unleashed upon our world.

Somehow it was up to the four of us, Henry and Natalie and Keir and me, to stop it. And I thought sixth grade was hard.

"What's our plan, Webster?" said Henry.

"Well," I said, looking into the long underground chamber and pretending I had it all under control, "the first thing we need to do is get a count of the stolen ghosts. Let's assume each lit globe is one ghost. Maybe we can create some sort of math equation to come up with an estimate."

I looked at each of them—no Katherine Johnson in this group, that's for sure—but one was head and shoulders above the other two.

"I guess that means Henry," I said, "whose math is way better than he pretends."

"Now you're ruining my rep," said Henry.

"I'll help with the counting," said Keir.

"Don't take too long," I said. "Meanwhile Natalie and I will try to find the globes with Janelle and Sydney's family and free at least one of them."

"Are you sure?" said Natalie. "I mean, they are ghosts, after all."

"Nice ghosts," I said, "if the story is true. And we need at least one of them to sign the complaint if we want to free the rest."

We turned together and stood side by side, facing the now-open door of the immense hidden chamber, all of us hesitating for a moment until Henry said, "Let's do it."

Walking into that cavern, surrounded by the rows of dazzling globes, was like walking into a sea of static. The sound of bubbling liquids burbled all about us, and little sparks danced along our skin like tadpoles with teeth. Oh, and yeah, it smelled as if some weird fish was burning.

As Henry and Keir went about their counting, Natalie

and I looked closely at the spirit-storage machines, their power cords plugged into a line of outlets. On the base of each, written with marker on a flat piece of metal, was a combination of numbers and letters. Assuming the letters were initials, and knowing that the last names of Janelle and Sydney's stolen ghosts were all Burton, we started searching for three machines in a row with numbers ending with the letter B. Easy, peasy, right?

But even with Natalie reading the numbers on one side and me reading them on the other, about a quarter of the way through the chamber we had still found nothing. My frustration was growing when Natalie, the bloodhound, piped up.

"Here," she said. "Three swirling globes all with serial numbers that end with B. Now what?"

"To get a signature," I said, "we're going to need to let one out."

"How do we do that?"

"Keir told us Ramsberger screwed the globes off his car like a light bulb."

"Be my guest," said Natalie, pointing to one of the globes.

The liquid inside the vials was bubbling, the lights inside the globe were swirling and sparking. Did the lights look sweet? Sour? Helpful? Dangerous? It didn't matter.

When I grabbed hold of the globe, the swirling lights moved toward my hands as if they were magnets. It felt as if frogs were jumping inside glass. I unscrewed the globe to the left, to the left. There were little squeaks above the bubbling sound before the globe came free. As I slowly pulled it away from the machine, the lights darted from one edge of the globe to the other, as if trying to figure out what had just happened. It took them a moment, and then—*Bam!*

The lights dashed out the bottom in a wave of sparks that bit the globe right out of my hands. As the glass shattered on the floor of the cavern, each color sprinted its own way about the chamber, a rainbow having a nervous breakdown. Along with the startling light show, a breeze began whooshing, a breeze that smelled like Ben Gay smoking a cheap cigar.

Then the colors came together and danced around each other in rippling ribbons of light, shooting showers of sparks into the air whenever the different colors touched, until everything combined into a bluish haze that spun around like a spinning cloud of cotton candy. As it spun, the haze formed into an old man in rumpled clothes with a sour mouth and eyes so dark they seemed to suck the light right out of the room. He stared at us as if he had eaten a rotten peach and we had been the ones to sell it to him.

"What do you fools want?" said the old ghost in an echoing voice. "I was dreaming sweet dreams when you woke me."

I looked around at my friends, all of them staring at the ghost, and then took a hesitant step forward. "Are you Mr. Burton? Mr. Silas Burton?"

"Why you asking, child?" said the ghost.

"Because if so, your granddaughters Janelle and Sydney asked us to help you. That's why we're here, and why we freed you from the machine."

"So you know my little grandchildren," the ghost said, and even as he said it I could hear an echo behind him, as his voice was joined by a bunch of others. "Couple of trou-blemakers, them two. How do you intend to help the likes of me?"

I took another step forward, my sneakers crunching on the broken glass. "Through the law," I said as I took off my backpack. "We can file a complaint to free you and all the other ghosts stored here if you sign our complaint. Do you want to see it?"

"I don't need to see it. If you were sent by Janelle and Syd-ney, then you...then you...you..."

"Is everything okay, Mr. Burton?"

His ghost mouth started strangely jerking. "You... You...You..."

His eyes snapped on, like two televisions tuned to noth-ing. He raised his arms as his mouth kept jerking and he said, "You don't belong here. You don't belong here. You don't belong here."

All along that tunnel of globes, sparks now fired and col-ors now zoomed and ghosts now appeared, dozens in all kinds of clothes from all different eras, with their arms out as they chanted along with the ghost of Silas Burton.

"You don't belong here," said a woman in a long red robe.

"You don't belong here," said a man in a straw hat.

"You don't belong here," said a girl in a fluffy white dress.

"I don't think we belong here," said Natalie as the ghosts massed behind Silas Burton, a brigade of ghosts with their arms outstretched and their mouths jerking strangely with every word.

"Time to go!" I shouted.

"I'm right behind you!" said Henry.

"And I'm behind Henry!" said Keir.

We turned and ran as fast as we could run along the long tunnel, our sneakers pounding as the ghost crew came for us.

"YOU DON'T BELONG HERE! YOU DON'T BELONG HERE! YOU DON'T BELONG HERE!"

Even though I was sprinting, Natalie was now far ahead and Henry shot by me like I was standing still. When Keir caught up, he slowed down just enough to tell me to speed up.

"This is as fast as I can go," I said.

"Now I know why you're in Debate Club and not the track team," he said.

"Get through the door and start flipping back the letters."

"Got it," said Keir before zooming ahead.

I glanced behind me and the ghosts were gaining, gaining. I tried not to think of what would happen if they caught me as I rushed through the chamber and out the entrance. Natalie grabbed hold of me to stop my momentum. I pressed my head into her shoulder as I caught my breath.

Keir was back at the wall, frantically flipping up the last letters in R. Edwina Ramsberger's name. Henry stood with his flashlight raised, as if about to battle the ghosts. I turned to look at the horror behind us.

But the ghosts had stopped. They floated about ten yards away from the edge of the tunnel, arms still outstretched, staring, but no longer moving, no longer shouting with those strange mouth movements. It was as if whatever was controlling them had released them from their globes to protect the chamber but wouldn't let them leave. At least not yet.

The sight of them, quiet and unmoving, gave me a shot of courage. I called out, "Mr. Burton, do you want to sign the complaint now?"

"Didn't you get the message, young'un?" he said, with the ornery back in his tone. "You don't belong here."

And then the last letter in Ramsberger was flipped and the panel with Edwina's sculpture slowly moved to the right until the chamber of stolen ghosts was once again sealed off.

There was a moment of quiet when the four of us looked around the still-lit mausoleum, and then at each other, and we started laughing. We were laughing with relief, laughing at the adventure, laughing at the fear we had felt. We were still laughing when the marble door started rumbling as it slid open to let us out of that cursed mausoleum and into the quiet safety of the night.

And that's when the laughter died in our throats.

For in the doorway to the cemetery now stood the two Martha Washington dogs, leaning forward in their cement dresses, teeth bared.

"Why don't you Websters ever listen to warnings?" said one of the Marthas in a voice all too familiar, the harsh triple voice of the demon Redwing.

"What are those things?" said Henry, pointing his flashlight at the Marthas.

"They're animates," said Natalie. "Remember the Pilgrim in City Hall after your trial?"

"Oh yeah," said Henry as he raised his flashlight. "I hated that Pilgrim."

"Are you ready for a horror show, little Elizabeth?" said the second Martha with the same demon's voice.

"The price for all your meddling," said the first Martha, taking a step forward and pausing for a brief moment before leaping with her cement eyes wide and her cement mouth open, leaping at my throat.

Before she could reach me, Henry stepped forward and clocked the animate on the jaw with his flashlight, sending her crashing noisily into a marble wall with a loud and horrible "Ooof!"

Henry was still following through on the blow, his body defenseless, when the second Martha sprang at him. In the ferocity of the animate's leap and the alarm in Henry's face you could see the future unroll, something terrible and bloody and irrevocable.

And then a blur shot out from the back of the mausoleum, something with a speed that was as inhuman as the cement dogs. The blur met the Martha midflight and the two figures, dog and tackler, gripped each other as they tumbled through the air before smashing onto the stone floor. When the wrestling commenced, as the dog tried to force its jaws upon the tackler's face, we could finally make out what the animate was fighting.

Keir. Of course it was Keir. But also not Keir.

He wasn't the sweet little boy who played video games with Petey and sauntered the halls of Willing Middle School West. Keir had become the thing he had been keeping under control all this time, the fierce beast I had spotted once out my bedroom window terrorizing the neighborhood squirrels. Keir had unleashed the monster within to save his friends.

As vampire and animate wrestled in front of us, the other

Martha rose unsteadily and shook her head as she gained her bearings. Natalie threw her flashlight at the dog, but the Martha ducked from its path, and in the next instant she had joined the fight of the monsters on the mausoleum floor, forming a terrifying tangle of violence.

We didn't know what to do, how to help. We were frozen, until out of the mess and the tumble we heard a voice.

"You might want to be getting out of here now," said Keir to us as he punched one of the animates in the jaw. "I'll hold these ladies as long as I can, and then I'll be running, too."

"We're not going to just leave you!" I shouted.

"Oh, these things can't hurt me," he said. "Not without a wooden stake or a fire to burn me to ashes. We're merely playing now, like pals." He slugged the Martha again as the other snapped its jaws. "Go on, Elizabeth, run. All of you, run. I'll lose them among the dead and then meet you at the gap in the fence where we climbed inside."

I grabbed hold of Natalie and looked at Henry, who smiled at Keir with gratitude and admiration as the battle continued.

"And one more thing," said Keir, as each of the dogs started ripping at his arms with their sharp cement teeth. "After this, I'll be needing a new coat."

CHECKLIST

It was well after dark in Redwing's domain, with the three moons painting the landscape with their ghostly greenish light, when the work gangs gathered on the banks of the River of Retribution. Beyond the wide plain, the castle blocked out the stars like an outstretched claw.

Mel, Juniper, and Leonora skipped unseen across the edge of the forest until they were facing the bridge that crossed the river. There they hugged goodbye. It was an awkward dance with Leonora struggling onto her backward-facing feet and the girls grabbing hold as best they could—but it felt sweet and true.

"I have a gift for you two," said Leonora before reaching into a pocket of her dress and pulling out two leather necklaces. Each necklace held a tiny cage housing a little worm, brown with red spots.

"Cute," said Mel.

"It's a glowworm," said Leonora. "A reminder of the glow of our friendship. They eat leaves. Now go quickly before I cry."

Juniper and Mel put the leather cords around their necks and tucked the little cages beneath their shirts.

"Thank you for everything," said Juniper. "We'll never be able to repay you."

"I have two new friends," said Leonora. "What payment could be better than that?"

"I wish we could hang out longer," said Mel.

"Me too," said Leonora. "There's still so much I want to talk about."

They laughed, the three of them, before Juniper and Mel left their new friend and slid out of the forest.

The girls waited for the last group of workers to reach the bridge, and then slowly, carefully, staying as low as they could manage, they followed at a distance. At the foot of the bridge, they squatted amid the stink of the sewage and waited. They could feel the footsteps of the workers reverberating on the wooden planks. When the sound disappeared as the gang was marched off, they made their own way across the bridge, staying low and holding their noses to keep from gagging. Once over, they waited until the gangs were far enough away before running to the right.

The directions they had received from the General were very specific. First cross the forest. Check.

Then cross the bridge. Check.

Then head to the right side of the castle. Check.

Then, while avoiding the guards on their rounds, find a

drainage tunnel at the mouth of a stream that led into the river.

It took a bit of hunting to find what they were looking for—twice they had to throw themselves to the ground and hold their breaths as rangers walked around the castle not fifty feet from where they lay—but eventually they found the stream bed. Protected by its banks, they followed it toward the castle until they reached the tunnel's circular opening, blocked off by a rusted metal gate. Check.

Above them the castle rose like a steep, unassailable mountain.

The gate, about Mel's height, was kept closed by a thick metal chain linked into a loop by a heavy padlock. But, as the instructions promised, the padlock was open. They unhooked the padlock, carefully pulled the chain through the metal bars so it wouldn't clank, and pried opened the wings of the gate.

The hinges squealed with the caw of a raven.

They stood stock-still, frozen by that raven's cry. And in the quiet they heard the footsteps and jangling metal of rangers on patrol.

Jolted by fear, they jumped into the tunnel, first Mel, then Juniper, and shut the gate behind them with a clang. Juniper slid the chain through the metal bars and around again so it looked to be padlocked from the inside. They waited, unmoving, in the shadows of the tunnel.

Atop one of the banks they saw a brown cap rise in the moonlight and then the shadowy silhouette of its ranger. The ranger brushed the beam of her flashlight back and forth across the riverbed as if she was painting it with light.

The girls shrank away from the entrance and leaned into each other as the flashlight beam jumped to their end of the riverbed. It hit the chain, then the gate. A slash of light fell onto Juniper's jeans.

Not a word, not a breath.

And then the light darted back to the riverbed before dying as the footsteps and jangle of metal moved away.

Juniper squeezed Mel's arm before turning and beginning a bent-back march through the tunnel, using the scraps of moonlight leaking through the entrance to guide her way. Mel followed.

It wasn't long before the tunnel slanted to the right, the leak of the moonlight died, and they were in utter darkness. Juniper moved slowly forward, and more slowly still, until she bumped her head on an overhanging piece of stone. "Ow!"

"Are you okay?" said Mel.

"No," said Juniper. "I'm not okay. I can't see a thing."

Then something caught Mel's attention, the tiniest glint on the wet floor of the tunnel before her. "The glowworms," said Mel.

They freed the necklaces from beneath their shirts and let the little cages dangle. The light from the worms, so soft and so yellow, was at first useless in the tunnel. The darkness around them was still complete. Even so, Juniper started moving forward. As Mel followed the sound of her friend, slowly, vaguely, the contours of the walls started appearing. The farther they traveled, the more their eyes grew accustomed to the darkness and the brighter the little worms glowed, until it seemed as if the girls had great lanterns hanging from their necks, or so my mother said.

With the light from Leonora's gift they found the metal ladder embedded in the stone. Check.

The rungs were slippery, so the girls wrapped their arms around the rails as they climbed. And they counted. One rung, two rungs. According to my mother, with each rung she felt somehow lighter. Twenty-seven rungs, twenty-eight rungs. The regret and despair of the Stormlands were left at the bottom of the ladder as she climbed into a sense of anticipation and hope. Fifty-six rungs. This was going to happen. Fifty-seven rungs. They were going to get home. Fifty-eight rungs. And everything was going to be just the way it was before.

At exactly fifty-nine rungs Juniper stopped. In the light of the glowworms they could see a stone ledge to the left that led to an old wooden door. There was a gap between the ladder and the ledge. Juniper reached out one of her long legs. Her foot landed uneasily on the stone. She swung her weight back and forth and then threw herself off the ladder onto the narrow ledge, landing with a stagger and a fall, one foot slipping over the side of the ledge.

After she picked herself up, she helped Mel across. Check.

They stood together now before a wooden door. Somewhere on the other side, according to the instructions, lay the Lens of Fate. They looked at each other. Juniper smiled at her friend, stepped forward, and took hold of the latch. A moment later they closed the door behind them.

Check.

29

BARNABAS MAKES A SUGGESTION

I was walking to the train station the next afternoon when I again heard the ice cream tinkle-linkle.

By the time I arrived at the white truck, a short line of short people was snaking back from the order window, kids from my old elementary school, which sat next to my current middle school. I was tempted to brush the little kids out of the way—the middle school rule book gave me that power—but I restrained myself and let the tykes have their fun.

The line had disappeared, and there was no one coming up the street, when I finally approached the truck.

"Lizbeth, Lizbeth," said Josiah Goodheart through the truck's window. "I heard you had quite the evening last night."

"Your client threatened me with a horror show."

"It does that, yes. Nothing to worry about."

"It sent its animates to rip out my throat."

"And yet here you are, hale and hearty. Even a demon is no match for the likes of Elizabeth Webster. Did you tell anyone about our last little meeting?"

"No one."

"I knew it. You can always tell a trustworthy soul by her thumbs. You have trustworthy thumbs."

I looked down at my thumbs, wiggled them a bit. Trustworthy? When I looked up, Josiah Goodheart's eyes were laughing at me.

"What will you be having today?" he said. "Your usual?"

"I was thinking maybe—"

"Stick with the Choco Taco," said Josiah Goodheart. "It's such a tasty treat. And you'll want a napkin with it, I presume."

"Another napkin?"

"Neatness counts, I've always said. That and an abacus."

He lifted one of the freezer lids in front of him, took out a Choco Taco already wrapped in a napkin, and handed it over.

"I understand you visited an abandoned power plant the other day," he said. "What did you think?"

"Creepy."

"Abandoned power plants tend in that direction."

"Not the power plant," I said. "I'm talking about Dr. Shevski. She was creating all these horrible machines to torture and kill ghosts, but she didn't know they were horrible."

"No matter how dreadful people might act, my dear

Lizbeth, they are always able to convince themselves it comes from the goodness in their hearts."

"And hence your name."

"Exactly right, as usual," said Josiah Goodheart. "None of us, I say, none of us is immune. But I am of the belief that you, and you alone, might change the good doctor's heart."

"How am I supposed to do that?"

"Ah, here come some more of the little darlings looking for their after-school treats."

I turned and saw a crowd meandering toward the truck from the middle school. As usual it was a crowd I wanted nothing to do with.

"It warms the cockles of my heart to see the young with all their innocence and hope," he said. "If you want to understand the vine that wraps about the heart of an adult, look closely at the sweet school days of her youth and there you will find the seed."

"Can I ask one more question before you get swarmed with middle-school rats?" I said.

"Ask away, Lizbeth."

"What's a cockle?"

He laughed without answering, which only meant he didn't know, either.

As I walked away from the kids suddenly lining up at the truck, I ripped open the wrapper, took a bite, and then glanced at the napkin.

Hazelwood Orphanage
Bellmawr, New Jersey
Paola Fiore

I immediately sensed what that was all about—as I'm sure you do, too. I would have to find some way to venture into New Jersey tomorrow. But first I had to go to the offices of Webster & Spawn and report my findings and failures in the chamber of stolen ghosts.

"Five thousand?" said my grandfather when we all met in his office. "Are you sure, girl? Five thousand?"

"Give or take," I said.

"Why, Elizabeth, that's astounding," said my grandfather. "Five thousand is much too many for a joint action. A group litigation it has to be."

"And quite a classy action it will be, I'm sure," said Barnabas, raising an eyebrow without a smile.

"I assume you have a good-faith basis for that estimate, Elizabeth," said my father. "We can't put any old number we want in a court document."

"In the time we had in the chamber, we did a rough count," I said, "based on a pretty clever equation Henry created. He figured out the number of ghost-storage machines per shelf, the number of shelves per yard, and then created an estimate based on the length of a hundred-yard butterfly."

"That's a surprising multiplier," said Barnabas. "I didn't know butterflies got that big."

"Is that a record, Barnabas?" I said. "Two jokes in one minute?"

"A butterfly a hundred yards long is no joke, Mistress

Elizabeth," said Barnabas. "Why, with the flap of a single wing, it could wreak untold devastation."

"Three!" I said. "Henry was state champion in his age group in the hundred-yard butterfly swimming stroke, so estimating its length was easy enough for him."

"With five thousand ghosts we're not talking about a gang anymore," said my grandfather. "We're talking about an army."

"Precisely," said Barnabas.

"Now tell us, Elizabeth," said my grandfather. "Who is our plaintiff? One is enough. More than one is better. But for whomever it is we will work tirelessly."

"Well, that's the thing," I said, squinting as I looked at my father, already anticipating his disappointment. "I couldn't get any of the ghosts to sign."

"And why not?" said my grandfather. "Was our fee agreement too onerous?"

"No, Grandpop. When I found the right ghost, and he was about to agree, his eyes started getting all staticky and all he could say over and over again was that I didn't belong there."

They all looked at me as I spoke, and I could tell that Barnabas and my grandfather were trying hard not to look at my father.

"Then a bunch of other ghosts showed up saying the same thing," I said, "and that's when we all ran."

"Splendid idea," said my grandfather. "Running, I mean."

"Ramsberger was somehow controlling their minds," said my father, "just as he controlled mine when we visited his house. And if that's the situation, then how can we bring the general litigation? First, we have no plaintiff. And second, any ghost witnesses we call will only say what Ramsberger wants them to say."

I thought about the napkin Josiah Goodheart had given me. "I think I have a lead that might help us take care of the witness issue," I said.

My father looked at me suspiciously. "What kind of lead?" he asked. "And where did you get it?"

"More ice cream, is it?" said my grandfather. "Your last cone found us the scientist behind all this, if I remember correctly."

"You do," I said. "And it was. I was eating the ice cream when I remembered there was a ghost the scientist was storing who I think might help us. I was planning to look into it tomorrow."

"Splendid," said my grandfather.

"As a matter of fact, Grandpop, I was hoping you could drive us in the Sturdy Baker."

"Me? Why, of course. I am always up for a delightful cruise in the Studebaker. Where are we off to?"

"New Jersey," I said.

"New Jersey? There is nothing delightful about a cruise into New Jersey. Come to think of it, I might be busy tomorrow, Elizabeth. I might be busy for a month."

I looked at him.

"Yes, yes, yes. I'll take you to New Jersey tomorrow if I must. Though I warn you, if it is to New Jersey we are traveling, I will have to wear a hat."

"That still leaves the task of finding ourselves a plaintiff," said my father.

"But won't the very presence of all those stolen ghosts be enough?" I said.

"Of course not," said my grandfather. "We need a plaintiff ghost with a concrete injury to get the relief we seek. Standing, child. How many times must we say it? Every action, every case."

"And what is the exact relief we are asking for?" said my father.

"Freedom, of course," said Barnabas. "But possibly— and I'm just seeing it now—if we expand the relief we want, it might be easier to find a plaintiff."

"What do you mean by that, Barnabas?" said my grandfather. "Spit it out."

"What if we ask not only for freedom from the ghost thief?" said Barnabas. "What if we also ask for each spirit's return to their natural state if they so choose, so that all those illegally imprisoned by the ghost thief would be free to return to their proper domains? That would prevent any of these poor spirit creatures from being forced to remain in this world against their will."

"Why, of course," said my grandfather. "That would only be right and proper."

My father squinted a bit. "How would that help us find a plaintiff whose mind is not controlled by Ramsberger?"

"I perceive a possibility here," said Barnabas. "If it's all right with the partners, it is a possibility I'd like to pursue."

"Pursue away," said my grandfather. "With all deliberate speed. If Elizabeth can counteract the ghost thief's mind control and Barnabas can find us a plaintiff to sign the complaint, then we are in business. And be sure to ask for attorneys' fees in the complaint, Barnabas. We are not in business for our health, after all."

"Indeed not," said Barnabas.

I stared for a bit, trying to figure it all out, and when I did I started smiling. Barnabas caught my smile and raised an eyebrow before he turned away. My father glanced at me, then at Barnabas, and then back at me, looking puzzled. But my grandfather took his pocket watch from his vest and opened it—a moth flew out, as it often did—and something in the gesture led me to believe he also suspected what was going on, as you might suspect, too.

"Well, let's not tarry," said my grandfather. "There is much to be done and I've received word the court will be in session any day now. Any day."

We all jumped up to get to work, but I had stopped smiling. I was suddenly feeling a little queasy. In fact, my stomach was buzzing as if I had eaten a swarm of bees. Trust me when I say don't do that. But I knew why the bees were buzzing. The Case of the Dastardly Ghost Thief had grown even bigger, now reaching not only into the chamber of stolen ghosts but into Redwing's castle itself.

REDWING'S GARDEN

The stone corridors of Redwing's castle were endless and cold, decorated with tapestries showing a triumphant red demon with hooves for feet and claws for hands and giant ram's horns jutting from its oversized head. In each tapestry the demon, with one giant red wing unfurled behind it, was ravaging a village, or being cheered by thousands, or standing atop a mountain as it peered through a golden telescope.

And now, hurrying down those corridors, wearing long gowns that had been laid out for them on a table on the other side of the wooden door—one gown blue and embroidered with flowers, and one gown green and embroidered with birds—were Juniper and Mel, heads down and hands clasping elbows within the gowns' long flowing sleeves.

They passed servants dressed in the same simple gowns,

men and women both. They passed guards with high leather boots and curved swords and plume feathers sticking out of their ridiculous hats. They passed officials in velvet coats talking about serious matters as they walked together down the long corridors.

The girls turned left. The girls turned right. Juniper held the map within the sleeves of her gown and checked it secretly as they walked. The girls climbed stairs.

"You two," said one of the plume-feathered guards.

They stopped, turned, smiled.

"Which way is the conservatory?"

"Down that way and to the right," said Mel, confidently pointing down the stairway they were climbing even though she had no idea what a conservatory even was.

Every step that took them deeper into the castle was a step closer to home. Every time a guard or official passed without looking twice, their confidence rose. It was as if a path strewn with flowers had been laid for them by the resistance. Then they turned the corner and saw the door.

It was low and round, covered with bright green moss and a thick vine with purple flowers. It was a door that promised a Garden of Eden beyond its simple barrier, with only the two guards with their curved swords and plumed hats standing in their way.

Guards? There was no mention of guards in the instructions.

Juniper and Mel should have been terrified at the sight, they should have felt lost and discouraged. Guards! But ever since they'd crossed the river into the forest everything had been so perfectly laid out for them by the General—Leonora,

and the instructions, and the glowworms, and the robes—
that they simply expected that the doorway would be cleared
for them, too. They were walking on with that expectation
when they heard the crash.

It came from behind, something loud and clattery, along
with shouts and calls and curses. The two guards rushed off
and then around a corner to do whatever guards do when a
fight breaks out. The girls looked at each other.

A moment later they were on the other side of the
unguarded door.

Before them now were trees, and patches of grass, and a
burbling little river. On the high blue ceiling golden clouds
floated across the painted surface while little birds flitted
back and forth. And in the middle of it all, on a high tuft of
grass beyond the river, stood a tall wooden chair, intricately
carved like a priest's chair in a church. The chair was too
big for a regular person, too big for someone twice the size
of a regular person, and on the back, where a giant's head
might rest, two burnt crescents were shaped like two horns
rising.

Beside the great throne, on a golden table, sat a rectangular box, inlaid with jewels.

"Is that it?" said Mel, pointing at the box. "I think that
might be it."

"Do you remember the summoning spell?" said Juniper.

"*Evoco Gaap, a septem spiritibus—*"

"Not now," said Juniper, grabbing hold of Mel's arm.
"Not until we know we have it."

Juniper stepped over a little bridge onto the tuft where
the throne and table stood. Before the box, she knelt. That

seemed strange to Mel, but then Juniper took off her necklace, opened the little cage, and gently took hold of the glowworm. She talked to it quietly before placing it on a little shrub growing beside the river. Then she stood, unlatched the box, and raised the top.

"It's just a stupid telescope," said Juniper.

"Look through it," said Mel.

Juniper lifted a golden telescope out of the box, brought it to her eye, and twisted the end this way and that. "Nothing."

"Maybe you have to tell it who you want to see. Remember, if it's the Lens of Fate it can look onto our world."

Juniper thought for a moment and then brought it back to her eye. "I want to see my mom," she said, "Marian Jelani." Juniper twisted the telescope again, as if bringing it into focus, and then, slowly, her face went slack and her jaw began to tremble.

She was looking back into the world of the living, Mel knew, seeing her mother, feeling so much love and want. For Mel, the change in Juniper's expression filled her with her own feelings of fear and loss, along with the need to go home.

"How's your mother doing there, Junie?" came a gravelly voice from the far edge of the garden room. "I miss her so much it's like a toothache in my heart."

Juniper lowered the Lens of Fate and turned to stare at a man in a gray suit and gray hat who had stepped out from one of the thick tree trunks behind the chair.

"Daddy!"

As Juniper started running to give her father a hug, Mel stood staring, one eye closed, wondering what Tommy Lee Jelani was doing right then in the middle of Redwing's castle.

THE ORPHANAGE

My grandfather did indeed wear a hat as he drove the Sturdy Baker into the wilds of New Jersey.

His car was big and black and older than my father, with chrome highlights and a lever on the floor that my grandfather kept pushing back and forth as we drove through the city and then over the Whitman Bridge, named, I suppose, for the chocolates. His hat was a floppy beige thing that looked like an upside-down porta-potty on his head. On the other side of the bridge there was a WELCOME TO NEW JERSEY sign and my grandfather harrumphed.

"What do you have against New Jersey, Grandpop?" I asked.

"It's a long story," said my grandfather, "involving a horse, a bushel of cranberries, and a female specter named Blaze."

"She sounds like trouble," I said.

"Five-alarm trouble," said my grandfather.

"You can take the next exit, Mr. Webster," said Natalie, who was directing us with her phone from the backseat.

Yes, I had asked Natalie to join us—did I beg, no, not really, unless begging means clasping your hands together and pleading. I wanted her along because that whole heart-wrapping vine thing Josiah Goodheart had laid on me from the ice cream truck gave me the idea that whatever problems Natalie and I might be having in our friendship could some-how be relevant to what had happened between Dr. Shevski and her Paola.

"Where are we going, again, Elizabeth?" said my grand-father after taking the exit.

"The Hazelwood Orphanage," I said. "We need to ask about a ghost."

"We're in the right state for that," said my grandfather.

The Hazelwood Orphanage, founded in 1887, was an ugly monstrosity with thick stone walls. According to the internet, Oliver Hazelwood, some rich railroad guy, died at the age of forty-one by choking on a chicken bone. Two years later the family, stuck with a house too big and too creepy, left it to the state with a provision that it be used to take care of the poor and the unfortunate. The building that had once housed a single family now took care of thirty-seven orphan girls left in the care of the state, all under the directorship of Ms. Adele Demerit.

"And how can I help you today, Mr. Webster?" said Ms. Demerit in her wood-paneled office. She was thin and tall, and her glasses were attached to a little chain around her neck as if she was afraid someone was going to steal them.

"My granddaughter, Elizabeth," said my grandfather, "and her friend Natalie have some questions we hope you'll be able to answer."

"Questions about what?"

"We're doing a paper on the ghosts of New Jersey for our history class," lied Natalie, "and we were most anxious to write about the ghost of the Hazelwood Orphanage."

"A ghost?" said Ms. Demerit. "Oh please, Mr. Webster, you shouldn't allow your granddaughter and her friend to have such flights of fancy. We don't waste our time here with such ghostly nonsense. Math and Shakespeare are the way forward."

"But there are ghosts in both," I said.

Ms. Demerit looked at me as if I was a piece of lint on her purple suit jacket.

"Do you know a Professor Ramsberger," said Natalie, "or the Ramsberger Institute of the Paranormal?"

"No, of course not. What a ridiculous-sounding name." She turned her eyeglasses back to my grandfather as if we didn't matter in the least to her or her day. "I'm sorry I can't help you, Mr. Webster, but I have quite a busy schedule and I must—"

"How about a Dr. Shevski?" I said.

Ms. Demerit slowly turned her attention from my grandfather to me. "How do you know one of our most esteemed alumnae?"

"She's the one who suggested we talk to you about the ghost," said Natalie. Another lie! "That's why we've come.

There's no literature about this specific ghost, so we'd be the first to write about it. Isn't that exciting?"

"I can say with utter confidence that there is no longer any ghost at this facility," said Ms. Demerit.

"No longer?" I said.

"I meant to say there is no ghost and never was a ghost."

"Then Dr. Shevski was lying?" said Natalie, which as far as I could figure, since Dr. Shevski had said nothing to us about the orphanage, was a lie about a lie. Natalie squared! If we weren't in the middle of an even bigger lie, I think I would have given her a cheer.

Ms. Demerit looked at us like we were worms, and then at my grandfather like he was the apple where we had been hiding. "There wasn't a ghost, I assure you, but there were, well, let us call them sightings."

"Sightings but no ghost?" said Natalie.

"As you no doubt know, Mr. Webster, young girls can be quite excitable. There have been sightings of a ghost in the West Wing since well before I started at Hazelwood as a teacher, but it is all about the power of suggestion. No matter how much we tried to squelch the ghostly tales, the story kept getting passed on."

"Is that how Dr. Shevski learned of it?" I said.

"She heard the stories when she was a student here and felt enough was enough. So about a year ago she paid us a visit and brought a machine of hers, quite an amusing contraption with a horn sticking out and a globe on top. At an assembly, she told all the students it was a ghost-trapping machine that would finally rid the orphanage of the Spirit of the West Wing and, with everyone watching, she turned it on. It was all very exciting."

"What happened?"

"Oh, there was a light show of sorts. She was somehow able to create a cloud of bright smoke that twittered and shrieked, and then she sucked the smoke into her machine. Suddenly a bunch of lights started blinking inside the globe. Everyone clapped and cheered. And since that time, there has not been a single ghost sighting at Hazelwood Orphanage. Does that answer your questions?"

"Did the ghost have a name?" I asked.

"Of course not. It was a nameless fiction, first created and then crushed by the power of suggestion. I'm sorry I don't have a better ghost story for you, children. Maybe stick to Shakespeare. The ghost in *Hamlet* is quite amusing." And then in a scary wavering voice, "*I am thy father's spirit.*"

She started bubbling with laughter, which I interrupted with a question. "Was there ever a student here named Paola Fiore?"

Her laughing stopped abruptly. "Not that I know of."

"Could you look her up?"

"Our files are private," she said. "And with that taken care of, I think it is time for you all to leave."

"Madame director," said my grandfather, "let me give you my card."

He reached his fingers into his vest pocket and pulled out his watch, a photograph, a set of stamps, a tiny screwdriver, and then a bent and folded business card, which he smoothed out before handing over.

"As you can see, I am an attorney with the firm of Webster and Spawn. We specialize in, let us say, unusual matters. I must confess that the girls' interest in the ghost of Hazelwood springs from one of our cases. We can subpoena this information, which will create a large amount of legal fees on both sides, along with an unfortunate flood of bad press. You know how much the scandal sheets enjoy writing about scandal."

"Scandal?"

"Yes. How do you think they got their name? Scandal sheets. What isn't clear about that? Or, you can simply answer my granddaughter's question and we'll be out of your quite impressive hair without a breath mentioned about Hazelwood to the press or to the court. It is, of course, your choice."

Ms. Demerit stared at my grandfather with a touch of hatred in her eyes. "What is really going on with you three?"

"Her name was Paola," said Natalie with the sweetest smile. "Paola Fiore."

Ms. Demerit's lips tightened as if she had just sucked on a bushel of lemons. Then, with an expression that made it clear she never, ever wanted to see any of us again, she stood and walked to a row of filing cabinets in the corner of her office.

"Yes," she said as she examined an old and dusty file. "Paola Fiore was a Hazelwood resident well before my time. She entered the orphanage in 1918 after both her parents died from the influenza."

"Like Keir," said Natalie.

"Who?" said Ms. Demerit.

"We wrote a paper about a boy whose mother died in the 1918 pandemic," I said.

"You write a lot of papers," she said with a squint. She carried the file to her desk. "Paola was twelve when she came here and stayed at Hazelwood, apparently, until 1922. The record of her classes ends midway through the year."

"Was she adopted?" I said. "It might help if we learned her new last name."

"It's unlikely she's still alive, dear. She'd be well over a hundred by now."

"Even so, the name might help," I said. "A grandchild might have a fond memory."

"That happens on rare occasions, I've found," said my grandfather.

"Very rare," I said.

"She wasn't the best of students, I must say," said Ms. Demerit as she paged through the file. "Her grades, well… And for some reason she didn't get along with the other children. But I don't see an adoption form in—wait a second." She picked up a newspaper article so old it fell apart in her fingers. "Oh my, that's terrible."

"What did you find?" said Natalie.

"There was a tragic accident," said Ms. Demerit. "The poor girl, she fell off the roof into the rose garden. Her neck snapped in the fall."

"What was she doing on the roof?" said Natalie.

"It doesn't say. Poor Paola."

"Did it say which part of the roof she fell off?" I said.

Ms. Demerit kept reading the article and then stopped and put it down without saying anything.

"Can I guess, please, please, please?" I said, raising my hand as if I was in Mr. Armbruster's class, even though I never raised my hand in Mr. Armbruster's class. "Did she fall off the roof of the West Wing?"

When she looked at me, Ms. Demerit's face was frozen in an expression of terror. So much for the power of suggestion.

THE DEMON'S DEAL

"Junie, oh, Junie, it heals my heart to see you," said Tommy Lee Jelani as he hugged his daughter beneath the twittering painted birds of Redwing's garden room.

"Daddy, I missed you so much," said Juniper, still holding the Lens of Fate her left hand.

"When I saw you in the corridor of my building," said Juniper's father, "I thought I was dreaming, like I'd dreamed of you a thousand times. And when the voices told me you were merely a remembrance of my old life, I believed them. But Junie, to see you now, to hold you in my arms, my heart is so full of love and hope it is ripping apart."

As Juniper's father made his sweet declaration, Mel looked on with suspicion. Mel and Juniper had slipped into the castle with utter secrecy and made their way into the garden room undetected. But somehow, and for some reason,

Juniper's father had beaten them to it. Mel wondered if Juniper was asking the same questions, before her friend pulled away from her father.

"What are you doing here, Daddy?"

"Sit down with me, girl," said Juniper's father as he gently led his daughter to a bench overlooking the little stream.

As they sat together, he held her free hand in his. A dogwood stood behind them, bending forward to embrace them with arms full of white blossoms.

"I've come to help," he said. "When I learned that you truly were in this world and stepping into danger, well, I just couldn't stay in my little room."

"How did you get here?" said Juniper.

"Does the how really matter? All that matters is that I can make sure you get back to the world of the living, you and your friend. And the fortune you were looking for? I can tell you where that is, too. You'll be rich, Junie, and you'll get to go to that college you want to go to. You'll do all the great things I dreamed for you, I know you will."

"You didn't say how you got here, Mr. Jelani," said Mel, still full of suspicion. If it was only the Lens of Fate he was after, he could have snatched it right out of his daughter's hand. But what else could Juniper, a living girl from the other world, do in this world for her father?

Juniper's father turned his eyes to Mel and she saw a lick of flame in them. "What's your name, girl?"

"Melinda," said Mel. "Melinda Weintraub."

"You were her little kindergarten friend."

"That's right," said Mel. "And I need to know..." She

glanced at Juniper. "We need to know how you got here, how you can help us, and what you are getting out of it."

"Mel, stop," said Juniper. "He's my father."

"Oh no, Junie. Your friend's as sharp as a flatted fifth. You have a right to know all this, and more. What did you think, girl," he said to Mel, "that you could traipse in here and take their most precious object without them knowing?"

"Redwing knows?" said Juniper.

"Don't you realize where you are, Junie? You're in the mouth of its power. With a snap of its claw it could send you to the Island of Lost Souls, or give you a century's worth of toil on the River of Retribution, or leave you hanging by your wrists in the dungeons of this very castle. But with the same snap it can save you, and save me at the same time."

"How can Redwing save you?" said Mel. "You can't go back to our world, can you?"

"No, thank goodness," said Tommy Lee Jelani, focusing not on Mel but on his daughter. "Who would want to? But listen up, child. That one-winged demon is offering a deal and it brought me here to make the offer. If you agree, Junie, you get everything I promised. And as for me? Well, I get myself a one-way ticket to the Gate of Light. I don't deserve it—I admit, I did things in my life. But that is the great good you can do for your father, Junie. Think of the glory of it. And the food! I'll be dancing all the way up that hill, I will."

There was something in his voice just then that my mother noticed as she stood in the garden room. It was as if there was a flaw in a recording and a second voice had been over-dubbed onto the first. But Juniper seemed to hear nothing other than her father's croon, seemed to see nothing but the need in her father's eyes.

"I want that, too, Daddy," said Juniper. "Oh, I want that so much for you."

"And all you have to do," said her father, "is tell me about the General. What does she look like? What does she sound like? Replay it all for me, Junie, everything that happened from the moment they broke you from that jail until you showed up in this room. Tell it all and all our dreams come true."

Juniper and Mel both understood the terms that were laid out. He was asking for betrayal. And my mother admitted to me that she was so scared, and so desperate to get home, that she was almost willing. Except there was something in that double voice, something in the lick of fire she had seen in his eyes. If betrayal of the General was being asked, it only made sense that betrayal of Juniper and Mel would be part of the answer. No matter how starry-eyed Juniper was at this reunion with her father, my mother didn't trust anything about it.

And then she realized she didn't need to trust it. That was when she started speaking. "*Evoco Gaap, a septem spiritibus de ventis.*"

Juniper looked at Mel with understanding in her eyes as she tightened her grip on the golden telescope. At the same time, Juniper's father looked at Mel with a puzzled expression as she continued chanting Gaap's conjuring spell. But before she could get out the last of the summoning words, Tommy Lee Jelani waved a hand at her in a dismissive gesture and the words were suddenly caught in her throat like an unruly knot of frogs.

Mel put her hand to her mouth and there was no mouth.
NO MOUTH!

Where her mouth had been was now a smooth flap of flesh. With her tongue she could still feel her teeth, and her vocal cords could still vocalize, but the sounds that came out were not smooth-sounding Latin words but the grunts and groans of a barnyard animal.

Juniper pulled her hand away from her father's grip and stared wide-eyed as Mel frantically fell to her knees, grunting in terror as her hands grabbed at where her mouth should have been.

"What do you say, Junie?" said Juniper's father, ignoring what was going on with Mel. "Can you do this one thing for me, this one simple thing? Please, baby. All you have to do is tell them what they want to know."

"You want me to betray the people who helped us?" said Juniper.

"That's it exactly."

"I can't."

"Of course you can. They betrayed you first."

"What do you mean?"

"The resistance betrayed you," said Juniper's father. "How else did I know you would be here?"

Juniper looked at her friend, spinning around in panic, and then back at her father. "I don't believe you," she said.

Suddenly the door behind Mel opened with a bang and two guards with their fancy hats entered. The guards halted on either side of the entrance as a great black bird flew into the room and circled before landing heavily on one of the trees.

After the bird, a woman entered, a tall haughty woman with a long nose and the stiff bearing of a queen. She wore a sweeping black dress trimmed in gold and some sort of silver crown in her hair. The Raven Master.

"You don't believe you've been betrayed?" said the Raven Master to the girls, her sneering voice as haughty as her face. "How innocent you are. All of life is a betrayal. But maybe you'll believe this."

She snapped her fingers and another woman entered the room. This woman was young, a girl really. She wore a long red dress, tight and shimmery, and stood with her head bowed. At first Mel couldn't quite place her, but when the young woman raised her head and smiled with utter misery, Mel understood immediately why she looked so sad.

"What else could I do?" said Leonora. "I had been crab-walking for over a hundred years. Do you know what that does to your back?"

Mel grunted at her, and Leonora turned to her as if she understood every word.

"I don't want your forgiveness," said Leonora. "Walk a mile like they made me walk, and then you can judge."

It was all enough to break both girls' hearts, even as they knew that her confession was designed to do exactly that, to break their hearts as well as their wills. Can you really betray those who have betrayed you? It all would have been too much to bear on its own, until a man was led into the room with a third guard holding tight to his arm.

Juniper's father?

Both girls stared at Tommy Lee Jelani before turning to look at the creature who was still holding Juniper's hand.

Juniper yanked away her hand as the creature stretched its neck and began to grow. Its wrists bulged out of jacket cuffs, its hands melted into huge claws, leather shoes split apart as its feet formed into great pointed hooves. Great horns spiraled out of its forehead, and its skin changed to a fiery red as a single red wing stretched and fluttered from its back.

There it stood, tall and arrogant, the lord of the domain, the demon Redwing in all its bitter glory.

"What have ye to say, girl?" said the demon in a strange triple voice, as if three strangers were all talking at once.

Juniper looked at the demon, then at her real father, who shook his head with sadness.

"It's better to go along," said Leonora. "Trust me."

"We don't," said Juniper. "And we never will again."

She turned to Mel, who was still grappling at her mouthless face, and Juniper gave a silent *I'm sorry* before facing the demon. "No deal," said Juniper, her voice shaky but sure. "No betrayal."

"That's my Junie," said the real Tommy Lee Jelani.

"What about you, silent one?" said the Raven Master to Mel. "If the demon gives you back your mouth, will you give us what we need?"

Mel looked at Juniper—calm, brave, defiant, everything Mel herself wanted to be. Mel's mouth had been stolen, and she was trembling with fear, but in the presence of Juniper's bravery she could only answer one way. Her words were an unintelligible grunt, two short vowels, but the meaning was clear as glass.

"We can wait," said the Raven Master. "You'll enjoy the

dungeons. Filthy and cold, like your world. And watch out for the rats. We breed them with two rows of teeth. A few decades will loosen your lips. Well, maybe not your lips, Melinda Weintraub, since you don't have them anymore."

And then she laughed the strangest of laughs. Whatever the Raven Master had once been, this laugh was no longer a human laugh. Her laughter was like the endless expanse of space, cold and empty and promising nothing but death itself.

"Before you go to the dungeons," said Redwing, "I'll take back what's mine."

At that the demon stepped toward the now-shaking Juniper and grabbed the Lens of Fate right out of her hands.

"Oh, I missed you so," said the demon to the golden telescope.

"Take them away," said the Raven Master.

As the guards grabbed hold of Mel and Juniper, the demon Redwing caressed the Lens of Fate. "We have so much to see, you and I," said Redwing. "So much to learn."

"So much to conquer," said the Raven Master.

The Ghost in the Globe

W as I supposed to know what that was all about back there in the orphanage?" said my grandfather as he drove the Sturdy Baker back toward the chocolate bridge.

"Not really," I said.

"That's a relief," said my grandfather.

"But even so, Mr. Webster," said Natalie, "the way you threatened that old lady and got her to show us the file? That was amazing."

"I've forgotten a lot, my dear, but a lawyer never forgets how to lay on a good threat. That's what the second year of law school is all about."

"What's the first year about?" I said.

"Billable hours," said my grandfather. "The third year I've forgotten entirely."

"And I loved the way you took so long to fish the card

from your vest pocket," said Natalie. "The suspense! I'm going to have to learn that trick."

"So where to now?" said my grandfather.

"I think it's time," I said, "for a fond reunion."

It wasn't long before my grandfather parked the car in front of the fence surrounding the ragged power plant with its yellow windows, its twisting ducts running this way and that, its three smokestacks pointing to the sky, and all of it covered with amazing graffiti.

"I know, I know," I said as my grandfather peered over the steering wheel at what was left of the building. "It's a bit of a wreck."

"Don't be ridiculous," said my grandfather. "It's in perfectly adequate shape. Maybe I should get in touch with the management company. We could save some pennies on our place, don't you think?"

"I don't think," I said. "I don't think at all."

"And according to your debate coach, that's your problem right there, Lizzie," said Natalie. "Right there."

Funny how much I didn't laugh at that.

I led my grandfather through the gap in the fence and the barely open door into that landscape of rust and gunk and scurrying rats. The pounding of my grandfather's cane echoed through the cavernous interior as we crossed the cement floors and then climbed the metal stairway. *Tink tink tink tink tink.* When we came to a stop at the brickwork arch, Ygor looked up from the table where he was working with Dr. Shevski and stared, his huge pale face hard and unwelcoming.

"What you cheeldren want now?" said Ygor after slowly

making his way to the entrance, his hands squeezing at the air as he approached.

"We came to talk," I said.

"We are too busy to jabber," said Ygor. "We are close on SEG. Almost ready to test."

"On Paola?" said Natalie.

"What do the children want, Ygor?" called out Dr. Shevski, still at the table.

"They want talk," called back Ygor.

"About Paola," I said.

Ygor looked at me and tilted his head. "They want talk about Paola."

"Who is the man with them?"

"Ebenezer Webster of the law firm of Webster and Spawn," said my grandfather. "Perhaps you've heard of us?"

"Perhaps I have," said Dr. Shevski.

A few minutes later, the five of us were standing around a Spirit Storage Globe that was sitting on a table. Inside the globe, lit up with all kinds of swirling lights, was the spirit of Paola Fiore.

"She was horrible ghost," said Ygor. "In middle of night would float into dormitory and scare all the orphan cheeldren."

"Including you, Dr. Shevski?" I asked.

The doctor's gray face turned to me and closed in on itself, like a hand becoming a fist.

"The ghost's cruelty was very bad," said Ygor. "Without Dr. Shevski taking action, she would still be haunting. Young orphan girls at mercy of cruel and heartless spirit. That is why we work so hard."

"To create the machine that will destroy her?" I said.

"To free the living from the curse of the dead," said Ygor.

"The dead are not a curse, young man," said my grandfather as he tapped his cane on the floor. "No, no, no. In my experience, it is quite the opposite, actually."

Dr. Shevski turned her closed face to look at my grandfather. "My understanding is that Webster and Spawn often sues the dead, isn't that right, Mr. Webster?"

"I won't deny that."

"So you know they are a scourge on our world."

"I know no such thing. We also sue the living, and we wouldn't call them a scourge, though there are some neighbors I can do without. But I actually find the plight of the dead in our world to be quite poignant."

"Poignant?"

"Indeed. In the course of our practice we often put the dead on the witness stand. They are surprisingly chatty. You can learn much by listening to their stories."

"What have you learned, Mr. Webster?" she asked.

"That if the dead are in our world haunting the living," said my grandfather, "it is only because some task of theirs remains uncompleted. Once that is taken care of, poof, they leave this world to continue their journey."

"Poof?" said Dr. Shevski.

"Poof," said my grandfather.

"And we were wondering," I said, "what remains uncompleted for Paola?"

"Why were you wondering, child?" said Dr. Shevski. "What is Paola to you?"

"The real question," said Natalie, "is what is Paola to you?"

Dr. Shevski looked at us and we looked at each other. I had asked Natalie along for this very moment. What was she to me and I to her and why did I think Paola had the answer to so many mysteries? But whatever we were after, it was time to get to it.

"We've come for your help, Doctor," I said. "Fred Ramsberger is holding thousands of ghosts as prisoners with your machines. He is using your Spirit Psychic Drive to control them. The law firm of Webster and Spawn is suing to have them freed."

"Why would we help you free thousand ghosts?" said Ygor. "Ramsberger is doing world great service."

"But those ghosts were all once alive," I said. "They felt the dawn, saw the glow of the sunset, loved and were loved. If you kill the ghosts, you're killing all of that."

"If Webster and Spawn wins its case," said Natalie, "the ghosts will be free to finish what they need to finish in this world and then move on."

"When we learned that Paola was a ghost that haunted the orphanage where you grew up," I said, "we thought that maybe talking to her might convince you to help our case. Someone once told me that if you want to understand the vine that wraps about the heart of an adult, look closely at the sweet school days of her youth and there you'll find the seed."

"You think there's a vine wrapped around my heart?"

"A vine of hate that is strangling it," I said. "And I think Paola is the seed."

"And so you want us to chat with Paola?" said Dr. Shevski. "I'd sooner chat with a porcupine."

"It is perfectly understandable to be afraid," said my grandfather. "A ghost is a frightening thing for most people."

"I am not most people, Mr. Webster, and I am not afraid."

"Splendid. Then we can put your Paola on something like a witness stand to hear her story. You can ask questions, Doctor, and then my granddaughter will ask questions."

"Your granddaughter?" said Doctor Shevski.

"Oh yes. Elizabeth is quite the sparkling questioner."

"Not so sparkling," I said.

"A little flat, to be truthful," said Natalie. "But with a nice touch of citrus."

"Really?" I said. "Was that necessary?"

"And what would be the result of all this nonsense?" said Dr. Shevski. "Who would decide Paola's fate? You, Mr. Webster? Or some court of dubious law?"

"You can decide," I said.

"Me?"

"This isn't only about Paola," I said. "It's also about you."

"What do you say?" said Natalie. "Just a little chat among friends?"

"Hardly friends," said the doctor slowly, and then she paused for a time, thinking it through. I couldn't then imagine what she was thinking, though I have a better idea now. Finally she said, "As you wish. Let's have our talk with the ghost."

"As long as we can do it without your psychic drive controlling her," said Natalie.

"Oh, you won't have to worry about the psychic drive," said Dr. Shevski. "Truth is, I've never been able to control Paola Fiore."

34

PAOLA FIORE

Ygor set six chairs around the table. Dr. Shevski sat on one side next to Ygor, who held a long steel pole with a large circle at the end. Natalie, my grandfather, and I sat across from them. At the head of the table sat the ghost of Paola Fiore.

She had flown wild around the factory floor when first freed from the globe, releasing a high cackle as a breeze kicked up that smelled of hot asphalt and roses. But Ygor was able to catch her in midair with one of the doctor's newest inventions, the SSN-7, or Spirit-Snatching Net, and deposit her at the table. She tried to flit away once more and Ygor simply snatched her out of the air and dropped her once again onto the chair. Paola looked around angrily, gave Dr. Shevski a hiss, and then sat back in the chair, looking down at the floor, her arms clasped petulantly as if she was in detention.

About the same age as Natalie and me, she was a ghostly green, wearing a party dress with a bright red stain on its white lace collar, high white socks, and black buckled shoes. Her neck was set at a strange and disconcerting angle.

"The ghost of Paola Fiore, I assume?" said my grandfather.

The ghost gave a dismissive shrug.

"My name is Ebenezer Webster, and my understanding is that you have been kept prisoner in this machine for months and months. A troubling state of affairs indeed. It is also my understanding that before your imprisonment, you had been haunting the Hazelwood Orphanage, the location of your untimely and tragic death. All of this is undisputed, I believe."

He looked around the table and received only nods.

"In view of your situation, we thought we ought to hear your story. It is nothing official, of course, but it might help you get out of that globe on a more permanent basis."

"And if I tell you to go chase yourself instead?" said the ghost. Her voice was a whistling wind with vowels and consonants, all with a strong Italian accent, as if the wind had come straight from Rome.

"Back to the globe, I suppose," said my grandfather with a shrug. "But if you do agree to participate, all we ask is that you tell us nothing but the truth."

"That might be hard for Paola," said Dr. Shevski.

The ghost glared at her own thumb before giving a rather grumpy "Fine."

"Splendid," said my grandfather. "Dr. Shevski, you said you had some questions."

"I do," said Dr. Shevski. "I'm not a lawyer, just a simple scientist, but the beauty of science is that the observable world is often so clear anyone can see the truth. Paola, you were already dead for many years when I arrived at the orphanage."

"I suppose," said the ghost.

"And I had nothing to do with your death."

"Not a thing," said Paola.

"But still you engaged in a brutal crusade to ruin my life at the orphanage and afterward."

"I'm a ghost," said the ghost. "That's what ghosts do."

"When I started getting close to Sylvie Glendale—doing our homework together and combing each other's hair—you swooped in and shrieked at her so consistently, she started running in the opposite direction whenever she saw me."

"Sylvie was a sleepyhead," said Paola. "Not to mention those shoes."

"And you did the same thing with Delores Gump."

"She spat whenever she talked. You had to wear a raincoat around her."

"And Abigail Thompkins, who was the most popular girl in our grade."

The ghost stared at the floor with that petulant look of hers, which I was starting to really enjoy, when she said calmly, "I was saving you from the heartbreak of betrayal."

"And then later, when I held the hand of Peter Decatur at the Halloween hop with Bellmawr Prep," said Dr. Shevski, "you managed to dump an ice cube down his pants."

"It was the best he danced all night."

"But I liked him. His hair had a swoop to it."

"You should be thanking me," said the ghost. "He's bald as a boiled egg now."

"And when the Edmonsons were thinking of adopting me, you spilled my soda over my dress at our introductory meeting and touched my eye so I started wiping at my dress and at the same time winking, touching and winking."

"They lived in Sicklerville," said the ghost. "What else needs to be said?"

"I had no friends because of you," said the doctor. "I had no boyfriend because of you. And I was never adopted because of you."

Paola, looking down, said softly, "And still you left me."

"You ruined my life. How many other little orphan girls have you terrified and bullied? How many other lives have you ruined?"

For the first time the ghost looked directly at Dr. Shevski. "Only yours," she said.

The two stared at each other for a long moment, as if something deep and deeply painful was being shared. Then Dr. Shevski broke eye contact and said to the rest of us, "We've heard enough. Ygor, return this blight on the living to the SS-G."

"Not so fast, Doctor," said my grandfather.

"What more must we hear?" said Dr. Shevski.

"One never knows until one hears it. Elizabeth, do you have any questions for Ms. Fiore?"

Any questions? What was I going to do with Paola Fiore?

Josiah Goodheart made it seem all I had to do was release Paola's ghost back into the world and Dr. Shevski would be changed just like that. *¡Snap!* That's why I agreed to this whole stupid ghost story thing. But the ghost had sat there and admitted to behaving so brutally to the young and orphaned Dr. Shevski it made me gulp. Yet there was also something familiar about the whole back-and-forth. Paola wasn't simply a mean ghost to young Dr. Shevski, she was far worse, the BFF who turns on you just because.

I looked at Natalie, remembered the way I felt when she chose nail polish and Debbie Benner over me, and sensed where this had to go.

"How did you die, Paola?" I asked.

"There was an accident."

"On the roof? Did you trip over a shoelace?"

"I was wearing buckle shoes," said the ghost.

"The same ones you're wearing now? Along with the same party dress? Pretty fancy."

She shifted awkwardly in her seat. "There was a dance."

"What happened at the dance?"

"Nothing."

"Remember, Paola," I said. "The truth. You promised."

She stared down for a moment and then said, "They yanked up my skirt and laughed at me."

"Who did that?"

"The other girls. The fancy girls. Abigail."

"It couldn't be the same Abigail as when Dr. Shevski was at Hazelwood."

"There is always an Abigail," said the ghost. "And this one poured a glass of punch over my head."

"Is the stain on your collar blood or punch?"

"Punch. The blood didn't come until I was dead."

"And what happened after they laughed at you and poured punch over your head?"

"I ran away crying. Like I always ran away when they were mean to me, which was always."

"You ran to the roof?"

"My secret place, where they couldn't find me and tell me that I looked wrong, or talked wrong, or was dirty-faced because of where I was born."

"And then, on the roof, you slipped."

"Sort of."

"How do you sort of slip?"

"You begin to slip, and try to stop slipping, and then you decide maybe with everything, it is easier not to try so hard."

"Oh, Paola!"

"Go sit on your hat," said the ghost. "I want no girl's pity."

I smiled. I was liking Paola more and more. "After you fell, Paola, why didn't you pass to the other side?"

"I wasn't finished."

"What did you need to finish at the orphanage?"

"There was one thing I'd always wanted. I still hoped to find it."

"And did you?"

"I thought I did."

"Enough," said Dr. Shevski. "She goes back into the globe. That is my decision. You said it was my decision."

"It is your decision after we hear the story," said my grandfather. "You may continue, Elizabeth."

And so I did. Bit by bit, surly answer by surly answer, I pulled out Paola's sad story, so tragic and so familiar at the same time.

35

FRENEMIES

When the newly born ghost of Paola Fiore rose from the West Wing garden, she surveyed the landscape of the living with a searing regret. The regret was not that she was dead, but that in what had been her life she had never found a friend.

It was this regret that kept her spirit at the orphanage even as the high voices sang to her that it was time to move on, a female chorus with a strange and urgent power compelling her forward. She could even see other wisps of spirit following the voices, as if passing to the next world was not a choice at all. But in her short painful life Paola had learned to trust no one, especially a high-voiced chorus of girls. So instead she stayed in the place of her humiliation and her death, with a single goal.

No matter how long it took, she would make a true friend

before she passed. She thought it wouldn't be too hard. All she had to do was find someone lonely and different and not afraid of ghosts.

Louise was shy and quiet, with long black hair, and wanted all the other girls to think she was mysterious. Paola waited for a moment when Louise was alone in the library before she shimmered to life in front of her. "Hi," said Paola. "Will you be my friend?"

Louise jumped from her chair and ran out of the library screaming. The nurse had to give her a shot to calm her. But Paola kept trying.

Tina was a bully whose only so-called friends were those who were nice to her out of fear. *She is tough enough*, thought Paola. Simi was an artist who drew trees with squiggly lines that made them seem alive. *She is strange enough*, thought Paola. Alison looked under rocks for bugs and spiders and let them run all across her fingers. *She is brave enough*, thought Paola. Paola appeared before each girl and made her simple request, "Will you be my friend?" Though each reacted in a different way—fear, curiosity, laughter—they all ended up rejecting her.

Though no real friendship was formed, the stories that spread about the Spirit of the West Wing made Paola's attempts ever more futile. One girl, an ethereal little monster named Catherine, even tried to summon the Spirit of the West Wing with chants and potions. When Paola appeared, Catherine ordered the ghost to terrorize one of the other girls. It wasn't long before Catherine's strange outbursts forced the headmistress to send her to a special place for very special children.

After years of failure, Paola began to wonder if she was the problem. Maybe she didn't understand what friendship was really all about. For the next bundle of years, she hung upside down from ceilings and lay under rugs all over the orphanage, listening, learning, studying friendships among the girls at Hazelwood. She discovered that the game of catching friends, like every other game, depended on rules. And these are the rules she came up with.

PAOLA FIORE'S FIVE RULES FOR CATCHING AND KEEPING A TRUE FRIEND

(1) A friend-catcher is always asking for your help, your attention, your reassurance. The more you give her, the more needy she becomes.

(2) A friend-catcher makes you a part of the grand drama of her life. This makes it clear that her life is so much more interesting than yours and makes you ever more devoted.

(3) A friend-catcher is always looking for a better friend, which is how you know she really likes you, because that means you're the highest-rated friend she could have at the moment. Highest-rated! Also, it keeps you working ever so hard to be a better friend to her than she could find elsewhere.

(4) A friend-catcher will sometimes make fun of you, call you by an uncomfortable nickname, sarcastically explain to you why the clothes you are wearing or the things you are thinking are wrong. This is called joking and is what true friends do. She

will also tell you to stop being so sensitive about her jokes, which is such good training for life!

(5) And finally, and most importantly, a friend-catcher wants you all to herself.

After Paola had formulated her rules, she tried them out on various girls, perfecting her approach even as she lost interest in the girls themselves. The rules were working, which was exciting, and many of the girls became enamored of their new ghost friend—obsessed, even—but none of it felt like true friendship. Paola figured the problem was simply that she hadn't picked the right girl. As she had learned, a clever friend-catcher was always looking for a better friend. So even as she practiced with and later ghosted a series of girls, she waited for the one true friend to arrive.

And then it happened. A new girl was brought to the orphanage, an immigrant like her, whose father had been hit and killed by a streetcar in Camden, leaving her without family in this country. The girl was small and shy, keeping to herself and her books. She talked with an accent, made no friends, sulked about the grounds at night in her heavy black shoes.

Perfect!

Paola bided her time, watching and learning, not wanting to rush things. And then one moonless night, she shimmered to life on the path the new girl was walking and said, "Can you help me?"

The girl stopped, hesitated. "Are you a ghost?" she said finally, strangely calm at the sight.

"Yes!" said Paola, excited by the calm.

"Interesting," said the girl. "How does that work?"

"I don't know," said Paola. "It just does. But I lost my shoe somewhere in the rosebushes in the West Wing and now I can't find it."

The new girl looked down at one ghostly Mary Jane and one stockinged foot. "I'll help you look," said the girl. "My name's Irina."

"I'm Paola," said Paola.

"Nice to meet you, Paola," said Irina, as if the ghost was any other girl. "Let's find your shoe."

In the rose garden, when Irina pointed at the ghostly shoe Paola had planted beneath one of the bushes, Paola clapped excitedly, as if Irina had solved the greatest mystery of all time. And so it began.

They met regularly on those nightly walks. Irina talked about the books she was reading and the science she was studying. Paola talked about the troubles of the undead, how the other girls had been so mean to her when she was alive, and how everyone was scared of her now—everyone but Irina.

"I don't know what I'd do without you," said Paola.

"I like having you around, too," said Irina.

"Promise you won't tell anyone about me or bring anyone else on these walks," said Paola.

"I promise," said Irina.

"Good," said Paola. "I don't want to share you."

Over the following months, Paola grew more and more attached to Irina, but Irina's manner with her was a little too formal for a true friend. Paola tried to break Irina out of her shell by doubling down on the rules, making up funny nicknames for her—calling her Glasses because of her large spectacles, or Clod because of her heavy black shoes—and laughing at some of the things she said. "That's why you don't have any friends," she would say, or "If all you're going to do is talk about silly old science, maybe I should find someone new to walk with."

"Why do you always say things like that to me?" Irina said one evening.

"You're too sensitive," replied Paola. "I'm only making a joke."

"I don't like those kinds of jokes," said Irina.

"Then maybe I should get a different friend, someone who thinks I'm funny," said Paola with a laugh.

Irina didn't join in the laughter, as if she didn't get the joke, as if it wasn't a joke at all. Which, in truth, it wasn't.

Something was going wrong, Paola could feel it. She loved Irina's calm, Irina's seriousness. She loved the way Irina dismissed the gossip Paola tried to share as if it was less interesting than what Irina found in her schoolbooks. She loved Irina. But she could feel her one true friend becoming more distant with every late-night walk.

For a moment Paola wondered if she had gotten the rules all wrong. Or, more frighteningly, she wondered if there were no rules at all. Maybe true friendship required honesty instead of manipulation, loyalty instead of tricks, acceptance, acceptance, acceptance instead of judgment and sarcasm and constant insecurity. The possibility of it filled Paola with a strange hope even as it terrified her to her ghostly bones. What if all these years she had been so, so wrong? She trembled over this moment of revelation, as if balancing on the edge of a knife, before landing on an inescapable conclusion.

No, she had not been wrong. That was impossible. A world that took her parents in a pandemic and tortured her in the confines of this orphanage and then allowed her life to end on a slip and a whim could not be survived with honesty and loyalty and acceptance.

The rules ruled, and to keep Irina's friendship she only needed to be better at following them.

"So how did it go?" I asked Paola at the table on the Phantasm International factory floor.

"The harder I tried, the more Irina pulled away," said Paola. "It made me sad, so I told her she was dressing wrong and should stop caring so much about science. I kept on demanding more of her attention. I tried to create more and more drama. But none of it seemed to work. And then I caught her."

"Caught who?" I asked.

"Irina," said Paola. "One night I waited for her on the path and when she didn't show I swooped into the orphanage and caught her betraying me with that sleepyhead Sylvie and her stupid pink shoes. They were doing their homework together, and Irina was laughing in a way she didn't laugh with me anymore. Rule five was very clear. I couldn't let that happen."

"So you shrieked at her, as Dr. Shevski described in her question?"

"Irina was being kind," said Paola. "I did more than shriek."

I looked at Paola, who stared down at the floor as if that was where her own beating heart lay. And then I looked at

Dr. Shevski, whose face was again a closed fist, even as her eyes were glistening. We had ended where Dr. Shevski had started. There wasn't anything more to say—or was there? I looked at Natalie, who was staring at Paola with a curious expression.

"Can I have a moment to consult with Natalie, Grand-pop?" I asked, as if he was a judge on the bench and I was asking for a short recess. Recess!

"Of course, my dear, take your time."

I grabbed Natalie and pulled her away from the table. We huddled where we couldn't be heard and stared at Dr. Shevski and the ghost of Paola Fiore, each trying oh so hard to ignore the other.

"What should I do now?" I asked.

"I don't know," said Natalie. "What were you trying to do in the first place?"

"Make them like each other again, maybe?"

"How's that going?" said Natalie.

As we examined the bitter old friends sitting at the table, I recognized something in the way they looked beyond each other, something heartbreaking. Their misery was so clear I could feel the tears pressing against my eyes.

"Is that going to be us in twenty years?" I asked.

"The way we're going," said Natalie, "that's going to be us in high school. I hate rules."

"You always did," I said. "But without rules, how do we not end up like them?"

"We decide," said Natalie.

"As simple as that?"

"Why not," said Natalie. "We decide we won't let

anything get between us. Even other friendships. Especially other friendships."

"Can it really be that easy?"

"Let's find out," said Natalie with a smile that reached into my heart.

Back at the table, I glanced at Natalie, who was now looking at Dr. Shevski, who was looking at Paola, who was still staring at the floor. And it was something in Natalie's eyes that pointed me toward the question that had been hanging in that room like an overripe peach.

"Why did you stay at the orphanage after Irina left, Paola?" I said.

"I still wanted what I wanted," said Paola the ghost. "But it never worked. Rule three kept coming into play and no matter how nice or pleasant a girl was, I always knew there was someone better."

"And was there?" I said.

"Yes, of course," said Paola. "Irina."

"And so now you regret how you treated her, don't you?" I said.

Paola pursed her lips and thought for a moment before saying, "I regret nothing."

"And you want to apologize for following all your rules with her," I said, barreling on like a fool.

"I apologize for nothing," said Paola. "The rules are the rules. Where would we be without rules?"

Well, that didn't turn out as I expected. I looked at Dr. Shevski. Her eyes behind her glasses were narrowed, her jaw was locked, her hands on the table were squeezed into fists.

"But I will also say this about Irina," continued Paola,

still staring at the floor. "I wasn't wrong about her, either. She was perfect. And I loved her. I still do. She betrayed me, and however she treats me now I can't forget that, but she was the closest I had ever come, the closest I will ever come, to having a true friend in this world. And for that she will always have the biggest piece of my heart."

I turned to Natalie and saw the very same thing. But the question was, what now did Dr. Shevski see when she looked at Paola, and was it enough to unlock her jaw, unclench her fists, and save the world?

We wouldn't know until we brought our case to the Court of Uncommon Pleas.

36

THE DEMON'S DUNGEON

My mother was still missing her mouth when my father flew through the air and landed on the floor of their dungeon cell. The superhero vibe was minimized somewhat by the fact that two guards had tossed him in like a sack of garbage, but all in all it was still a pretty cool entrance by my dad.

He sat up and fixed his glasses as he looked around the stone-walled cell with its arched ceiling and piles of hay on the floor for beds. His gaze first landed on Juniper, then on Juniper's dad, and then on my mouthless mother, his eyes widening behind his glasses at the sight of her bizarre, simplified face.

"Oohoohiihiih," my mother grunted.

He put on a consoling smile and said, "Hi?"

My mother had been in the cell for almost a full day with Juniper and Juniper's dad, who was no longer plagued with the voices. Father and daughter were in the midst of a tearful reunion, with hugs and laughter and long quiet talks. My mother had kept her distance, sitting at the opposite end of the cell, wanting to give them privacy as she dealt with the spiraling anxiety caused by her still-missing mouth.

(It will always feel wrong for me to describe my mother missing her mouth. How horrible! And yet, why am I imagining vacation shots of Hawaii with a waterfall behind me and an umbrella drink in my hand?)

My father stood and dusted the dirt off his suit, said hello to Juniper, introduced himself to Juniper's father, and then walked over and sat down on the floor next to my mother.

"So, about the mouth thing," said my father. "When I heard what happened to you, I ran right to the Court of Uncommon Pleas and filed an emergency motion. Normally the demon is allowed to manipulate the physical appearance of those under his dominion as he sees fit. But I made it clear that first, you are not under his dominion, and second, going mouthless for any length of time would be disastrous for your health. Have you been eating?"

"Ahuouih?"

"No, of course not. I had quite the spirited argument with the demon's counsel, but the judge ruled in your favor. Yay! She ordered the demon to solve this very serious situation within a week."

"Aee? Aheuaiooaeeh?"

"I understand," said my father, jumping up and backing away with his hands raised as if he was suddenly facing a wild badger—a mouthless badger, true, but with claws nonetheless. "And when I started demanding that she force the demon to take care of this situation immediately or sooner, banging my fist on the table and shouting 'Forth-with!' with each bang, the judge slammed her gavel and held me in contempt. And so here I am."

"Of all the cells in the dungeon," said Juniper, her eyes narrowing in suspicion—and how could they not after what Redwing had pulled—"how did you end up in ours?"

"It turns out I have a client in the castle with some influence," said my father, smiling at Juniper. "She arranged for me to be sent to your cell, and she's already working to get Mel back her mouth even more quickly than the judge ordered—though I'm not sure I want to hear what comes out of it."

"Ohooheeeh," said my mother.

"Exactly," said my father, backing away from my mother until he was on Juniper's side of the cell. "So," he said to Juniper as casually as possible as he slid to sit next to her, "anything fun happen since I saw you guys last?"

Juniper laughed.

My mother sat back, crossed her arms, and stewed in her anger and fear as my father and Juniper chatted like old and dear friends. Unable to be part of the conversation, she was forced into a role she wasn't used to, silent observer. And this is what she observed.

Juniper's father was strangely happy, even in the confines of a dungeon cell. Sometimes he held on to his daughter and laughed at her jokes, and other times he leaned back and closed his eyes and hummed to himself. Even in his gray clothes, there was nothing gray about Tommy Lee Jelani anymore. My mother hadn't realized the cost of having your own inner voice droning and droning, criticizing, warning.

And my father didn't seem frightened at being locked up.

Instead, he seemed to be enjoying himself. He had a cocky sort of bravery, like the crazy stuff was exactly the stuff that made him feel alive. And she began to suspect that all his banging and forthwithing was simply a device to spend more time with them. Or, to be precise, to spend more time with Juniper.

But the real revelation was Juniper herself. What she saw in Juniper was confidence, and excitement, and a strange and marvelous calm. This was not the same nervous and insecure girl who had been her dearest friend for so many years. On this side of whatever divide they had passed, Juniper had become someone new, someone stronger and braver and, yes, happier.

And it pissed my mother off.

My mom was supposed to be the bold one, but over here that was Juniper. My mom was supposed to be the rebel, but here it was Juniper who was enamored with the resistance. My mom was supposed to be the flirty one, but here was Juniper flirting with the strangely cute teen lawyer. And while Juniper was normally the homebody, it was my mother who was desperate to get home, while Juniper wasn't so desperate to get home at all.

And then it hit my mother, what had been bugging her so much, and right there she expressed all her annoyance and anger at her friend.

"You're not coming home with me, are you, Juniper?" said my mother.

They all turned to her, and smiles broke out, which confused my mother until she slapped her hand to her face and realized she had actually spoken the words through an opening surrounded by lips. She was mouthless no more!

There was a moment when Juniper and my mother hugged and danced around the cell at the same time, laughing, both touching my mother's mouth, and then they stopped and stared at each other as my mother's question hung between them.

Then Juniper turned to the baby lawyer, as if looking at my mother, her friend, had become too hard, and said, "Thank you, Eli."

"Yeah, from me, too, I guess," said my mom.

My father shrugged and said, "My dad always taught me that it never hurts to make a fuss. He's a great one for banging on the table."

"We should celebrate," said Juniper's father. "Who's up for champagne?"

"You have champagne?" said my father.

"I just asked who's up for it," said Tommy Lee Jelani. "We're in a dungeon here, but we can imagine the crisp taste, the sparks of the bubbles. Can you hear the *thwap* of the popping cork? Can you smell the dry beauty of it? And the way the bubbles pour out of the bottle like joy itself. What about you, Junie? Champagne?"

"I've never had any," said Juniper.

"We've got to change that, don't we?" said her father.

"What we need to do is get out of here," said my mother.

"We will," said my father. "Give it time."

Right then they heard footsteps walking down the dungeon hall and the jangle of keys.

"I guess time's up," said my father as he stood and looked nervous.

Two guards burst into the dungeon cell with their curved swords and ridiculous feathered hats. One of the guards, a tall man, pointed first at Juniper and then at Mel. "You two come with us," he said.

The other guard, a woman, pulled out her sword and flashed it at my father.

"I'm the attorney for these two prisoners," said my father, taking a step forward. "I demand to be allowed to accompany them."

The woman guard stuck the point of her sword into my father's tie. She took a step forward and my father backed up the same distance. "Sit down," said the woman, her eyes fierce, "or you'll be missing more than your ugly tie."

"Ugly?" said my father.

My mother was about to say something when Juniper gave her a look—a keep-your-mouth-shut-please-please-please look—and my mother bowed her head and obeyed even as my father backed away from the sword and sat down beside Juniper's father.

"Where are you taking my daughter?" said Juniper's father.

"You don't want to know," said the man as he grabbed Juniper's arm and shoved her toward the door.

Juniper looked at her father and patted the air with her palm—a stay-calm sign—before being pushed out the door. My mother, head still lowered, followed her friend. The two guards trailed the prisoners, slamming the cell door behind them.

As soon as they were out of the cell, Juniper and my mother looked behind them as Astrid put her finger over her lips.

From the very first, Juniper and Mel had recognized Astrid, who had led them to the edge of the Stormlands, and the other guard, Kofi, from the diner. Seeing them was like seeing old friends. Silently they passed two unconscious guards slumped against a wall beside the door of the dungeon hallway, each missing their stupid hat.

Once the four were out of the dungeons, Juniper stopped and turned. "What about my father?"

"We had to get you out," said Astrid. "He's not in the same kind of danger."

"What danger?"

"All will be explained," said Kofi, "but we don't have much time. Follow us, be quiet, and be happy. You're going home."

Juniper turned to Mel with a panic on her face. Mel turned away as if she didn't see a thing. "Good," she said. "Let's go."

The four marched through the corridors of the dungeon level, then up flights of stairs. Astrid's sword was unsheathed and whenever they passed servants or guards she gave one of the girls a little poke for effect.

"Stop it," said Juniper when she got a poke that was a bit too hard.

"Shut up and keep walking," said Astrid, who maybe was enjoying the playacting all too much.

Finally, Kofi, who was leading the procession, stopped at a nondescript door, knocked once, looked left, looked right, and then pushed the door open. He gestured for the girls to go inside. Once they passed through the doorway, Kofi, who stayed in the corridor with Astrid, shut the door behind them.

And suddenly Juniper and Mel were alone in a dressing chamber with the General.

37

No Exit

The General stood in the center of the chamber, dressed not in gray city clothes speckled with brick dust but in a beautiful black dress with a high collar, long sleeves, and a tight black corset like a piece of armor around her waist. In her pale hands she held the ornately decorated rectangular box that held the Lens of Fate.

"It is time for you two to go home," said the General in her crisp British accent. "We have all admired your perseverance. We are also grateful that you gave up no information about our group despite the pressure they applied. But the powers arrayed against you have become too great for us to control."

"You mean that woman with the bird," said Juniper.

"The ambitions of the Raven Master know no bounds," said the General. "She sees in two living mortals a road for achieving even more power. We can't let that happen. At great cost we have obtained the Lens of Fate from the garden room. Take it and summon the wayward demon who brought you here. Trade the lens for your trip back home and your freedom. Go with our gratitude and our blessings."

"What about my father?" said Juniper.

"You had a moment with the dead that the living have dreamed of for millennia," said the General. "Did you speak to your father of the fortune you are seeking?"

"Yes," said Juniper, "I did."

"You did?" said Mel, eyes widening. "So?"

Juniper shrugged.

"Then tell me, child. What more could you want?"

"To protect him."

The General tilted her head as if she was examining a painting. "That is not the role of the living."

"To fight what is being done to him and the people around him," said Juniper.

"That is our role. Life on the other side is a gift. To have it taken from you is a crime, and I know of what I speak. Live your life. You will have time enough on this side of the line."

"But not in my father's domain."

"Hopefully not. There are much finer levels, with finer caretakers. You might even be sent right off to the Gate of Light."

"But on any other level I would not be with my father," said Juniper. "And I wouldn't be with you or the resistance. I feel so much purpose here. I'm not ready to go."

"Think carefully, child," said the General. "I can't force you to leave, but the costs of staying could be unimaginable."

"I feel like I didn't just find my father, I found my place," said Juniper. "I want to stay."

My mother stared at her friend as she made her declaration. Juniper was the one who waited for the light to change before crossing the street, but now she was some cape-swirling superhero ready to face off against a demon. And it made my mother so...so...

"What about me?" said Mel in a voice suspiciously like a whine.

Juniper and the General both turned to look at Mel as if a stray dust bunny on the floor had started to talk.

"Gaap told us we have to go back together, so how do I get home?" said Mel. "If you stay, I feel like I should stay, too, but I can't. This place has done terrible things to me. I'm sorry, but I need to get back and I need you to come with me. I need everything to be exactly as it was before."

The General and Juniper looked at Mel with pity on their faces. Juniper walked over to give my mother a hug, and the emotions overwhelmed her and she started weeping. My mother was weeping because she was scared, and she was sad, and because she'd known this would happen. The truth was, she had known it that day on the raft as they crossed over into the Stormlands and were each looking in different directions, known that everything ever after would be different.

"I love you," said Juniper softly into my mother's ear.

"I know."

"And I won't do anything to make you stay."

"I know that, too. I see what you've become here and I'm happy for you."

"Of course you are," said Juniper.

"And I'm mad at you. And I'm jealous. And I'm angry. And I'm lonely. And I'm scared."

"You brought me here to find my destiny, and I'll be forever grateful. I'll join you on the other side when I can."

"Promise?"

"I do," said Juniper, before she let go of my mother and turned to face the General. "Mel needs to go home. If for her to get home I have to go, too, I will. But if there's another way..."

The expression on the General's face, both sad and admiring, was answer enough.

A short time later Juniper and her father were headed to a safe house in the Stormlands on the Island of Lost Souls, where they both would be trained for roles in the resistance. Their guide through the forest was—wait for it—Leonora. She was again crab-walking, her punishment for disclosing to the resistance all she had learned in her short time as a collaborator with the Raven Master and the demon. It seemed that one night joining the demon's army was one night too much for someone who wasn't a joiner.

"I don't know what came over me," said Leonora. "Standing straight was such a shiny object, it became the most important thing to me in the universe. But as soon as it happened, I immediately regretted everything. I even like walking like this. It's so steady! I felt so bad I went right to Astrid and told her everything. Do you forgive me? I hope you forgive me. And the worst thing was, they don't chat here. What kind of monsters don't chat?"

Before Juniper left for good, the girls, back in the wet, muddy clothes they had left upon first entering the castle, stepped off to the side so they couldn't be heard by the others.

"So," said Juniper.

"Yeah," said Mel.

Juniper pulled an envelope out of her pocket and handed it to Mel. "Can you deliver this to my mom?"

"What do I say to her? How can I explain anything?"

"You don't have to," said Juniper. "I explain it all in here. Just tell her I love her."

Mel glanced at the baby lawyer standing now to the side. "The lawyer says he can work it so you can come home whenever you want. He likes you, you know. The way he was looking at you, it was obvious."

"Really? I hadn't noticed."

"Yeah, right," my mother said, and they both laughed as they hugged goodbye.

"I'm sorry," said Mel as the tears came.

"Me too," said Juniper.

"I'll be waiting," said Mel.

"We have to go," said Juniper, and that was it.

A moment later, as Juniper and her father were following Leonora to their new lives, Juniper turned and gave my mother a last, lingering look. It was my mother's final glimpse of the best friend she would ever have. And Juniper was absolutely radiant.

Then my mother was off on a journey of her own, following the baby lawyer down and down the narrow stone steps, down and down some more to the portal set in a cavern deep beneath Redwing's castle. My father was convinced that he could make a deal with the Portal Keeper on the other side to send my mother back to her world without a court order. All it would take, my father said, would be something of great value to a Portal Keeper, which is why he was now holding the ornate box that held the Lens of Fate.

"The portal's through the door at the bottom," said my father as they climbed down and down. "There's a clerk who checks the paperwork and then the Portal Keeper. I'll go through first and arrange things with Portal Keeper Topper on the other side."

"It sounds easy," said Mel.

"It always sounds easy," said my father as they climbed down and down, "until your stomach starts talking."

Eventually, after seeming to descend into the center of the earth, they approached a landing at the very bottom, which led to a large wooden door. As the landing came into view a breeze raced past them down the stairs and suddenly, in front of the door, with his arms crossed and his eyes narrow, stood the demon Gaap, in his old-man persona, dressed in the white toga trimmed in purple and gold.

"Going somewhere?" he said in his high twittery voice. "And with the Lens of Fate in your clutches?" His hands clasped together. "How wonderful! When you didn't summon me, girl, I grew worried, but you are indeed persistent and have come through in the end. Where is your friend? She must be here, too. A deal is a deal. Where is she? Where?"

The demon tilted his old man's head and stared at my mother for a moment, before his mouth turned down at the edges and his body began to swell in size. Great bat wings unfurled behind his back, horns spiraled out of his forehead, and his face twisted into that impossible bat face, with sharp teeth and pointed ears.

"Don't tell me you were trying to steal the lens from me," he said in a voice not so twittery. "You wouldn't dare. But it appears that you would. As if you didn't know that Gaap is the thirty-third spirit of Solomon and commands sixty-six legions of demons. It is a good thing, then, for you, little one, that Gaap arrived in the nick of time."

UNCOMMON PLEAS

When my mother came to the part of her story where the demon Gaap blocked her route home, she told me you never know when you might surprise yourself. I wasn't sure what she meant until the day I took the ghost thief to trial.

I was wearing my black robe with purple stripes, waiting in the City Hall courtyard with Janelle, and Sydney, and my mother—yes, my mother!—when Barnabas hurried in the south gate before stopping short at the sight of us.

"Mistress Elizabeth?" said Barnabas. "Why aren't you in the courtroom? The session is about to start."

"I was waiting for you."

"But you don't need to wait for me anymore. You have your own keys."

"Yeah, about that," I said.

"No time for explanations. We must get you to court right away, especially with your father's condition. Hello, Melinda, good to see you as always."

"Hello, Barnabas."

"And these, I assume, are the Burton children."

I did the introductions, along with serious handshakes all around.

"It is a pleasure to meet you both," said Barnabas, "but now we must hurry."

It was already a familiar route to me—through the basement maze, into the hidden doorway, up the endless flight of stairs in the City Hall tower lit by flaming torches—but to see it through Janelle's and Sydney's eyes was to remember how cool and terrifying this whole courtroom of the undead thing was.

"Should we be scared?" said Janelle softly as we climbed the tower.

"I'm always scared when I go to court, afraid that I'm going to mess up somehow," I said, "but all you guys have to do is answer questions."

"So, it's like a math test?" said Sydney.

"Maybe not that easy," I said.

In order to make this late-night court appearance, Janelle and Sydney had told their aunt and uncle they were sleeping over at a friend's house, which was sort of true since Petey was sort of a friend. They had survived one of my mother's dinners—no sure thing, that—and were set up to sleep in Petey's room. He was sleeping on my floor, and not too happy about it, but I reminded him that this whole case came about because he couldn't keep a secret, and that shut him right up. Which might have explained why my mom was with us.

"If they're staying in my house, they are my responsibility," she had said, a decent enough explanation, but not the whole truth, I suspected.

At the top of the long stairway, we faced the huge wooden door that led to the courtroom. Barnabas slammed the gavel-shaped knocker once, twice, three times, and a horizontal plank high on the door swung open. In the gap appeared a huge, monstrous face that caused Janelle and Sydney to back up and gasp.

"Barnabas," said the man behind the door.

"Ivanov," said Barnabas.

"Case?"

"*Burton v. Ramsberger*," said Barnabas, "along with a group litigation titled *Cutbush v. Ramsberger*."

"Counsel?"

"Eli Webster, who I expect is already in the courtroom, and Elizabeth Webster. These are two of our plaintiffs, the Burton children."

"Nice to meet you ladies," said Ivanov before sticking his head out and looking around. "What about Cutbush? I don't see Cutbush."

"She'll be summoned," said Barnabas.

"Let's hope so," said Ivanov. "When Judge Jeffries saw that the Websters were on the docket today he was in quite the mood. It won't take much for him to order me to toss you all out of the courtroom." Then Ivanov looked at me and smiled. "Hello, Elizabeth. Always a pleasure. How goes it?"

"It goes well, Ivanov, thank you," I said. "And thank you for the keys. I was honored."

"You're very welcome, but you've earned your keys. The Burton children are very lucky to have you on their side. And Melinda, so good to see you, too. I wore the hat you knitted all through the winter. But hurry on now, all of you. Court is about to be called into session and whatever you do, Elizabeth, you don't want to be late for the rehanging judge."

The plank was slammed shut and a moment later the door opened. Now off his ladder, Ivanov, only as tall as a guitar, nodded his big old head at us as we passed.

When we entered the courtroom, I heard a little laugh and saw Janelle and Sydney staring around, slack-jawed. I looked around myself and took it all in. The crowded benches full of the weird and the wonderful. The ram's head on the wall behind the judge's bench, staring and chewing. The tall green court clerk with the bolts coming out of her neck. The great iron cage hanging by a chain from the ceiling and hovering over a huge round hole in the floor. The little diapered babies painted on the domed ceiling, flying around, pointing and twittering. And all of it bathed in the sharp scent of licorice.

"This is the strangest place I've ever seen," said Sydney.

"It's fantastic," said Janelle. "Like Disneyland without the mice."

"Welcome to the Court of Uncommon Pleas," I said. "And don't worry, Janelle, there are enough rodents in here to keep you on your toes."

On one of the back benches I spotted my grandfather sitting with—surprise, surprise—Avis. I led our group on over.

"Hello, Avis," I said. "I haven't seen you in court before."

"Oh, it's a big day, Elizabeth," she blurted out, her hands jerking with excitement. "A big day. I wouldn't miss it. Good luck, dear. Good luck."

"I'll need it," I said.

"Melinda, what are you doing here?" said my grandfather.

"I thought I'd help take care of the girls," said my mother. "Janelle and Sydney, this is the esteemed Mr. Ebenezer Webster the Third."

"We're pleased to meet you," said Sydney.

"You'll stay here for the time being," I said to the girls. "My grandfather will tell you when to go to the table at the front."

"I most certainly will," said my grandfather. "Now, which one of you is the fourth grader?"

"That's me," said Janelle.

"It's best if you sit next to Barnabas," said my grandfather. "I just had my suit cleaned."

On my way to the barristers' bench up front, I spotted Ramsberger sitting beside one of his masked workers, who was holding a box on his lap. Today Ramsberger was in his professor clothes, all tweedy and bow-tied, but still quite frightening. Maybe it was the bow tie that sent the shiver up my spine, thinking he might ask me about the root causes of World War I.

And sitting on the other side of the masked worker was Dr. Shevski. I tried to give her a smile and sort of failed. I still didn't know if our little frenemy intervention had changed Dr. Shevski's mind about anything. I figured I'd find out eventually. Sitting next to Dr. Shevski, Ygor nodded at me and then patted a fat briefcase. What did that mean? Mysteries upon mysteries.

At the front of the courtroom I walked down the row of barristers, ignoring the annoyed faces under their white wigs snuffing at the presence of a mere girl on their sacred little bench, and plopped down between my father and Josiah Goodheart.

"How do you feel?" I said to my father. He looked quite official in his robe and wig, but his face had a tint of green to it.

"A bit queasy," he said. "I'm not sure why."

"Sitting next to Mr. Goodheart will do that to you," I said.

"I heard that, Lizbeth," said Josiah Goodheart, "and I would be insulted, mightily insulted, if that wasn't precisely the effect I hope to have on my opponents in court. And how are you feeling this evening?"

"Better than my father," I said, "since he's the one handling our trial today. I saw Dr. Shevski in the courtroom. Is she one of your witnesses?"

"Know her, do you?" said Mr. Goodheart, his eyes widening deviously. "I've been told she's an interested party and nothing more. I believe my client Mr. Ramsberger asked her to come."

Right then the ram on the wall, chewing on a stick of black licorice, bellowed his trumpet blast and neighed out, "All rise!"

We all rose.

"*Oyez, oyez, oyez,*" he proclaimed. "The Court of Uncommon Pleas, sitting now in the land of Penn's Dominion, is hereby called to order, with the Right Honorable George Jeffries, First Baron Jeffries of Wem, presiding. All persons having business before this court are ordered to draw near and give their attention or give their necks. May the Lord Demon save this honorable court."

With a burst of smoke, the judge appeared with his scraggly white wig and bloodred eyes, coughing and waving at the smoke still swirling around him. After a few more horrifying words, the court was in session.

"The clerk will call the first case," said the judge.

The tall green woman stood from behind her desk and shouted out in a garbled voice, "*Simpson v. Lilah.*"

As the parties lined up at the tables set before the judge and began their arguments—it seemed to be a case about a really bad haircut—I turned to see Ramsberger nodding at something Dr. Shevski said, grinning and nodding.

"They probably amped up the mind control on you to make sure it's working," I said quietly to my father. "That must be what is making you sick. Or maybe it's because Mom's in the courtroom."

"Mystery solved."

"Are you going to be okay?"

"I'll be fine," he said. "The carpet maybe not so much. But this means it's all on you, as we suspected."

"Yikes," I said softly. "Do you have it in you for one summoning?"

"I hope so," he said.

We listened for a bit as the court case droned on and my

father turned a darker shade of green. What started out as mint was becoming closer to pickle.

"I've heard enough," said Judge Jeffries, "and enough is more than enough. In the case of *Simpson v. Lilah*, I find for the defendant. You miss your hair, Mr. Simpson, and the power contained therein? Get a wig like the rest of us. Case dismissed," he said with a bang of his gavel. "Call the next case."

The clerk stood up and called out in her garbled voice, "*Burton v. Ramsberger* and *Cutbush v. Ramsberger*."

The ram's head bellowed.

"Quiet, Bailiff," said the judge, turning around and pointing his gavel at the ram's head, "or I'll make a burger out of you."

The ram stared and chewed and stared some more, but he stopped his bellowing.

"I understand this foul concoction of cases has been brought into my court by the pack of miscreants known as Webster and Spawn," said the judge after turning again to face the courtroom. "Well, I know how to handle that crew. Counsel, come before the court and announce yourselves before I scrape this barnacle of a case off the hull of my docket."

Standing and Shaking

"Elizabeth Webster for the plaintiffs Burton and Cutbush," I said, standing at the plaintiffs' table.

"And who are those young scoundrels with you, Ms. Webster?" said the judge.

"Janelle and Sydney Burton, Your Honor. The defendant stole the ghosts of their mother, father, and grandfather."

"Your Honor, if I may," said Mr. Goodheart. "Josiah Goodheart for the defense, along with the defendant Professor Frederic B. Ramsberger."

The ram's head on the wall behind the judge let out a nervous snicker at the name. The judge's marble eyes rolled.

"We are simply asking at this point," continued Mr. Goodheart, "that you save the court's valuable time and dismiss these frivolous complaints for lack of standing. Was the freedom of these children compromised in any way?

Nay. Can they prove lawful ownership of the ghosts in question? Nay. Do they have any concrete injury that gives them the right to stand before this court and complain about the defendant's conduct? Nay, nay, and, I say, nay."

"Am I to understand, Mr. Goodheart," said the judge, "that you are saying nay?"

"Aye, sir," said Josiah Goodheart. "Nay."

"Well, Ms. Webster, I think Mr. Goodheart has a point. No one owns a ghost. And so as to the case of *Burton v. Ramsberger*, I find these plaintiffs have no standing and the case, therefore, is—"

"What about universal succession, Your Honor?" I said.

"Universal what?" said the judge.

I turned and looked at my grandfather in the back row. He nodded and smiled. "Universal succession?" I said.

"Is that a question?" said the judge.

"I don't think so," I said. "Maybe it's an answer?"

"Explain yourself, Counsel."

"These children are the rightful heirs of their dead mother and father and grandfather. Under the ancient common-law doctrine of universal succession, in effect since the Romans were running around in togas, they inherit all the rights of the family. It hardly seems proper that universal succession would give the children the right to recover any of the family's stolen land or stolen money, as well as the stolen buried bones of their ancestors, while not giving them standing to recover the stolen ghosts of their family members."

"What an extraordinary argument," said the judge. "I never heard of such a thing. Have you any case law in support?"

"As to stolen ghosts, there is none, one way or the other," I said. "If you ruled for the plaintiffs it would create new law in the Court of Uncommon Pleas."

"New law, you say?"

"You'd be blazing a trail," I said with a little fist pump.

"Blazing a trail, you say?"

"Statues will be built," I said.

"Oh please," said Josiah Goodheart.

"You don't believe I'm a trailblazer, Mr. Goodheart?" said the judge. "You don't believe I warrant a statue?"

"I believe you are an avid adherent to the ancient traditions of the law, Your Honor," said Mr. Goodheart with a slight bow.

"And what could be more ancient," I said, "than the Roman doctrine of universal succession?"

The judge closed his red-marble eyes and put his hands over his mouth. It was a good look for him. That should be the portrait on his Christmas card. When he finally opened his eyes again, he stared at me with a squint. "No matter how disappointed I am to say it, Ms. Webster, I find the universal succession argument to be strangely compelling. Did you come up with that yourself?"

"My grandfather helped."

"Even so," said the judge, "I'm going to allow this case to proceed."

"Thank you, sir," I said.

"Don't thank me. You still must prove your case. Now where is this Cutbush woman in the joined action? As a rule, I'm not inclined to allow a group litigation. It is a device of the rabble and so should be discouraged at every turn, as should the rabble itself. But Cutbush must be in court if we are to take any step forward or I'll dismiss that one right off."

"Cutbush is a ghost," I said.

"Then summon her, Ms. Webster."

"We can't, sir. She was stolen and is being held captive by the defendant."

"Objection," shouted Josiah Goodheart. "Ms. Webster is slandering my client's good name."

"His name is Ramsberger," said Judge Jeffries. "Hardly a good name, Mr. Goodheart. Is your client in possession of this Cutbush ghost?"

"My client was hired by one Avis Picklefeather to rid her premises of a ghost, who turned out to be this Cutbush entity," said Goodheart. "Since then, the Cutbush ghost has been very happily maintained by the Ramsberger Institute of the Paranormal."

"Happily, you say?" said the judge.

"Immensely, Your Honor," said Goodheart. "She has no complaint."

"But she signed the complaint. Right there. See?"

"She signed before she attained her current status."

"Then put her on the stand to say so," said the judge, "and I'll dismiss this case with extreme prejudice."

"Prejudice?" I said. "Isn't that bad?"

"It means, child, that once I dismiss the case, it is dead, now and forever. Call your witness, Mr. Goodheart."

"The defense," said Josiah Goodheart, "calls Ms. Cutbush to the stand."

At the announcement, Ramsberger's masked worker

brought the box he had been holding up to the front of the court and set it on the defense table before floating back to his place next to Dr. Shevski.

Ramsberger stood, opened the box, and lifted out one of the storage machines from his chamber of stolen ghosts, with its small motor, its vials filled with bubbling liquids, and its globe alive with the swirl of multicolored lights, all connected to a car battery. Slowly, with the scritching sound of metal scraping glass, he unscrewed the globe.

Just as when I unscrewed Silas Burton's globe, colors shot out from the machine and twisted around each other with showers of sparks until they combined into a spinning bluish haze. From this spinning haze a figure emerged, a tall, thin woman in a long-sleeved black dress. And floating with her, along with the scent of jasmine, were the telltale sounds of voices, or should I say a singular British voice, whispering, whispering into the ghost-woman's ear.

I turned and saw Barnabas gazing with love at the spirit, as my mother sat stock-still next to him, her eyes wide and a hand at her mouth.

"Are you Cutbush?" said the judge.

"I am," said the ghost in a hushed British voice.

"Then take the stand and be sworn in."

"As you seek," said the ghost, floating now toward the witness stand. The clerk brought over a pillow on which sat the gold-plated skull of a beheaded king, and the ghost placed a hand on the skull, swearing to tell the truth, the whole truth, and nothing but the truth even as the voices whispered.

"State your name for the record, please," said Josiah Goodheart.

"I am Isabel Cutbush," said the ghost. Cool, right? But you knew that already, didn't you?

"You are the named plaintiff in a group litigation styled *Cutbush v. Ramsberger*, is that correct?"

"I signed the document, yes," said the ghost.

"And you signed that complaint when you were still floating free before you ever met my client."

"Before I met your client, yes."

"And where are you lodged now?"

"With the Ramsberger Institute of the Paranormal."

"And how are you being treated?"

"I am being treated…wonderfully," she said, her voice flat as slate.

"And are you happy?"

"Oh so happy," she said with the same flat voice.

"Would you like to be freed?"

"I am being treated wonderfully," she said. "I am oh so happy."

"And if you don't want to be freed, then I assume you would want the complaint withdrawn. Is that right, Ms. Cutbush?"

"I am being treated wonderfully," she said. "I am oh so happy."

"With great respect, Your Honor," said Josiah Goodheart, "we ask that the complaint be dismissed with prejudice. Along with, I suppose, the usual sanctions for a plaintiff's counsel that has a plaintiff sign a disingenuous complaint even before any offense is committed."

"Though it pains me to say it," said Judge Jeffries with an un-pained smile, "I believe all of that is appropriate here. In the matter of *Cutbush v. Ramsberger*, I find—"

"Really, Judge?" I said. "Can't you hear the voices that are badgering the witness? Can't you see that she is being mind-controlled?"

"Mind-controlled?" the judge said with his voice full of astonishment. "Is that your paltry argument? Mind control?"

"It's not just my argument," I said, "it's the truth of what is happening here."

"Are you asking for the right to cross-examine your own plaintiff?"

"Why would I do that when all she is allowed to say is that she is being treated wonderfully and is oh so happy?"

"Then what am I to do, Ms. Webster? Your plaintiff herself has asked for the complaint to be withdrawn."

"She didn't say that," I said. "She only repeated what they told her to say. Mind control is a significant part of our complaint and is being suffered by each member of the group litigation. Now Mr. Goodheart is using that very thing to have the complaint dismissed. What I ask for is a witness to prove that element."

"Your Honor," said Josiah Goodheart. "That this case was ever brought is a travesty. That Ms. Webster now asks this court to examine the most ridiculous, I say the most ridiculous, of her allegations is a mockery. She is seeking to turn this entire proceeding into a sham. A sham, Your Honor."

"Yes, I know, Mr. Goodheart, a shammy sham, as you would have it," said the judge. "But I believe we owe it to Ms. Cutbush and the other group plaintiffs to get to the bottom of this mind-control allegation. If true, it is a stake in the heart of the very idea of justice. Ms. Cutbush, please take your place at the plaintiffs' table."

Isabel floated out of the witness stand and around the courtroom until she was hovering beside Sydney and Janelle. The girls smiled at the ghost while Isabel simply stared dazedly forward.

"You may call your witness, Ms. Webster," said the judge.

I looked over at Fred Ramsberger, who smiled slightly as he twiddled his bow tie. He didn't seem worried. I was sure Goodheart had prepared him for this very possibility. I turned around and looked at Dr. Shevski. Would she cooperate? Would her truthful testimony be enough? And what about Ygor? I wouldn't be surprised if there was a Spirit Psychic Drive sitting in his briefcase. Maybe I could show that to the judge, but what if I opened the case in dramatic fashion and there was only a ham sandwich inside?

Those three seemed my most obvious options, but my mother's story was still echoing in my mind, along with things I had heard from both Ramsberger and the doctor. This would be my last chance to get to the bottom of the mind-control thing, as well as the chamber-of-stolen-ghosts thing. I needed a witness who was behind everything, and I knew who it would have to be. I'm sure you know who it had to be, too.

I took a deep breath and the air in my lungs seemed alive with fear, which might explain the shake in my voice when I said, "Your Honor, plaintiffs call to the stand R. Edwina Ramsberger."

40

THE RAVEN MASTER

Josiah Goodheart bellowed his objections, and Fred Ramsberger shouted out in horror even as his great orange head turned pale, and the ram neighed, and the babies on the ceiling twittered at the fuss. Even Bittman, the troll recording the court session beneath the judge's desk, opened his door and commanded everyone to speak one at a time or there would be no proper record of the proceeding.

Finally, the judge pounded his gavel once, twice, three times for effect and then stared at me with his hard red eyes. "Who is this witness of yours, Ms. Webster, and why all the fuss?"

"The witness is the defendant's grandmother, Your Honor," I said. "She is a former spy who we believe is responsible for the mind control of our plaintiffs."

"A spy, you say?" said the judge. "Astonishing. Is she in the courtroom?"

"No, Your Honor. She now resides on the other side, level eight, in the domain of the demon Abezethibou, also known as Redwing. We would have to summon her."

"We object most strenuously, Judge," said Josiah Goodheart. "This witness is not a party to this complaint, she could only muddy, I say muddy, the issue at hand, which is that the named plaintiff wants to withdraw her complaint."

"Did I mention that the witness was a spy?" I said.

"You did," said the judge.

"Spies are pretty cool," I said.

"I once knew a Spanish saboteur named Adoncia," said the judge. "Quite a charming dancer. We did a minuet together at Lord Dunson's estate that I still remember. Ah, the shape of her hand and smell of the posies... Where was I? Oh yes, now I remember. I think it appropriate to hear from this witness. Mind control is a serious allegation that is central to the plaintiffs' claims. And the relation to the defendant is quite close. Summon your witness, Ms. Webster."

"My father will do the honors," I said.

My father stood unsteadily at the barristers' bench, took a step forward, and staggered back again as if to stop himself from falling. Then he closed his eyes and started muttering to himself as he waved his hands back and forth, like a conductor leading a chorus of seals.

And nothing happened.

His hands waved and he gagged and his hands waved some more and nothing happened.

I looked up at the judge and he tilted his undead head at me.

At that moment a breeze arose in the courtroom, a breeze smelling of green leaves and dead mice, and a small cloud zoomed past, circling and diving before it landed on one of the ram's horns. The ram's eyes rose to stare at the cloud as it turned into a huge shining raven. At that point my father put both hands over his mouth and bolted toward the back of the courtroom. We all turned to follow his desperate run.

When the raven cawed, we turned around again and the witness stand was filled.

As the clerk lurched to the witness chair, and as the glowing figure now sitting there swore on the gold-plated skull, I stared at the ghost of R. Edwina Ramsberger.

I recognized her, of course, from that painting in Ramsberger's library. She was tall and haughty and wore a formal black dress with thin silvery straps that left her shoulders bare. But that painting, and the sculpture in the crypt, had not done justice to her strongest feature, her nose, so triangular, so sturdy, so unapologetic. My nose was bigger than I would like—I mean just look at the cover of this book—but it was a bud to her blossom. Her nose was the proud prow of a great ocean liner. I suddenly wanted to grow up fierce enough to earn such a nose.

As she gave her oath, the ghost of R. Edwina Ramsberger stared back at me with a look so cold I felt I would freeze, and cracks would appear all over my frozen body, and I would disintegrate into little Elizabeth ice cubes bouncing all over the courtroom floor. *Careful*, I heard a voice, my own voice, say. *Careful, girl.*

"Well, Ms. Webster?" said the judge.

I gazed down at the table and said, "Could you, uh, please state your, uh, name for the record?"

"Look at me, child," said the ghost.

My head still down, seeing her only in the edges of my vision, I said, "Answer the question."

She put her hand on her shoulder and the ghost raven swooped down and landed on her fingers. She looked up at it with a kissy face before saying, "I am Radclyffe Edwina Ramsberger. Look at me, child, and you will understand what that means."

She pulled her hand away from her shoulder and the bird remained, gripping her ghostly flesh with its ghostly claws, its head turning this way and that as if hunting for a pigeon.

"Afraid to look?" said the ghost. "Smarter than you appear. Tell me, girl, who is that floating behind your table? Is that Isabel Cutbush? We were wondering what happened to you, Isabel. The mood in the castle has been so much cheerier without you moping around. Are things going well, dear?"

"I am being treated wonderfully," said Isabel. "I am oh so happy."

"I'll be sure to tell our lord and demon," said Edwina. "It has been so worried."

"Ms. Ramsberger," I said, still avoiding that freezing stare, "the defendant, Fred Ramsberger, is your grandson, isn't that right?"

"We sadly don't get to pick our descendants," she said, "as your parents are no doubt aware."

I glanced at Ramsberger at the defense table. His face looked stricken, like he had just been bashed with a baseball bat. That, at least, was fun.

"According to your grandson," I said, "you were in the CIA."

"Is that what the loose-lipped fool said?"

"He also said of you, and I quote, 'She overthrew more regimes than you have teeth.'"

"He loves to hear himself talk," said Edwina. "And that tweed, Frederick. Really?"

"But I'm a professor," said Ramsberger.

"That's no excuse," said his grandmother.

"I'd like to talk about this whole overthrowing regimes thing," I said. "How do you go about that?"

"It is a complicated effort, difficult to describe."

"Try," I said, with the right amount of sass.

"Must I?" she said to the judge. "Is this even pertinent?"

"The term is 'relevant,'" he said back. "And yes it is, and yes you must, and I'll have no more objections from the witness stand."

"Fine," she said. "But, little Elizabeth Webster, I'll keep it simple for a simple mind like yours. Think of it as a three-step waltz. First step, find a group you can control. Second step, have your group create mayhem that destabilizes the regime. Third step, make sure that you are the solution."

"Let's start at the beginning of the dance," I said. "How do you control the group in the first step?"

"Money. Passion. Politics."

"What about mind control? Ever try that with the CIA?"

"There were techniques being investigated at the agency, wild ideas. But we used mostly money. You'd be surprised how effective money can be."

"I would not, actually," I said. "And next comes the mayhem, isn't that right?"

"The best part. It's fizzy, like champagne."

"And finally, the solution. I suppose that's your specialty."

"You're such a bright little parrot," said the ghost. "I bet your mother is proud."

I turned around and glanced at my mother, sitting next to Barnabas. For maybe the first time in my life I saw fear in her eyes as she stared at the witness. That was quite alarming, but it also reminded me it was time to bring in my mother's story.

"Where do you currently reside, Ms. Ramsberger?" I said.

"Upon my early and tragic death, I was sent to Redwing's domain."

"Yes, we know. But where in Redwing's domain do you reside? Are you in the city, where all newly dead are first sent? Were you punished by being exiled to the Stormlands? Or did you somehow manage to find your way into the glorious corridors of Redwing's castle?"

"You seem to know much of Redwing's domain, child. In fact, you remind me of someone I met many years ago. A girl as insolent as you. You have her eyes."

"How's the food in the castle?" I said.

"Delicious," she said. "We feed off impertinence."

Do you know how sometimes you can't help but let loose a burst of laughter in the middle of a horror movie? Yeah, well, there it came, like a hiccup of fear and merriment.

"I'm glad you find me amusing," said the ghost as I popped a hand over my mouth.

"Sorry about that, it's just so—demonic. But from the answer, I assume you are living quite happily in the castle. Parties? Dancing? Servants feeding you grapes?"

"Have no doubt, child, I was given nothing in the afterlife. I earned every step of my way to that castle."

"It's funny how they all say that. But you owe it all, I presume, to making sure you were the solution to some mayhem you created. So please tell the court the solution you proposed for the demon Redwing. Was it one of the mind-control techniques you learned from the CIA? Was it the voices?"

She turned to her grandson. "How much did you tell her?"

"Nothing, I swear."

"Your foolish mouth will doom us all."

"But, Grammy, I didn't say—"

"Psychic driving, it's called, isn't that right?" I said, interrupting Fred Ramsberger's little grandchild snit. "I read all about it in the library. You bombard the victim with their own voice, creating some kind of psychotic break. It was a technique perfected by the CIA at the same time you were overthrowing regimes."

"Don't be so clever, dear, it's unbecoming."

"Answer the question," said the judge. "Were you aware of this mind-control technique when you were on this side?"

"I was, yes."

"And you taught the technique to the demon, isn't that right?" I said. "You taught it how to control the dead by breaking their minds with their own voices, all so you could live in luxury in its castle."

"Their little minds needed breaking, dear. Before, when there were only wooden clubs to keep them in line, they were so miserable and troublesome. Now they are nothing but happy."

"Happy?"

"Oh yes, dear. You should see them whistling as they work."

"And that is why there is a resistance movement in the city?" I asked.

"Communist jackdaws, nothing more. There are always complainers."

"Led by the General?"

"How do you know that?" Her voice rose in shock. "Who are you in touch with, child?"

"Why is your grandson stealing ghosts?" I said.

"Why don't you ask him?"

"I'm asking you. It is all part of Redwing's plan to expand its dominion, isn't it?"

"What plan is that, dear?"

"The plan you hatched for it. The plan for the demon to overthrow the regime of our world and put itself in charge. The plan to make Redwing the ruler over all the living. The plan that would—"

"Your Honor, haven't we had enough!" shouted Josiah Goodheart, standing now as he interrupted me. "All this talk about plots and plans and a domain on the other side of that greatest of all dividing lines has nothing, I say, nothing to do with the case at hand. I repeat that the plaintiff wants to withdraw her complaint. What more is there to discuss?"

"I'm getting to it, Judge," I said.

"Well, get there faster, Ms. Webster," barked the judge.

"Isn't it true, Ms. Ramsberger," I said, "that you taught the same CIA mind-control technique you gave the demon Redwing to your grandson so he could control the ghosts he captured?"

"Not exactly the same technique," said Edwina. "In this world, without the demon's power to apply it, we must rely on the less-reliable power of physics."

"You're talking about Dr. Shevski and the machines she has built to capture and control these ghosts. But the result is the same, isn't it? Broken minds?"

"The result is the same, yes. Happy souls. Isabel was once a complainer, weren't you, Isabel? Always the sad one, the lost one, pining for her betrothed on the other side of the line. And look at her now. Look how happy she is."

"I am being treated wonderfully," said Isabel. "I am oh so happy."

"This is exactly the point of our case, Your Honor," I said. "This group litigation is about freedom, and not only about being freed from the prisons of the ghost catcher. We are also asking for freedom of thought, which is the key to every other freedom. How is a plaintiff to bring a case to regain her freedom if her freedom of thought has been stolen? How can the group plaintiffs testify about the crimes against them if they are mind-controlled so they can only say they are happy, so happy, forever happy?"

"Are you asking for relief, Ms. Webster?" said the judge. "What would you have the court do?"

"Yes, dear Elizabeth," said the ghost. "What would you have the poor man do?"

I looked right at the ghost of Radclyffe Edwina Ramsberger when I said, "Tell the witness and the defendant to knock it off, to cancel the mind control, and let Isabel Cutbush and our other plaintiffs think and talk for themselves." I kept staring as if my stare alone would be enough to make her crack and admit all.

Big mistake.

41

THE VOICES

The cold slipped into my chest and surrounded my heart like the claw of a giant raven.

As I stared into Edwina's spectral eyes, I could feel frost creeping its way down my veins. The blood in my arms and legs turned into a frigid sludge and my brain ached as if I had just taken a huge slurp of a purple Slurpee. I tried to look away but the ghost's gaze held me in a prison of ice.

It's cold, so cold, I heard myself saying. *Why did you have to bait her like that? Why are you always such a troublemaker?*

The words were coming from my freezing brain, tapping the inside of my skull like a knuckle. The ghost's smile grew brighter until it was all I could see. Even her brilliant nose disappeared in the bright light of that smile. And the knuckle kept tap-tapping.

This is why you have no friends. Would it have killed you to be nice for once? Then maybe everyone wouldn't hate you.

There was a noise in the courtroom. Someone was speaking, but it was hard to hear with that knuckle tap-tapping in my skull. I pried my gaze away from the ghost of Edwina Ramsberger and aimed it at the judge, who was staring at me with those bloodred eyes as his mouth moved.

Why is his mouth moving? Is he yelling at you about the ghost on the witness stand? Calling her to the stand was such a mistake. This whole case is a mistake. You're a mistake.

I shook my head and took a deep breath and stared at the judge's flapping lips. His sharp unpleasant voice started cutting through the static.

"Are you there, Ms. Webster?" said the judge. "Are you listening?"

"I...I think so," I said.

"You think so?"

"No, yes, I'm here."

Why are you playing at being something you're not? You're not a lawyer. You're not even a decent student. The pariah of Debate Club. Talk about disasters.

"Tell me now, Ms. Webster," said the judge. "Do you have a request of the court?"

"I think so," I said.

Just shut up, Elizabeth. Just stop talking so much. They're all staring at you. You're making such a fool of yourself.

"Then as to the cases now before the court," said the judge, "what it is you want?"

You want to go home. You want to climb into your bed and hide under your covers.

"I want to go home," I said.

"What is that you say?" said the judge.

Dismiss the case before it all gets worse. Dismiss the case so you can go home and stop making such a fool of yourself. Dismiss the case.

"I want to go home. Dismiss the case."

"Dismiss the case?" said the judge. "Both cases, I assume?"

"Yes, Your Honor." *Dismiss the case.* "Please, Your Honor." *Dismiss the case.* "Dismiss the case." *Dismiss both cases!* "Dismiss both cases."

"Well, that's extraordinary, I must say," said the judge.

From the back of the courtroom came a shout. "I object!"

I turned around and saw my grandfather banging his cane as he made his way to the front of the courtroom.

"Why it's Ebe-wheezer Webster come to play the jester," said the judge. "Well, it is not in your power to object. You are no longer allowed to stand before this court, as well you know. Sit down, you rapscallion, or I'll put you in the cage."

"Then I ask for a brief adjournment so I can talk to my granddaughter. Can't you see it? Something has gone awry!"

"All I see is a pompous old fool trying to delay the inevitable. My time is too precious to give an adjournment to the likes of you. Sit down, now, or I'll have Ivanov sit you down."

As my grandfather stood still and stared at me with pained eyes, the judge slammed his gavel. *Look how sad you made him. You bring nothing but sadness. You're a failure, have always been a failure, will always be a failure.*

"Counsel for plaintiff has made a very clear request to dismiss her cases and clear my docket," said the judge, "and I am of a mind to grant her motion. Any objection, Mr. Goodheart?"

Josiah Goodheart stood and looked at me and there was, for the first time since I've known him, a look of pity on his face. "No, Judge," he said. "No objection."

"Well, this is quite extraordinary, but I suppose I have no choice. In the matters of *Burton v. Ramsberger* and *Cutbush v. Ramsberger*, I hereby—what is that knocking?"

Everyone looked to the back of the courtroom, and though I couldn't hear a thing with the voices battering my skull, I turned to follow the gazes of everyone else. We were all staring at the rear door of the courtroom, the one my father had dashed out of with his hands over his mouth.

Slowly the door opened and into the courtroom came three figures, each holding a machine with a globe the size of a basketball. The globes were wild with spinning, swirling lights.

Don't look at them. They don't matter. Dismiss the cases.

"What is this interruption?" shouted the judge. "Is this your doing, Ms. Webster?"

It's time to go home, to bed, to leave all your foolishness behind. Dismiss the cases.

It took all my strength to lift my gaze from the lights spinning and swirling in the globes to the three figures carrying them.

They're nobody. Ignore them. Dismiss the cases and go home and stop being such a mistake.

But whatever the voices were saying, the faces of the figures said more. They smiled with friendship, they smiled with love. Henry, who had leaped into a shed that dark fall night to save me from some unknown killer. And Keir, who had wrestled with the cement Martha Washington dogs to protect us all in Ramsberger's mausoleum. And Natalie, my bestest and oldest, my truest and dearest and, as we now agreed, my forever friend—at least till high school.

And it didn't matter if I looked cool or dorky, if I mastered the clarinet or slaughtered it. It didn't matter if I said something stupid and then something even stupider. I looked at my three great friends and saw nothing but love and support for whatever I was, and the sight dislodged a single word from deep inside my cold-clutched heart.

The word sounded like the voices that were battering my skull—it had the same pitch, the same tone—but this voice was not something being imposed upon me. This voice was rising from deep inside, ignited by the sight of my friends, something I instinctively knew to be true. As I heard the judge's voice, I turned around to face his bench.

"What is going on, Ms. Webster?" said the judge. "I recognize those three. Mr. Harrison, and Mr. McGoogan, and a witness from Mr. Harrison's case, Ms. Delgado. What is happening in my courtroom?"

"Freedom," I said. That was what the true voice of my heart was saying. "Freedom."

Apologize, you fool. The other voices battered at my skull. *Bow and scrape and beg for forgiveness and dismiss the cases. Dismiss the cases!*

"What are you asking for, Ms. Webster?"

"Freedom," I said.

And that's when I heard the commotion behind. I turned my head to see Henry and Natalie and Keir putting the machines on the floor of the courtroom and unscrewing the globes, turn by turn, until ribbons of color filled the courtroom.

The ribbons wrapped around each other, sending sparks into the air whenever they touched, a fireworks display on the Fourth of July, accompanied by a hum of voices like the buzzing of a thousand bees. The sparks finally formed into two columns of spinning blue clouds, from which emerged a squad of ghosts, floating in formation in the courtroom, their arms outstretched and their mouths jerking strangely as they said, in unison:

"WE ARE BEING TREATED WONDERFULLY. WE ARE OH SO HAPPY. WE ARE BEING TREATED WONDERFULLY. WE ARE OH SO HAPPY."

"Ms. Webster, what is the meaning of this?" shouted the judge.

"Freedom," I said.

"WE ARE BEING TREATED WONDERFULLY. WE ARE OH SO HAPPY."

"Stop all your blabbering and start making sense."

"Freedom."

"Are you saying that all these ghosts are suffering from the mind control perpetrated by the defendant? Is that what you're trying to prove? If so, this is not the way to do it." He banged his gavel. "We will have order in this court. Quiet, all of you."

The ram bellowed, and the judge pointed his gavel at the columns of ghosts, and they quieted their words to a whisper—*We are being treated wonderfully. We are oh so happy*—even as the sound of the bees surrounding them continued buzzing.

"Mr. Goodheart, if your client is mind-controlling these spirits, then he must stop, immediately."

Josiah Goodheart looked at his client, who shook his head, and then said, "Your Honor, we are not controlling these ghosts."

"Then who is it?" The judge stared down at the witness. "Is it you, Ms. Ramsberger?"

She looked up at the judge. "These specific ghosts? No, I am not controlling them. They are not worth my time. I make no promises about the girl."

"Well, whoever it is, it must stop now!" said the Judge. "Or there will be contempt declared! And you do not want to be found in contempt of my court, believe me."

As the judge kept shouting, a ghost detached itself from the squad and floated briefly around the courtroom. I hadn't noticed her within the crowd, but Paola Fiore gave me a wink before she drifted to the benches and sat down right beside Dr. Shevski. Dr. Shevski gave her a smile of her own and they clutched each other's hands, one human, one ghost.

At the same time, Ygor reached into his wide briefcase and suddenly something snapped in the courtroom and the whispering chants died, along with the buzzing of the bees, and the ghost platoon drifted out of their columns and floated free across the courtroom.

Joining them was Isabel.

Even as the judge pounded his gavel and called for order, the ghosts floated free.

There was something joyful about the swarm of ghosts celebrating their freedom, laughing and yelling as they floated like those lovely candle lanterns let loose in the night sky. Even the babies on the ceiling pointed gleefully at the scene. And was someone singing opera? Yes! Three of the ghosts swooped toward Janelle and Sydney. One I recognized, the old man I had seen in the Chamber of Stolen Ghosts, Silas Burton, the girls' grandfather. The other two were undoubtedly the girls' parents. The ghosts hugged the girls so tightly with their ghostly arms, the girls' breaths were squeezed out of their bodies with a whoosh.

As the ghosts continued their celebration, Josiah Goodheart caught my eye. He wasn't smiling—he didn't want a smile to be seen by his client or the judge—but he gave me the smallest of nods. As if this was exactly what he had wanted when he gave me that first Choco Taco. As if he was telling me, *Well done!*

The beauty of it all lasted only a few short moments before the spirit of Isabel Cutbush floated to the front of the court, turned to face the pack of ghosts, and said, "The time has come to take action. What do we want?"

"FREEDOM!" called out the ghosts.

"When do we want it?" asked Isabel.

"NOW!"

And then the ghosts attacked.

42

THE CAGE

The attack of the army of stolen ghosts in the Court of Uncommon Pleas was halted by Ygor with the flick of a switch, turning the Spirit Psychic Drive back on before too much blood was spilled.

And with that proof, the Judge immediately ordered the bailiff to place Ramsberger and the ghost of his grandmother in the iron cage hanging from the courtroom's ceiling.

Josiah Goodheart bellowed out his objections—"This is an outrage, an outrage, I say. What about the presumption of innocence? What about the fundamental rights of human and ghost to a fair hearing?"—but the judge overruled the objections, saying he was placing the Ramsbergers in the hanging prison for their own protection, since the cage was impenetrable by ghost attackers.

In a flash Ramsberger, his bow tie pulled off, his tweed

ripped, a line of blood leaking down his huge orange skull, sat whimpering on the floor of the hanging cage as the ghost of his grandmother floated by his side, looking down at him as if she was locked inside a coop with a mangy ferret dressed in tweed. The ghostly Raven stood on Ramsberger's head and cawed out in anger.

With the Ramsbergers safely imprisoned, Ygor once again turned off the Spirit Psychic Drive, and my father, suddenly sound of stomach and mind, took over the trial. As he put on his witnesses, first Janelle and Sydney, then Janelle and Sydney's mother, father, and grandfather, then Isabel and the other plaintiffs in the group litigation, I sat in the back with my friends, too chilled to talk, as Natalie tried to knead some warmth into my arms.

"Your hands feel like cold dead fish," said Natalie.

"I'll get the tartar sauce," said Keir.

"I loved how you won the case with a single word repeated over and over again," said Henry. "I used that same tactic when I was four."

"Yes, it was quite impressive, Elizabeth," said Keir. "A tip of my hat to you. One word and the judge agreed with everything you meant to say."

"There's a lesson in there somewhere," said Natalie, "but I'm sure we'll ignore it."

"We would have arrived a bit sooner," said Henry, "except for the dogs."

"But I took care of the critters," said Keir. "One of them likes me, I think. She's not bad-looking either, for a cement dog. Who knew Martha Washington was so cute?"

"George knew," said Natalie.

"Here, Webster," said Henry. "You'll want these back." He reached into his pocket and pulled out my courtroom keys.

As I took the keys from him, my tongue thawed enough for me to say, "Th-thanks."

"It was nothing," said Henry.

"It was everything," I said. "Thank you for showing up and knocking some sense into me."

"That's what friends do," said Natalie.

"I think I've heard enough," said the judge with a bang of his gavel, cutting off one of the ghost witnesses in midsentence. "I find the evidence to be overwhelming that these plaintiffs have indeed been illegally captured and mind-controlled by the defendant. Mr. Goodheart, do you have a defense?"

"Indeed we do, Your Honor," said Josiah Goodheart. "If this was a group litigation of mice against the Acme Mouse-trap Company, would you allow the action? If this was a group litigation of poison ivy plants against the Acme Weed Eradication Company, would you allow the action? These ghost pests have invaded the space of the living. We need more, I say, more Ramsbergers, not less, or we will be over-run. Look at my client in that cage, battered and bloodied by these invaders. His condition is proof of our defense. This case must be dismissed, I say, dismissed forthwith, with prejudice and with damages awarded."

"What say ye to that, Mr. Webster?" said the judge. "Sounds pretty convincing."

"Your Honor," said my father, "wasn't Mr. Goodheart,

when objecting to your putting the Ramsbergers in the cage, going on about the fundamental rights of human and ghost?"

"I believe he was," said the judge. "Mr. Goodheart, these ghosts are not pests to be controlled, they are the spirits of what were once living beings, who now continue on with all their joys and heartbreaks and yearnings. Do they overstep occasionally? Yes, they do. Is there a solution for that? Yes, there is. This very court. But we will have no unsanctioned ghost thief in my jurisdiction. I find for the plaintiffs here, both the Burton children and the Cutbush group litigation, and order all such ghosts released immediately."

A cheer went up from the ghosts and the crowd and the little babies floating around on the ceiling. My father looked around at the cheering crowd and then his gaze fixed on Barnabas, sitting between my mother and Avis. Barnabas nodded. My father nodded back and turned around again.

"Quiet," said the judge with a bang of his gavel. "I also order that the defendant, Frederick Ramsberger, and the ghost of his grandmother, Radclyffe Edwina Ramsberger, be held in the custody of the court, pending a proceeding before the Supreme Tribunal, regarding this plot of the demon Abezethibou, also known as Redwing, to use these ghosts to somehow gain dominion over the living world. The Lord Demon will need to get to the bottom of this and take appropriate action."

"You can't be serious," said the ghost of Edwina. "Do you not know who I am?"

"I know exactly who you are," said the judge. "Bailiff!"

The ram on the wall neighed and slowly, slowly, with the creak of a turning wheel, the cage with the Ramsbergers and the raven was lowered all the way through the hole in the floor, even as the two shouted out in complaint. There was a great flash of light and when the cage was brought back up again, it was empty.

"Is that all, Mr. Webster? Are we free of you now at last?"

"Your Honor," said my father, "I simply want to make sure that all the plaintiffs' requested relief is granted by your order, including where we asked that each spirit be allowed to return to their natural domain if they so choose. That would prevent any of these beleaguered plaintiffs from being forced to remain in a world not their own against their will."

"If I so grant, will you be through, sir? Will the whole pack of scoundrels going by the name of Webster and Spawn scurry out of this courtroom immediately, so I don't have to look at you again for the rest of this circuit?"

"We will leave with all deliberate speed," said my father.

"So it is ordered," said the judge. "So it is done. And don't be so deliberate about your leaving." He banged down his gavel and then called out, "Next case!"

43

THE FINAL WORD

I was back on the debate stage, sitting between Charlie and Doug Frayden, getting ready for my closing argument. Yes, Ms. Lin had given me another chance at the anchor position. Foolish woman! And this wasn't against the chumps from Pattson Middle School as before. On this day, Willing Middle School West was up against our archenemies, the Masters of Misery, the Despots of Despair, the Bad, the Rude, the Rudely Smelly, yes, the debate team from Willing Middle School East.

Talk about a bunch of losers.

Today's topic: Cell phones should be banned in schools. We were in opposition. Power to the people!

As Charlie and Doug and our opponents all made their points, I took notes, even as all the tips I had received after my last disastrous debate fluttered through my brain.

Everyone and their mother had a comment on my performance, including my mother and her mother. And it seemed as if everyone and their mother was also in the auditorium that day, watching.

Tragically, they had mentioned the debate contest in this morning's announcements and that seemed to have boosted attendance, which made no sense to me. Who were the kids who actually listened to the morning announcements?

Along with Charlie and Doug at the table, Henry and Keir and Natalie were in the house, which meant that they would have much to joke about after it all went sideways. My mother had left work early to catch my performance and sat alongside Stephen, who had also given me his sage advice. (Why is good advice supposed to be green and smelly? I don't know, either.) Beside the two of them sat my father, who seemed to be suddenly taking an interest in my life, which was weird and unpleasant. Petey was sitting beside Janelle Burton, the two having walked together from the elementary school right down the road. And because of the morning announcement hyping the debate death match, other friends had come, too. There were Young-Mee and Stacey and Juwan, and also Debbie Benner, who was sitting with Natalie. I don't know what rule might have applied to that situation, but Natalie and I had decided no more rules. So yeah.

Oh, and best of all, over there to the side was Mr. Armbruster.

If you're going to be humiliated, it might as well be in front of everyone!

But I wasn't as scared as I should have been. It turned out

that our Chamber of Stolen Ghosts case hadn't just helped the stolen ghosts.

We all dashed out of the courtroom that night as soon as the judge banged his gavel, running as fast as we could in case he considered changing his mind. I hugged Ivanov on the way out, and then it was down the stairs and through the maze, all of us meeting together in the locked-up City Hall courtyard. With the ghosts zooming back and forth in their court-ordered freedom, it was a party.

"Thank you so much, Elizabeth," said Sydney, as her sister, her parents and grandfather, and my grandfather, too, looked on while she gave me a hug. "We are so grateful, all of us."

"This was a wonderful victory," said my grandfather to the sisters. "All because of you two young ladies, and Elizabeth of course."

"And maybe also Petey," I said, "but don't spread it around."

"I won't, I promise," said Janelle. "But knowing Petey, he probably will."

"No offense about that thing in the chamber," said the ghost of Silas Burton. "I didn't know who you were at first, and I was being ornery."

"But even if he did know," said Janelle, "he'd be ornery just the same. That's what he is."

"True," said the old man.

"Teach me," I said.

"Please don't," said my grandfather, giving me a look of

pure love, "our Elizabeth is ornery enough," and everyone laughed.

While the Burton family was having their reunion, I glanced to the side and saw the strangest sight—Barnabas grinning. Who was this stranger smiling like a fool? I excused myself and headed over.

Barnabas was standing in the middle of the courtyard holding hands with Isabel Cutbush. But Isabel was no longer a ghost. The remedy Barnabas had slipped into the complaint had done its magic, and Isabel now was a living, breathing woman in her natural domain, the world of the living. After more than a hundred years separated by the dividing line of death, the two were finally together. The romance of it all was enough to take your breath.

"Oh, Mistress Elizabeth," said Barnabas, snatching his hands back from his betrothed as if he had been caught stealing cookies. "What a success your case was."

"Something's wrong with your face, Barnabas," I said. "Your mouth has somehow become strangely twisted at the edges. Have you eaten a bad fig?"

"Elizabeth Webster," said Barnabas, "may I formally introduce you to my fiancée, Isabel Cutbush."

"Barnabas has been gushing about you," said Isabel.

"Barnabas doesn't gush," I said.

"No, you're right," said Isabel. "But he said a few nice things, which constitutes a gush for him."

"I'm so happy you two are together at last," I said.

"Thank you," said Isabel. "Yet it feels peculiar. We've been away from each other for so long, it's as if we were strangers."

"Which means we get to court each other all over again," said Barnabas.

"And Isabel will be staying with me as they do," said Avis, dropping into our conversation. "With me."

"I hope I won't be a bother, Ms. Picklefeather," said Isabel.

"No bother," said Avis. "No bother. But remember, in my house everyone sweeps up their own feathers."

I looked up and saw my mother, slowly, hesitantly, making her way to us. When she arrived, she clutched my arm in congratulations for the win, but all the time she was staring at Isabel.

After a long awkward moment, Isabel said, "Nice to see you again, Melinda."

My mother was too flummoxed to reply.

"You know each other?" said Avis. "How? How?"

"It was a long time ago," said Isabel.

And then my mother took a step forward and in a low voice asked, "How is she, General?"

That was the first time I realized that Isabel was the General in my mother's story. I wouldn't be surprised if you'd figured it out already, what with the British accent, the Victorian dress, her presence in Redwing's castle. But my mother hadn't known, even though she'd heard the story of Barnabas and Isabel long before I ever came onto the scene.

Isabel smiled at my mother's question. "I am no longer the General," she said. "A while ago I passed on the role. It fits her perfectly. And she taught us all the chant. Did you recognize it?"

"I did," said my mother, and then, with something urgent in her voice, she said, "Is she happy?"

"Don't ask me, Melinda," said Isabel. "Ask him."

We all turned to see where Isabel indicated. And there stood my father. Yes, of course, my father. He was in a group with my friends, congratulating them on bringing in the ghosts and winning the case for us. He lifted his head when he caught us all staring at him. His expression was bewildered, as it usually was. But now I knew why he was often missing, traveling back and forth to the other side, and who he was traveling back and forth to see.

Love is weird.

My mother said the first time my father looked at her with anything other than annoyance in his eyes was in the stone stairwell in Redwing's castle, when the demon Gaap had blocked their way.

Instead of cowering before the great bat-winged demon, my mother, who had been pushed past her limit by everything, by every single thing, went right after Gaap, yelling at him for the way he had tricked them into making his bargain. Gaap knew the terrors of Redwing's dominion, she shouted at the demon, knew all the dangers they would face in their quest, and yet he had dropped them in the middle of a city street filled with traffic and forced them to brave the Stormlands and Redwing's castle to get his little toy for him. A simple matter, he had said, which was a lie to its bones. How dare he?

"I'm a demon," said Gaap. "What did you expect?"

If my mother wasn't so angry, she would have acknowledged the truth of what he said. But she was so angry, and his bat-faced smile only made her angrier. She couldn't help stalking forward, as if ready to punch the demon right in his nose.

That would not have ended well. I can imagine my mother scurrying as a mouse for all of eternity in the cellars of Redwing's castle if my father hadn't stepped in and calmly threatened a suit in the Supreme Tribunal, where demons bringing humans to the other side for their own selfish purposes is much frowned upon by the Lord Demon.

The fear in Gaap's eyes from the baby lawyer's calm words pulled something out of my mother, an emotion that stayed with her even after the demon fled, even after my father went over to the other side, came back with her papers, and brought her back to her life. Their relationship was forged in that moment, when my mother had enough righteous anger to attack a demon and my father had the calm and the smarts to make the demon disappear. What could be more romantic?

But in truth, my mother no longer had the stomach for questing in a strange and horrible domain or attacking demons. And my father never had the stomach for sweet domesticity when there was so much injustice, and, yes, adventure, on the other side. Whatever they felt for each other in that moment was doomed to turn, and so it did.

Okay, dab the tears and hear the final part of my mother's story, where she delivers the letter Juniper had given her to Juniper's mother. There were tears there, too, along with a promise that Juniper was okay, better than okay, was happy and with her father, and could come home whenever she wanted to. And then there was the thing about the treasure.

There was no buried chest filled with gold. Too bad, right? Instead, the letter talked of a small metal box that Tommy Lee Jelani had given to his wife to store and that she had dutifully taken along with her on every move after his death. It was just letters and photographs inside, she thought, stuff she couldn't bear to throw away. But according to the letter, there was also a notebook with songs. His songs.

That's a pretty pathetic ending for an otherworldly adventure, a stupid notebook with stupid songs that no one wants to hear. Except that when Juniper's mother showed the notebook to a local musician, who started playing one of the songs, the excitement in the musician's eyes was as real as the notebook itself.

You won't recognize the name of the song, but your parents would. The local musician recorded it, and it did okay, and then this famous band covered it and it became a thing. They even put it in a couple of movies. And all the time, Juniper's mother was raking in enough royalties to buy a house for her family, and cover Juniper's younger sister's medical treatments, and send both of Juniper's sisters to college. Juniper's mother still gets payments from the streaming services every time your mom plays it in the car, singing along like she was seventeen again, while you complain about having to listen to such stupid old stuff.

Right after my mother turned over the letter, she grabbed *The Book of Ill Omen* from the floor of the basement in Juniper's apartment building and returned it to Jack's Cauldron of the Odd in Olde City Philadelphia.

"I knew you'd be back," said Jack.

She slapped the book and a fifty-dollar bill onto the counter. "Now burn it like you promised," she said.

The old man inhaled from his cigarette. The tip sizzled. As he winked his milky-white eye and grabbed the fifty, the moonstone on the book's cover glowed.

The end. Maybe. Because I expect *The Book of Ill Omen* is still calling out to customers in search of something strange and miraculous. *I know what you want. Find me. Feed me. Use me.*

After my mom told me her story, I kept seeing Juniper in the street, or in crowds, or sitting in front of me on the train. Which was strange, because I didn't even know what she looked like. But each sighting gave me a shot of courage. She hadn't been doomed to stay what she was, careful, quiet, scared. She was able to change by listening to her own heart, no matter how surprising the direction it told her to travel. And, actually, the same thing happened to my mother. That they ended up on different paths means not a thing. What matters is it was a path they each chose, listening to their own inner voice.

"Opposition closing argument," said the debate judge. "Three minutes. Ms. Webster?"

I stood unsteadily, gave an *uh-oh* expression to Charlie and Doug, and took my place at the podium. As I looked out at the crowd, at all my people, I imagined I saw Juniper sitting somewhere not far from my father with the rest of my family and my friends.

I closed my eyes and stood there thinking of all the arguments that had been made by both sides, and all the advice I had been given after my last debate disaster. A spot in the district tournament was no longer at stake, I had taken care of that, but humiliation was still possible. And then the voices jabbering away in my head went calm and then quiet.

For the briefest moment there was silence, a beautiful empowering silence.

Slowly a word started forming, like the word that arose in court when I saw Henry and Natalie and Keir, a single word, blossoming like a golden flower. It wasn't anyone else's word. It was my word. And because of that it had the power of truth. One word, but one word can be enough.

I opened my eyes and began.

ACKNOWLEDGMENTS

E very novel is collaboration. I want to thank the incandescent Alexandra Hightower for the firm yet gentle way she guided this book and the whole series in the direction it needed to go. She has been a delight and revelation to work with, as have all the folks at Little, Brown who worked so hard on getting the details right, especially my copyeditor, Barbara Perris, and the managing editor in charge of everything, Annie McDonnell. I also want to thank Karl Kwasny for his amazing cover artwork, as well as Phil Buchanan and Angelie Yap for their epic design work. It wasn't long before I realized I had to raise the level of my writing to keep up with their covers. I also want to thank my agents, Wendy Sherman and Alex Glass, whose support and advice have meant everything every step of the way in my writing for young readers.

The poet Jon Silken, who literally wrote the book on the subject, taught me about the amazing poetry of World War I, which Mr. Armbruster teaches to Elizabeth. The information about the CIA's effort to mind control through psychic driving came from *Journey into Madness* by Gordon Thomas. Peter Cilio, one of our great designers of garden sculptures, gave me the lowdown on the Martha Washington dogs. They are apparently called sphynxes, come from France, and sport the face of Marie Antoinette. Who knew? But to Elizabeth they look like Martha Washington and who am I to argue with Elizabeth.

I also want to mention here one inspiration for Ebenezer Webster, III. I was lucky enough to clerk for the Honorable James B. Moran in the federal courthouse in Chicago. Along with being a wonderful man, a patient boss, and a jurist for whom the motto "Equal Justice Under Law" was not just something carved into stone but the animating spirit of his courtroom, Judge Moran was also the most brilliant lawyer I ever met. Like Ebenezer, he could hold a case up to the light and see all its facets. His good work continues with the James B. Moran Center for Youth Advocacy in Evanston, Illinois.

Finally, I want to thank Pam for her unconditional love and support when I decided to give up the law and try to write for a living. Watching our children grow into themselves has been the great adventure of our lives. All we ever wanted for Nora, Jack, and Michael is the same thing I want for Elizabeth and all of you: the courage to find your truth and the freedom to pursue it when you do. With that, and an ice cream truck on a summer afternoon, I think we'll all be okay.

WILLIAM LASHNER

is a *New York Times* bestselling author and a graduate of both the Iowa Writers' Workshop and the New York University School of Law. His novels have been published worldwide and nominated for two Edgar Awards, two Shamus Awards, and a Gumshoe Award for getting gum stuck on his shoe. When he was a kid, his favorite books were *The Count of Monte Cristo* and any comic with the Batman on the cover. Elizabeth Webster is his first series for younger readers. You can visit him online at williamlashner.com.